A Moment...to Love

A WHISTLE STOP ROMANCE

Jennifer Faye

Best Wishes,
Jennifer Faye

Published by Lazy Dazy Press
ISBN-13 (digital): 978-1-942680-00-0
ISBN-13 (paperback): 978-1-942680-01-7

Thanks & much appreciation to:
Cover Design & Formatting: The Killion Group
Content Editor: Tessa Shapcott
Copy Editor: Joyce Lamb

DEDICATION

To my real life hero, who has held my hand
every step of this amazing journey.

PRAISE FOR JENNIFER FAYE

"Faye's romance tugs at the heartstrings…"
—RT Book Reviews TOP Pick! & 2014 Nominee Reviewers' Choice Award for Best Harlequin Romance! *The Return of the Rebel*

"Romance fans will adore the characters Faye has created in her enchanting tale."
—RT Book Reviews TOP Pick! & 2013 Winner Reviewers' Choice Award for Best Harlequin Romance! *Snowbound With The Soldier*

"Fun, quirky and romantic"
—RT Book Reviews TOP Pick! & 2013 Nominee Reviewers' Choice Award for First Series Romance! *Rancher To The Rescue*

CHAPTER ONE

Alexis Greer had always been a little superstitious.

She especially believed the adage that bad things came in threes. So far today, her originating New York flight had been delayed, causing her to miss her connecting flight, leaving her stranded for hours, and when she'd finally arrived in New Mexico, her luggage had gone missing. At last count, that accounted for only two unfortunate events. The knot in her stomach wrenched tighter. She was due for one more bit of bad luck.

She inhaled a deep, calming breath as she stared out the dusty windshield of her rented SUV. The slanting desert sun added a glow to the red clay that stretched out on both sides of the two-lane road. The *ding-ding-ding* and flashing red lights of the railroad crossing had her tramping on the brakes.

First in line, she pulled to a stop as the passenger train rolled into view. The *woo-woo* of the whistle blew loud and clear. It wasn't a new streamlined one. No, this was an older train that had been lovingly restored to its former youth and beauty.

Just beyond the engine were two passenger cars. Faces, both young and old, dotted each window. What a novel way to bring tourists to this small desert town. But then her gaze settled on the train depot. She frowned. The weathered building had been boarded up. The gray walls were peeling and overgrown vegetation had it surrounded. The station had certainly seen its better days.

When the red warning lights stopped flashing and the metal gate lifted, she eased the car forward. The tires rumbled over the tracks as her gaze latched on to a large wooden sign standing prominently on the edge of town.

Welcome to Whistle Stop, New Mexico
Population: room for more
Atmosphere: downright friendly
Weather: bright and cheery

Alexis smiled. Someone had a terrific sense of humor.

In the blink of an eye, she'd passed a variety of rustic storefronts and a number of attractive adobe-style houses. If it weren't for the handful of modern pickups parked on either side of the paved road, she'd swear this quaint desert town had been cut off from the rest of the world for the last fifty or so years. She found something sweet and endearing in the thought. After growing up around the hustle and bustle of New York City, a slower pace was inviting.

Still edgy after the turbulent flight, she pulled to a stop along the curb in front of Sam's Hitchin' Post. She rubbed her temples. Her jangled nerves needed calming. She needed chocolate. More specifically, she needed a Choconut Bar—her favorite.

She'd jumped out of the car and stepped onto the sidewalk when *Beethoven's Fifth* sounded from her cell phone. She sighed. Only one person had that ring tone, Howard Samuel Greer III, CEO and majority stockholder of HSG Holdings Inc. Her boss. And her father.

She stopped outside the store to fish her phone out of her purse. "Hello, Father. I just arrived in Whistle Stop."

"Good. Did you make contact with the seller yet?"

Her shoulders sagged, allowing her purse strap to slip down her arm. "I had some delays getting here. I'll meet with him tomorrow. Now stop worrying and go get some rest."

"I've been resting for weeks." His voice held a sour tone. "Don't boss me around. Tell me again your plans."

"They haven't changed. I'm handling everything."

"Don't forget to negotiate for the buildings and the—"

"I told you, I've got this deal under control. I'll get the land and the buildings."

"This is so important. I don't have to tell you that."

Her stomach roiled. Little did he know how important. Their company was in trouble—big trouble. Ever since her father's massive heart attack, she'd stepped up at the office—filling his very large shoes. This New Mexico deal was going to make or break their land development enterprise. She'd kept the condition of its finances from her father for the past several months, knowing the truth of their precarious situation would put too much strain on his already fragile heart. She would do anything to protect the one person who'd always been a constant in her life.

"I've still got time to fly out there." His steely determination rang out in each syllable.

A shiver raced down her arms at the thought of him conducting an important business negotiation that had the potential to turn contentious. He didn't need to risk another heart attack. Whistle Stop was in the middle of nowhere, and she'd be willing to guess their medical facility wasn't state-of-the-art.

Alexis paced up and down the sidewalk. "I can handle this on my own. The doctor ordered you to rest, and besides, you have your physical therapy sessions. You can't miss them." She'd use any excuse possible to get him to give up the idea of joining her on this trip. "Just relax."

Her father heaved a disgruntled sigh. "A man can only watch so much television. I need to be doing something. And don't you dare suggest a crossword puzzle."

"I wouldn't dream of it," she said innocently, thinking of the four or five puzzle magazines she'd left on his bedside table.

"This doesn't mean you're the boss now. I'll be back at the office sooner than you think."

All the more reason for her to wrap up this deal quickly before he got released from his doctor's care and returned to the office, where he'd undoubtedly uncover the truth about the company's financial instability. She squelched the prick of fear jabbing at her chest.

The bank holding the note on the piece of land she needed had assured her the seller was desperate—they were about to foreclose on his property. Alexis planned to swoop in with an irresistible offer for the acreage, including the ghost town, and HSG's new Wild West-themed resort would be a sure deal. Her father would never have to know how close his illness had come to driving the business into bankruptcy.

She knew all too well the importance of this company. It was her father's life's work. When her mother had up and left her father, the only thing the woman had wanted was HSG Holdings—not her own daughter, her own flesh and blood. The memory slashed at the scars on Alexis's heart.

In the end, her mother had walked away without the company and without a backward glance at her only child. How could a mother do such a thing? Why didn't her mother love her?

No matter how many times Alexis contemplated those questions, she never got any closer to the answers. And now wasn't the time to be dredging up ugly family history. Thankfully, she did have one parent who loved her and cared for her—her father. Now it was her turn to care for him.

"Father, it's time you consider retiring. The company is too much for you, especially after what happened." She couldn't bring herself to mention how this latest coronary episode had caused permanent heart damage.

"No!" His voice vibrated the phone. "My life is HSG. Since when did you become so anxious to take over? Maybe you're more like your mother..."

Her father didn't have to finish the sentence for her to know what he meant. "I'm not like my mother. I'll never be cold and uncaring like her—"

"I know." He exhaled a weary sigh. "I'm sorry. I shouldn't have said such a thing."

Unable to let the subject drop, she had to make sure her father understood what drove her. "I don't want to push you out of HSG so I can take over." She stopped herself short of saying that she wasn't even sure she wanted to take over—ever. "I just want to take care of you. I...I couldn't bear it if...if anything happened to you."

"Hush now. I'm not going anywhere. And I know you're nothing like that woman. Forgive an old man for his careless ranting."

Alexis blinked repeatedly. "Already forgotten."

"But I still worry that you're not experienced enough to close this deal."

"I can do it."

Once she saved HSG, her father would never doubt her ability to run the company, and maybe then, he'd take a step back from the business. A crackle and hiss filled the line. "The connection is breaking up. Don't worry. This deal is in the bag."

She only wished she felt as confident as she sounded.

Her need for a Choconut Bar multiplied significantly as she ended the call. Her father had never been an easy man. He liked having things done his way.

She'd be the first to admit he'd been a loving father. He'd raised her as a single parent and was always there when she needed him. Whenever times got tough at school, he'd listen to her and then give her a Choconut Bar. Once she'd devoured the rich chocolate coating with a gooey caramel and pecan center, she'd unwind and things would work out. She needed that optimistic feeling now.

A little bell tinkled above her head as she stepped inside the Hitchin' Post. She glanced up to find a little brass bell. How quaint. Her stilettos clicked across the worn tiles. A menagerie of scents greeted her, from leather to cinnamon and cloves.

She glanced around, awed by the vast amount of food and other necessities crammed into every nook and cranny. Overhead, cowboy hats in earthen tones were suspended from the ceiling. How did someone squeeze so many goods into such a small area?

In no time at all, her gaze latched on to the candy rack at the front of the store. She rushed over and immediately spotted the familiar gold emblem of the Choconut Bar. Her mouth watered. She reached into the box but grasped nothing but air. Empty. No, this couldn't be happening. Not now.

Not ready to give up, she clutched the cardboard box and rushed to the checkout. She plunked it down on the worn linoleum counter. "Do you have any more of these?"

An older man behind the counter with a name tag that read Sam grabbed the box to read it. He was a tall, lanky man. A few strands of silver hair were combed across his balding head. Through gold, round-rimmed glasses, his kind eyes glanced at her, and then he pointed to the right. "Sold the last one to him."

Alexis followed the line of his finger to a cowboy headed for the door. "Hmm...thanks. Maybe I'll have a word with him—"

"I wouldn't. He's...he's not exactly social. Best to leave him be."

What a strange warning. Well, it wasn't like she wanted to strike up a friendship or anything. It'd be a simple business transaction, and then she'd be on her way.

Alexis's attention zeroed in on the cowboy's chambray shirt tucked into a pair of faded denim jeans that hugged his trim waist and firm backside. A breath hitched in her throat. Her gaze trailed down his long legs to his dusty cowboy boots. Her mouth grew noticeably dry. They sure had some mighty fine cowboys in these parts. She wrenched her gaze to the back of his hat.

Keep your mind on the task at hand. She'd never actually considered asking someone for their candy, but then again she'd never been under this much pressure. She started after him. Drat. Her black suede heels gave her some desperately needed height, but they prevented her from running after the man.

"Excuse me, sir."

The cowboy turned. He shot her a questioning look, and her brain stuttered at the intensity of his brown gaze. His golden tan and muscled physique reminded her of a drool-worthy model on the cover of a sexy romance novel. If she was interested in having a little bit of fun in the sun, this cowboy would definitely be her first choice—but she didn't have time to be entertained. She had a job to do. And everything would be so much easier with that candy bar.

Alexis moistened her dry lips and implored him with her most charming smile. "The clerk over there. He, um, said you bought the last Choconut Bar. It's the only kind I eat. I was hoping you'd consider selling it."

His brows arched up beneath the brim of his hat and then lowered into an uncompromising line. "No."

The familiar brown wrapper peeked out of the pocket of his shirt as though taunting her. If she were like either of her parents, it'd be her father because once she set her mind to something there was no backing down. Besides, if she couldn't persuade this man to sell her some candy, how on earth was she going to sew up the land deal?

The cowboy turned away.

"Please wait." She rushed to stand between him and the exit. "I can make it worth your time."

"I doubt it." The corner of his mouth lifted. "Is this some sort of *Candid Camera* bit? You're seriously going to haggle over a Choconut Bar?"

She yanked out her wallet and pulled out the smallest bill. "Here's ten dollars. You can keep the change."

He brushed aside her offer. "I don't want your money." He scowled. "I just want to be left in peace."

Heat swept up her neck and set her cheeks ablaze. She'd spent too much time at her father's land development company. She'd grown accustomed to negotiating for everything she wanted. Cowboys were a special breed. She would need a different approach.

She leveled her shoulders, ready to try again. "We didn't get off to a good start. It's been a long day with flight delays, and then the airlines lost my luggage—"

He held up a hand, halting her spiel. She hated how she'd let her guard down and played the oh-woe-is-me card.

He shoved his Stetson higher on his head while keeping a steady gaze on her. "You know, you aren't the only one who has had a rough day."

"Sorry." She lifted an apologetic smile to the cowboy, but even in her four-inch heels, she still had to crane her neck to gaze directly at him.

He surprised her when his eyes flickered with amusement. With the scowl erased from his face, he looked less intimidating and years younger. Thirtysomething would be her guess—not too old for her—if she were interested, that is. Not that she was in the market for a relationship. Her disastrous engagement had taken care of her foolish dream of finding true love.

"Is this candy really that important to you?" The cowboy's voice grew thin with exhaustion, making her regret her impulsiveness.

Not sure what to say, she shrugged. Her gaze strayed back to the familiar brown wrapper, but she couldn't bring herself to push the subject. He must share her preference for the rich chocolate. Something about this cowboy had her liking him already. Not that she "liked" him, but if she were looking for a sexy distraction, he wouldn't be such a bad choice.

The man crossed his arms. "If I agree to give you the candy bar, will you move aside and let me out the door?"

"Deal."

He yanked the chocolate from his pocket and held it out to her.

"Want to share?" She wasn't greedy, after all.

He shook his head. "Just take it."

"Thank you." Alexis snatched the bar and stuffed the money in his hand before he could refuse.

The cowboy cleared his throat, reminding her to move aside and let him pass.

He opened the door and muttered, "Women."

Heart pounding, Alexis grinned like a little kid. She ripped open the plastic wrapper from the bar. Her teeth sank into the thick chocolate layer before reaching the creamy caramel center lined with pecans. Her eyes drooped closed as the rich taste filled her mouth.

She'd pushed. She'd negotiated. And she hadn't given up. She'd achieved her goal. Tomorrow she would successfully negotiate the sale of a large tract of land encasing something very special—Haggerty, a genuine Wild West ghost town.

Holding her lucky Choconut Bar, she felt confidence well up inside her.

She would succeed.

CHAPTER TWO

Cord Lawson stepped out of the Hitchin' Post onto the sidewalk, anxious to head home to the Brazen H. His empty stomach rumbled. The warmth from the late-day sun only added to his discomfort. He'd missed his lunch, and now he'd forfeited his snack.

He didn't even know Ms. Business Suit's name, but she'd rubbed him like a burr, thorny and irritating. She might be a looker with her sleek, chin-length blond hair, pert nose, and lush lips, but she was definitely way out of this cowboy's league.

He stuffed his fingers in his pockets, searching for the keys to the truck. Too bad he couldn't rid himself of the vultures at the bank as easily as he got rid of her.

"Hey, Cord. Wait up," a male voice called out.

A quick glance over his shoulder revealed Mr. Forbes, his real estate agent, hustling down the sidewalk. Cord paused and turned. He hoped the man had chased him down to tell him the property had been sold and his troubles were now behind him.

Cord gazed down at the stout man gasping for air. "Do you have good news for me?"

"Well…" The man ran a hand over the short strands of white hair on the top of his head. His gaze lowered, avoiding Cord's expectant look. "I wish I did. I wanted to apologize for the mix-up and to assure you that everything has been cleared up."

"What are you talking about?" The muscles in Cord's neck bunched. The last thing he needed was another problem when he was poised to ask the bank for an extension on his loan. He couldn't afford for it to all go wrong now.

"Oh. I thought Melanie had kept you on top of everything." Mr. Forbes's round face puckered with worry lines. "She's probably just embarrassed by the whole matter since she's usually so thorough with her work."

Cord tapped his boot. He had a windmill to repair, as well as a fence line on the western boundary to inspect. If that wasn't enough, before he called it a night, there was a pile of bills on the kitchen table with his name on them. He did not have time to chitchat.

"Mr. Forbes, just spit out the problem."

"A while back, Melanie and I were discussing your account, and I filled her in on the unique aspects of your ranch. You know, about Haggerty. She was intrigued to find out it's a ghost town." Mr. Forbes searched his face as though looking for a sign of understanding. "When Melanie went to upload the information online about the couple hundred acres you're selling off, she misunderstood and included details about Haggerty being for sale too."

Cord fisted his hands. He knew what was coming next—someone wanted to buy Haggerty. In that moment, his mind strayed to the possibilities that could bring. If he were to forsake his heritage and sell the land, he wouldn't lose everything to the bank. He'd be able to save the house and barn. Yet he remembered the solemn vow he'd made to his grandfather that when Haggerty became his responsibility he'd respect and protect the land where his family had lived and died.

Cord always maintained he was nothing if not true to his word. Even though his short-lived marriage hadn't been the best, he'd have stuck it out and kept his vow till death do us part—but his ex-wife had had other plans. And when he hadn't complied, she'd taken her anger and frustration out on him by painting an ugly picture of him for the townsfolk. She'd claimed with on-demand-tears in her eyes that he was mean and stingy. The worst part was that most of Whistle Stop believed Susan's tall and malicious tales.

"Cord, you all right?" Mr. Forbes sent him a concerned look.

"Yeah, I'm fine." He couldn't let himself get distracted. The most important thing was saving the land. "You know I'm in the process of applying to have Haggerty listed with the National Register of Historic Places."

"I totally understand." The Realtor patted him on the arm.

"Do you?" Because the history of his family's land wasn't something people talked about, but Cord's grandfather had spent years teaching him about his ancestors. "As long as I'm alive and kicking, no one but a Lawson will own Haggerty."

Mr. Forbes's round face grew red like an heirloom tomato. "We have solid interest in the ghost town."

This news struck Cord like a sharp blow to the solar plexus. He didn't need this complication. What if the bank got wind of this and twisted his arm to force the sale? Those bankers wouldn't care about his heritage so long as they got their money. The thought soured his stomach.

Just then, Ms. Business Suit strolled out of the store. When their gazes connected, he noticed the deep-blue depths of her eyes. Okay, maybe she wasn't so bad. In fact, she was pretty hot. She flashed him a broad smile, and he forced himself not to smile back. He didn't have time to waste with flirting—that was a thing of his past.

He and Mr. Forbes moved aside to let her pass. Cord turned his head, allowing his gaze to linger on her, catching the sway of her rounded hips. It didn't hurt to look. And, oh boy, was Ms. Business Suit a fine sight.

Mr. Forbes cleared his throat. "About the ghost town—"

Cord turned back to find amusement in the man's eyes. "Yes...how far did this inquiry go before it became clear your office had made a mistake?"

"Well...information was forwarded about soil samples and water supplies."

"So you didn't bother to inform this person that Haggerty isn't for sale? You didn't take the time to tell them the listing is *only* for the two hundred acres on the eastern border of the Brazen H?"

"C'mon, Cord." Mr. Forbes grabbed a hanky from his pants pocket and dabbed it across his brow. "The property may have been in your family for generations, but selling it would keep you from losing everything. It's perfect."

Cord gritted his teeth. "Really? What about all those folks buried in the Haggerty family cemetery? Is it good for them? Would you sell out your grandmother's last resting place to earn a buck?"

Mr. Forbes tugged at his shirt collar. His forehead glistened again. "No. I...I'll have Melanie call the woman back and clarify which property is for sale."

"Make sure they know your office made the mistake. I want Melanie to convince this person to buy the two hundred acres. Time is running out for both of us to make this sale."

"I understand." The man swiped the hanky down his face. "I'm really sorry about this. I don't want to lose you as a client."

Cord inhaled a deep, calming breath. He hated being responsible for the pained look on the older man's weathered face. Not long ago he had made a monumental blunder himself by marrying Susan. His failed marriage had landed him in this difficult financial situation. He shouldn't be so hard on Mr. Forbes or Melanie. Neither of them would intentionally hurt this deal.

"That won't happen," Cord said, checking his anger.

Mr. Forbes rocked back on his heels. A weary smile puffed up his cheeks. "Thanks for understanding. We won't fail you."

They couldn't fail. As of right now, Cord didn't have a plan B.

Mr. Forbes met his gaze. "Melanie will be in touch as soon as she speaks with the potential buyer."

Cord yanked his key ring from his jeans pocket.

"Make it sooner rather than later. If I don't come up with the money for the balloon payment soon, the bank is going to foreclose."

"We won't let that happen. Have faith."

Cord's faith was really shaky at this point. He didn't even want to contemplate what he'd do if the worst-case scenario happened. Where would he go? What would he do for a living? Ranching was all he knew. And with his dyslexia, it was the only place he felt comfortable.

Besides, if he sold off half the ranch, it'd fix only part of his problem—paying off the mortgage. But at the same time, he'd lose too much grazing land to sustain his herd. Without enough cattle, he'd never be able to keep the place afloat. Talk about being stuck between a rock and a hard place. Somehow. Some way. He'd find the means to hold on to the only life he'd ever known—the place where he belonged.

♥♥♥

Surely, she hadn't heard them correctly.

Please say it isn't so.

Alexis blindly stared at a colorful poster for the area's high school talent contest taped to the windowpane of Evert Feed Store. Ever since she'd heard the men mention the ghost town, she'd been rooted to this spot on the sidewalk. What they were saying just couldn't be true—Haggerty had to be for sale.

When the conversation ceased, she turned to see the cowboy's retreating form. Her worried gaze lingered on his dusty tan Stetson with a brown leather band around the crown. A crop of light brown hair crept out from under it and curled against the nape of his tanned neck.

That was Cord Lawson—the man she'd flown across the country to meet? Her stomach plummeted into her suede heels. Getting on the cowboy's bad side by making a fuss over the candy definitely qualified in her book as her third piece of bad luck. Oh, what mess had she gotten herself into this time?

Standing around fretting wasn't going to rectify things. Alexis set off after the cowboy. She raced past the stuccoed storefronts with their brightly painted signs as fast as her high heels would allow. She had to catch up to him. She needed to smooth things over before the man dug his cowboy boots in any deeper about not selling the ghost town.

"Hey! Wait up!"

Cord slowed and turned. "You again. I already gave you my only candy bar." He pulled at his shirt pocket. "See? Empty."

She couldn't help but laugh. "That isn't why I stopped you. I was wondering if maybe I could repay your kindness by offering you dinner?"

She couldn't believe she'd just blurted out a dinner invitation to this sexy stranger. She'd written off men after Steven had lied and cheated on her. But then again, this invite was all about business and had absolutely nothing to do with the way his gaze made her stomach feel as though a dozen butterflies were fluttering around inside it.

The cowboy's brow creased as he considered her offer. "No, thank you."

"Come on. I just arrived in town, and I don't know a soul here." She once again flashed her most radiant smile, hoping to thaw his frosty exterior. If she couldn't establish friendly terms with him, launching straight into her business proposal could constitute a monumental disaster. "Besides, there's something I'd like to run past you."

He shook his head. "You can't take no for an answer, can you?"

"Not when saying yes can be so easy."

His warm brown eyes deepened to a shade of dark chocolate, alerting her to the fact that she'd once again chosen the wrong words.

"Are you implying I'm easy, Ms.—"

"Greer. Alexis Greer." She extended her hand to shake his, but when he didn't move, she lowered it back to her side. Not about to let his rebuff unnerve her, she lifted her chin and spoke with what she hoped was a confident voice. "And I wasn't implying anything."

He arched a disbelieving brow.

"Can we start over?" Why was he being so difficult? Was he always so distrusting? There had to be a way to get on his good side. "Join me for a friendly dinner. My treat."

"There's no need to start over, as I doubt we'll ever meet again. As for dinner, I can't. I'm not available." His matter-of-fact tone left no room for persuasion. Without giving her a chance to say another word, Cord turned and strode up the sidewalk past the handful of quaint shops with colorful awnings.

What was up with him? Her shoulders slumped. She'd certainly blown that encounter. Was this a sign of things to come? Was she on the verge of messing up the entire deal? If she failed, her father wouldn't waste time on words. He'd jump on the first plane westbound. Being a career-driven man, he'd disregard the risks to his life to save this deal for what would be the crowning jewel in his empire.

Alexis nervously fidgeted with one of her diamond stud earrings while worrying her lower lip. It wasn't so much the thought of HSG going bankrupt that had her body tensing. It was the knowledge of what it'd do to the one person she loved most in this world—her father. Sure, he could be demanding, contrary and stubborn, but he could also be understanding, encouraging, and loving. Howard S. Greer III was a complex man, and she loved him with all of her heart. Without him, she'd be all alone in this world. The thought chilled her to the bone. Life without her father in it was totally inconceivable to her.

She moved her hand to her forehead and rubbed it, hoping to ease the throbbing. Sure, she'd hit a stumbling block with the cowboy, but this wasn't her first challenge since taking charge of HSG, and it likely wouldn't be her last.

Determined to take care of her father to the best of her ability, she leveled her shoulders. She couldn't let this deal fall through. Correction: She wouldn't let it fall through. This encounter had only been a small defeat. She'd regroup and try again.

Alexis slipped her fingers into her purse, seeking out the remainder of the chocolate bar. After standing on the sidewalk in the hot sun, the chocolate had softened, but that didn't dampen her anticipation. She pulled back the plastic wrapper and sank her teeth into the now-creamy chocolate. As the rich taste spread on her tongue, her eyes drifted closed.

Tomorrow would be better.

She took another bite of the heavenly chocolate.

The cowboy had a price. Everyone did. She just had to figure out his.

CHAPTER THREE

What a beautiful morning!

Alexis stood outside the Three-Star Motel and stretched. There was no need for an alarm clock while staying here. The train whistle blew repeatedly at precisely six a.m.. With the motel being so close to the tracks, no one could sleep through that noise. Not a chance. But then again why would she want to miss such a glorious start to the day?

She gazed up at the clear blue sky and smiled. She had a good feeling that today her luck was about to turn around. Just then, a bubblegum-pink and vibrant-blue hot air balloon drifted into her line of vision. *How beautiful.* Alexis watched, fascinated, as it lazily floated over the edge of town. *What must it be like to ride in one?*

She stood there watching until the balloon drifted out of view. Then she realized that she'd better get a move on. She had important business to attend to with one very sexy cowboy, but first she was going to get her morning run in. Just because she was away from home didn't mean that she could slack off on her exercise and diet routine.

All warmed up, she set off down Ponderosa Street toward the big mountain in the distance. If her memory served her right, when she'd researched Whistle Stop there had been a brief mention of the Rocky Mountains and this was…was Roca Mountain. It certainly was very impressive in size—very impressive.

At that hour of the morning, there was a distinct chill in the air, hinting at the cooler months that would soon be here. She jogged the length of Ponderosa Street and then swung north on Silver Avenue, using Roca Mountain to keep her oriented. This road led her to a residential area with colorful adobe bungalows. Unfortunately, there were a lot of for-sale signs. She recalled reading that the population had shrunk in the past few years as people were forced to move elsewhere for jobs. Hopefully, when the resort was built, it would turn the declining economy around for the residents of Whistle Stop.

After making her way around the outskirts of Whistle Stop, she turned onto Main Street and headed for the town square. The center of the town. The epicenter of activity. The heart of Whistle Stop.

Alexis stopped in her tracks.

What in the world?

She sucked in one deep breath after the other as her body cooled down. Her eyes scanned the town square. Someone had taken the time to trim the shrubs and cut the grass, but that's where the TLC abruptly ended. Some of the benches lining the cracked sidewalks were broken and wrapped with yellow caution tape. Her gaze moved to the gazebo that had white paint peeling from the pillars. Even some of the shingles were missing. And the tall clock that stood off to the side of the park no longer kept time.

If she looked hard, she could see the beauty beneath the years of neglect, but it didn't negate the sadness of seeing the park in such poor condition. Why had everyone given up on it? This was the place where the townsfolk should gather and share bits of their day. It should be the glue that made the town special—picnics, carnivals, farmers' markets, and the list went on.

A breeze rushed past her, sweeping some lose strands of hair into her face. Carried with the fresh air was the most delightful scent of cinnamon. Alexis inhaled a much deeper breath. Her empty stomach rumbled. If she were smart, she'd turn right around and head back to the motel. But she did need to seek out some coffee. The coffeemaker in her room would do in a moment of desperation, but she craved some really good java.

Her gaze moved around the town square and settled on Poppin' Fresh Bakery. Its candy-pink and frosting-white awning rustled in the breeze. And the name was scrolled over the big picture window in teal and white paint. It looked new and cheery.

Alexis gravitated across the town square to the cute bakery. She really shouldn't go in. It would take a lot more than her morning run to burn off the calories awaiting her. She was just about to turn away when a young man rushed out the door with a white box of goodies. The most enticing aroma of coffee mingled with baked sugary treats tempted and teased Alexis. How could she walk away now? After all, it was her duty to make sure that Whistle Stop would fit HSG's image for the resort.

She rushed inside and immediately spotted the coffee machine. Inwardly she cheered. Morning just wasn't right without a good cup of coffee. She promised herself that she'd stick to her diet. She'd get a large coffee and slip right back out the door. Easy peasy.

"Hi, can I help you?" A young woman with a friendly smile stood ready to fill her order.

"Just a tall coffee with cream."

"No problem." The woman, whose dark hair was pulled back in a braid that trailed midway down her back, turned to grab a cup. "Are you new to Whistle Stop?"

"Um…yes. I just got in last night."

The young woman lifted one of the coffee pots and steam billowed from it. "You'll like it here. Lots of great people."

"If you don't mind me asking, what happened to the town square?"

"The economy. Young people are moving away for work, and with less money coming in, the town council voted to cut back on the upkeep."

"That's a shame." Her research into the town hadn't turned up anything about the neglect of the town square. She'd make sure to mention in her presentation to the town council how revenue from the resort would help with its upkeep. "It looks like it was really quite a beautiful park in its day."

"It was."

"I also noticed the old train depot on my way into town. How long ago did the train stop servicing the area?"

"They did away with stopping here years ago when the town started to die off." The young woman reached into the fridge behind the counter and pulled out the creamer. "By the way, I'm Piper. I own this place."

Alexis made a mental note to add the train depot to her growing list projects. "Hi. I'm Alexis. I'm from New York."

"Oh, so you're the lady everyone's talking about." Piper smiled broadly.

"They're talking about me?" Somehow, that did not sound good, not good at all.

"Don't worry. The gossip mill is always talking about something or someone. I wouldn't worry. By this afternoon, they'll be on to something new." Piper placed the hot coffee on the counter. Her diamond ring sparkled beneath the bright lights. "What else can I get you?"

Alexis's gaze strayed to the glass display case that held cinnamon rolls. "Uh…nothing."

"Are you sure? I just frosted those cinnamon rolls. They're poppin' fresh."

Alexis's mouth watered. She really shouldn't. It would cost her a ton of calories for the day. But they looked so good. And it'd been ages since she'd indulged in a cinnamon roll. *Oh, what the heck?* "Okay, I'll take one."

"A girl after my own tastes." Piper smiled. "I think this is the beginning of a wonderful friendship."

"I'd like that." Alexis smiled back. "By the way, your engagement ring is beautiful."

"Thanks. The big day isn't until next year." Piper chatted a bit more about her wedding plans to a councilman's son.

It was nice to have a friend in this new town. She wasn't sure how long she'd be here, but after what she'd overheard the day before, Cord Lawson was going to take some serious persuading to get him to sell his ghost town.

When more people strolled through the door, Alexis paid her bill and moved to a table near the window. Piper hadn't been exaggerating. The cinnamon roll was still warm and soft. It practically melted in Alexis's mouth. A moan swelled in the back of her throat. This treat was definitely worth cheating on her diet.

While she enjoyed her treat, she gave some more thought to the train depot. She did know a top executive with the railroad. They'd worked well together on another HSG project. He had said if she ever needed anything to give him a call. Something told her that helping to revitalize a small town hadn't been what he'd meant, but it wouldn't hurt to run her idea past him.

After savoring the last bite of the roll, Alexis got to her feet. It was time to get to work. She'd grab a shower and then head to the Brazen H, the home of the handsome but stubborn cowboy who stood between her and building the resort. But what he didn't know yet was that he'd met his match. She wasn't about to jet back to New York until they hammered out a deal.

♥♥♥

Cord slammed the phone down on the desk in his study. He jumped to his feet, sending the leather chair careening back into the credenza that rested beneath the window. Unable to stand still, he started to pace.

He'd wasted more than an hour getting the royal runaround from the Internet bank holding his mortgage. Normally, he would have done business with Whistle Stop's Save-A-Penny Bank, where he could do business one-on-one, but his ex-wife had made sure to turn the bank president against him.

Cord's foreman, Manny, had been playing pool at Cactus Mike's Saloon when he'd witnessed Susan, half-drunk and rambling, telling the banker that Cord wouldn't let her leave the ranch and that she'd had to sneak around to make it into town. Nothing could have been further from the truth.

Cord drew his thoughts up short. There was no point in dwelling on the past. It wouldn't change a thing. What was done was done. He just had to deal with the cards he'd drawn.

He stormed out of the room, grabbed his hat from the round table in the entryway, and headed for the front door. It'd been five years since his ex-wife had strode out of the same doorway, and yet he was still working to piece his life back together. By letting his heart overrule his mind, he'd put the only way of life he'd ever known at risk.

Maybe if he hadn't been in such a rush—maybe if he had concentrated harder on reading the fine print on the mortgage—maybe then he wouldn't be in this mess. Or maybe he'd created this fiasco by marrying a girl with big dreams. He'd hoped the Brazen H would be enough for Susan, but he'd been so wrong. And when she'd found out that he wouldn't sell the ranch and move, she'd gone ballistic. If only he'd listened to his gut and not been rushed to the altar out of sympathy for Susan living in poverty. He'd wanted only to help her. Somehow, his good intentions had gotten all turned around. And now he might pay for it with his ranch.

Why did hindsight have to be so damned enlightening?

He jerked the front door closed with a loud *thwack*, followed by the *bang-bang* of the screen door. He'd started down the stairs when the crunch of gravel drew his attention. An unfamiliar tan SUV blazed up the lane, sweeping up a cloud of dust behind it. They certainly were in a mighty hurry.

Cord paused on the bottom step and waited until the vehicle skidded to a stop, throwing up a spray of dirt. He did a double take when he caught the sheen of honey-blond hair. The chocolate fiend. What was she doing here?

The woman smiled as she stepped out into the sunshine. He found himself smiling back. It was as though she'd sensed his thoughts—his loneliness—and shown up. In that instance, he realized he was being ridiculous. First of all, she was a stranger. And secondly, there was no such thing as intuition, or whatever you wanted to call it.

Could she be the interested buyer? His muscles bunched up. He recalled Mr. Forbes saying the person was female. If so, he'd have to start thinking a lot more clearly. No sexy smile or sweet talk was going to sway him—not ever again. Susan had taught him that lesson—the hard way.

Ms. Business Suit lifted her sunglasses and rested them on top of her golden hair. Good. He wanted to be able to look in her blue eyes when he talked with her. They were so expressive—so captivating.

"I didn't expect to see you this morning. If you're here for more chocolate…"

"No." Amusement reflected in her eyes. "You must think I'm some sort of crazed chocoholic."

"That wasn't exactly the description I had in mind." When she responded with warm laughter, the melodious tone eased the tension in his body. Drawn in by her good mood and not wanting it to end, he asked, "Are you sure you didn't stop by for directions to the next candy store?"

Her laughter faded into a friendly smile. "No need. A generous cowboy sacrificed his chocolate bar to satisfy my craving."

"Nice guy."

"Definitely."

Cord approached her, checking out the tailored business suit that hinted at her curves. *Wait a sec. Is that the same outfit she wore yesterday? Sure looks like it.* He expected a woman like her, with her perfectly styled hair and her long, polished nails, to be finicky about wearing an outfit two days in a row. Still, he found himself contemplating the curves lurking somewhere beneath the folds of her clothes.

"I'm surprised to see you're still in the area. From the looks of it, I'd say your luggage has yet to catch up with you."

Her smile faded. Color poured into her cheeks, causing him to regret his thoughtless remark. He stifled a frustrated sigh. He was completely out of practice when it came to making casual conversation with women—with anyone. He kept to himself on his ranch. It was better that way. It kept the gossip to a minimum.

The woman glanced down and moved a stone back and forth with the toe of one high heel. "The airline promised it would be here by this morning, but it isn't. All I had in my carry-on was some casual clothes. I plan to go shopping after my meeting."

"You have a meeting around here?"

She nodded. "With you."

With him. So he was right. She'd known who he was all along. His jaw clenched. "What do you want?"

She lifted her chin and looked him in the eyes. "Mr. Lawson—"

"Call me Cord. Mr. Lawson was my father."

"Okay. Cord, you can call me Alexis. I'm here because I'm interested in purchasing the land you've put up for sale."

He crossed his arms, sensing she was keeping something from him. "Lexi, how did you learn about my land being up for sale?"

Her eyes lit up, probably surprised by the way he'd shortened her name. Her mouth opened, but without a word, she snapped it shut again. He should have guessed a businesswoman like her would take herself too seriously to consider using a nickname. But he genuinely liked the name Lexi. It suited her.

"I saw an ad on the Internet and flew out here to see the property for myself."

He took a moment to glance at the corral next to the lane with its wooden fence and the few horses that soaked in the morning sun. Could this stranger be the answer to his problems? Maybe he should hear her out. What could it hurt? He turned his gaze back to her. When he noticed her eyeing the horses, he asked, "Do you like horses?"

"Yes, I do. Quite a lot, actually."

Some casual conversation before diving into business might loosen them both up. His mother used to tell him that you could catch more flies with honey than vinegar. He intended to get this particularly pesky fly snared in his trap before she opened up about her interest in his land. "Would you like to go check out my stallion? He's one of the finest-bred horses in the county."

Lexi didn't answer as her gaze remained on the horse. For someone who liked horses, her hesitant expression puzzled him.

"Come on. I'll introduce you."

She shook her head. "Thanks. But I...I don't think so."

He knew by the way she continued to stare at his prize stallion that she was tempted. So what was holding her back? He knew it was none of his business, but horses were a passion of his and no one should fear them—respect them, yes, but not fear them. And then her comment and reaction came together.

"Did you fall from a horse?"

Her surprised gaze moved to him. "How did you know?"

He shrugged, not wanting to admit that the sadness reflected in her big blue eyes got to him. "Have you been on a horse since then?"

At first, she didn't react. It was as though she hadn't heard him, but then she shook her head. "I wanted to ride again, but...well, it didn't work out."

"Then come say hi to Midnight Star." Cord led the way across the gravel parking area. The black stallion observed their approach. The horse remained perfectly still, as though curious about their intent. When Cord reached the fence, he glanced over to find Lexi a good five feet behind him. She stared in awe at the horse, but her shoulders formed a rigid line.

He had a hard time imagining being afraid of a horse. He'd always had a kinship with them, not that he was a horse whisper or anything, more like he had the patience other folks lacked. He liked to think that he was observant and open to their unspoken communications. More than anything, he took comfort in the fact that animals were not judgmental. They were accepting and loving, unlike most of the people who'd crossed his path.

The spirited stallion snorted, as though sensing the tension in the air. Cord let the horse and the woman keep their comfortable distance. Nothing good would come from rushing things.

"This is Midnight Star." Cord climbed up and perched on the wood rail.

Lexi gave the horse a wide-eyed perusal. "He's quite beautiful."

"Yes, he is. He was a gift from my uncle."

"You must be his favorite nephew."

"I'm his only nephew." Midnight Star approached Cord and allowed him to run a hand down his sleek neck. "After Uncle Pete's stroke, he had to sell off his ranch. He couldn't bear to part with the stallion, so I offered to board him. When my uncle passed away a few months ago, he left the horse to me."

Lexi's concerned gaze caught his. "I'm sorry about your loss, but it was kind of him to leave you the horse."

Her sympathy warmed a spot just beneath his ribs. It'd been a long time since he'd opened up to anyone, even about the broad strokes of his life. What was it about this woman that snuck past all of his carefully placed defenses and burrowed into his chest? If she were to purchase that spot of land, how would he keep her at a safe distance? Especially when he'd ride past her place every time he drove into town.

Lexi's gaze moved back to the horse. "Do you ride him much?"

"Not like I should. I just don't have the time." He studied the genuine curiosity in her bright eyes. "How long has it been since you were horseback riding?"

"I was a teenager." She paused as though wondering if she should say more, and he hoped she would. She licked her lips. "I tried talking my father into buying a horse farm, but he said our New York City town house was a lot shorter commute to the office. So instead, he got me a horse and boarded it. He hoped it'd get the notion of riding horses out of my system."

"And did it?"

A thoughtful expression filtered over her face. "Yes and no."

"Not very decisive, are you?"

"I rode for a number of years. I even took part in some competitions, but then I...I got busy doing other things."

The way she stumbled over her words and the way her gaze drifted off to the side, he'd lay odds there was more to her story than she was letting on, but it was none of his business.

"Why don't you come a little closer? Midnight Star won't bite. I promise."

She took a few hesitant steps forward, until she was standing next to him.

"Would you like to pet him?"

Her gaze darted between him and the horse. Then she cautiously raised her hand. Cord wrapped his fingers over the back of her hand and guided her fingers to Midnight Star's muzzle. Cord spoke to Midnight Star in a soft, hushed tone as Lexi petted the horse. After a few strokes, her shoulders started to ease, and she relaxed.

Cord pulled his hand back, realizing there was no need for him to keep touching her—enjoying the softness of her skin. She turned her gaze to him, and a strange sensation rose in his chest. He swallowed hard. It had to be dirt the breeze kicked up that caused the weird feeling within his ribs because there was nothing special about this woman.

It'd take a lot more than good looks and expensive clothes to impress him. A polished professional like Lexi would never understand a down-to-earth cowboy such as him—just like those suits at the bank didn't understand his desperate need to keep his ranch.

"Hey there, big boy," Lexi crooned to the horse as she continued to run her hand over him. "I think you and I could be good friends."

This was Cord's opening, his chance to sell her on the small parcel of land. "He likes you."

Lexi smiled, easing the stress lines from around her eyes. "Is that true?" she asked the horse as though the horse would answer her. "Do you like me?"

Cord stifled the urge to laugh. She was like a child having met a horse for the very first time. And what surprised him most of all was Midnight Star's tolerance of her fussing over him.

Cord cleared his throat. "You know, when you purchase the land, you could have some horses of your own."

There was an extended pause, as though she mulled over his words. "You've got a really big farm here."

"West of the Mississippi, we call them ranches."

"The ranch has an unusual name. How did you come up with it?"

"I didn't. The ranch has been in my family for generations. I'm not sure who actually came up with the name, but it's in honor of my great-great-grandfather. The way it was explained to me is that he'd brazenly set off for the then untamed Wild West to start up the mining town of Haggerty. Hence the name Brazen H."

"Interesting." She turned away from the horse and gazed around at the array of different-sized buildings. "Do you run this place by yourself?"

He shifted his weight from one foot to the other. "No. I have ranch hands who do a lot of the work."

"Still, it must be a huge responsibility."

"It is." His chest puffed up a little. Why did this stranger's words mean something to him? The knowledge unsettled him. He'd prided himself on being a loner, on not caring what others thought of him.

Besides, he couldn't afford to risk getting to know Lexi better. When she found out the truth about him— that he was just a dumb cowboy—she'd laugh at him. Voices from the past echoed in his mind. He'd been the butt of the kids' jokes while in school. *Cord the gourd! Cord the gourd! Dumb as a board!*

Finally all grown up, he'd thought those days of public ridicule were over. Then he'd become the target of gossip when his marriage crumbled. The fact that his thoughts were unearthing ancient history threw up all sorts of warning flares.

Cord hitched his thumbs in his jean pockets and pulled back his shoulders. "I have work to do. Can we get to the point of your visit?"

Lexi opened her mouth, but all that came out was a cough, followed by another.

"Are you okay?"

She nodded. Her voice was a bit raspy when she spoke. "My throat is dry and it tickles."

"Come sit on the porch. I'll get you a drink." He led her to the porch.

It'd been a long time since he'd had a woman here. Not that Lexi was his invited guest or anything. Soon she would be gone. The thought didn't comfort him like he thought it would. Maybe he was lonelier than he was willing to admit.

CHAPTER FOUR

This cowboy was certainly full of surprises.

Alexis swallowed hard, trying to soothe the dry tickle in the back of her throat. All the while her thoughts were on the compassionate side of Cord she'd just witnessed. He'd been so kind and friendly as he helped her work past her nervousness about being around horses again. How could a man who could be so patient with animals and humans have gained a reputation that had people hesitant to deal with him?

She leaned against the wooden porch rail. Something sure wasn't adding up. There was a lot more to Cord Lawson than she'd uncovered so far. And that only intrigued her all the more.

Her gaze sought out the man at the center of her thoughts as he headed for the door. His long legs covered the expansive porch in just a few steps. She couldn't help but notice his broad shoulders that narrowed down to his trim waist. When her gaze lowered to his firm backside, she swallowed hard again.

Checking out this very fine cowboy was the absolute last thing she should be doing. Men were nothing but eventual trouble. In her experience, they couldn't be trusted.

She forced herself to glance away. The hominess of the porch drew her in. She'd dreamed of one day

slowing down long enough to kick back on one of her

own. In the shade, she'd sip at a tall glass of fresh-squeezed lemonade while taking a moment to watch the world go by—but that wouldn't be happening any time soon. Her duty was back in New York, taking care of the one person in this world who'd always stuck by her—her father.

Still, her imagination strayed, conjuring up a similar image. Only this time, Cord and a smiling woman were the ones relaxing on the two matching white rockers, laughing at some private joke. Alexis frowned and turned away. Sometimes her imagination knew no bounds.

She forced her attention back to the ranch that seemed to spread off in every direction for miles and miles. Standing there with the wide-open range at her feet was so liberating. This was the perfect place for a person to forget their troubles and just take in the majestic wonder of New Mexico. When the resort was built, its guests would love this setting. She certainly did.

Cord strode out of the house with a tall glass in hand. She readily accepted the drink and lifted it to her parched lips. The ice-cold water rolled over her tongue, cooling her windpipe and soothing her cough.

He sent her a concerned look. "Better?"

"Much. Thank you. I'm sorry to have bothered you. I'm just not used to these hot, dry conditions."

"It's no problem."

The cloudless sky rained down an endless supply of sunshine. She refused the urge to fan herself. What in the world made her think a suit would be proper attire for standing around in the desert? But with her luggage missing, she couldn't exactly meet him in her running attire.

"It would help if I wasn't overdressed."

"Lexi, what I said earlier about your clothes, I didn't meant anything negative by it. You look good. Real good."

She lifted her chin and their gazes collided. "Thank you."

His brown eyes captivated her with their intensity. Alexis pressed her lips into a firm line, holding back her retort over him shortening her name. No one called her Lexi. But at this point, staying on the cowboy's good side overrode her burning desire to correct him.

With effort, she glanced away, shrugging off her crazy interest in this cowboy. No matter how striking his looks, she couldn't forget she was here for one thing and one thing only—to buy a ghost town.

She moved and set the glass on the table between the two rockers. "You must spend a lot of evenings out here, enjoying the view."

"I couldn't imagine living anywhere else."

The solitude, though foreign to a native New Yorker, actually appealed to her. Sometimes the hustle and bustle of city life could be so tiring. A glance out at the distant horizon, where the lonesome landscape butted up against the reddish outcrop, made her feel like she was on a different planet from the one she'd known all her life.

Cord crossed his arms and shifted his weight against the railing. "Let's get down to business. Are you here because you've decided to hang up your designer heels in exchange for a pair of scuffed-up cowboy boots?"

"Not exactly."

"But you are interested in the acreage I have for sale, aren't you?"

"The thing is…" She hesitated, searching for just the right words.

"If it's the price, it's non-negotiable."

"It's not that."

Concern flickered in his dark eyes. "You do want the land, don't you?"

"Yes, I do." Alexis strove for a strong, confident tone. "The thing is, I'm not interested in buying it for personal reasons. I'm a land developer."

"What?" A whole host of expressions filtered across his face. "You mean, like those people who divvy up huge tracts of land to turn it into residential property?"

"Well, yes, but that's not what we want to do here." She reached into her purse, pulled out one of her business cards, and handed it over.

"What *do* you want to do here?" He accepted the card, but he didn't so much as glance at it before stuffing it in his pocket.

"Does it matter as long as you get your money?" When his brows furrowed together, she decided to take a different approach. "Normally I'd make this offer through your real estate agent, but this project is very personal to me. I thought if we could talk one-on-one, we could reach a quick and equitable agreement."

"I don't know about this." He ran a hand over the back of his neck. "This isn't what I'd been expecting."

"My company is prepared to meet your asking price." The way his brows furrowed into a dark, formidable line, she hesitated to say more. She worried that if she mentioned the ghost town now, he'd balk.

"Yesterday at the store you knew who I was, but you didn't let on." His narrowed gaze held hers. "You make me wonder what you're really up to."

Gone was the kind, thoughtful cowboy who'd teased her about her craving for chocolate and who'd taken time out of his day to show her his impressive stallion. She narrowed her gaze in on him. She just couldn't make up her mind about him.

She glanced away, breaking their connection. "I didn't know who you were at first. It wasn't until we were on the sidewalk that I heard the ghost town mentioned and put two and two together. I tried inviting you to dinner to explain things, but you shot down my offer, more than once."

He glowered at her. "You should have said something as soon as you realized who I was."

No matter what she said now, he'd take exception to it. He was definitely in no frame of mind to be receptive to her plans. Time to back off and let him absorb her offer. "I'm simply offering you what no one else has, the full asking price for the land."

"And you haven't denied that there's something you're hiding from me."

She crossed her arms, not about to be bullied into an admission. She was tired of men who thought she should cave in to their demands. First, her father and then her ex-fiancé. And look where that had gotten her—her father didn't believe she was capable of running HSG without him, and her ex had had the nerve to replace her without even bothering to tell her that they were over. Well, things would be different with Cord. Of that she was certain.

She straightened her shoulders and tilted her chin upward, meeting the cowboy's hard stare. She refused to let him intimidate her. He'd get his answers, but not like this. Past experience had taught her that sometimes the two negotiating parties needed to part company mid-negotiation. The downtime allowed common sense to settle in before they met again and tried to resolve any lingering issues. That's exactly what was needed here—a chance for Cord to cool down.

"You need me," she said, knowing about his financial bind. "And when you come to that conclusion, you can reach me at the motel in town. Good day, Mr. Lawson."

Alexis lowered her sunglasses to the bridge of her nose. Without another word, she marched down the steps. She could feel Cord's glare poking her in the back, but she refused to acknowledge him.

Had she made the right move? Or had she taken too hard of an edge with him? Was she walking away from her only opportunity to successfully complete this project? She envisioned how the news of her failure would send her father's heart rate soaring through the roof. Her stomach churned. She'd already come too close to losing him. She'd do her best to keep it from happening again.

The knowledge that the contrary cowboy couldn't afford to be egotistical for long gave her some peace of mind. Soon, reality would settle in, and then the stubborn Mr. Cord Lawson would be more agreeable to her terms.

And if not...she was working on a backup plan.

Before she'd left New York, Alexis had set up a meeting with one of New Mexico's leading real estate agents to talk about other prospective properties for HSG's ghost-town resort. Not about to take any chances upsetting her father when his health was so precarious, she wanted to have something to show him if she couldn't make the Haggerty deal work. Luckily, the Realtor had mentioned he'd be passing by Whistle Stop today and they'd made arrangements to meet at the Poppin' Fresh Bakery at ten. Apparently, the bakery's reputation for divine baked goods was known far and wide.

Minutes later, Alexis eased the SUV into the town square, which had one-way traffic circling the park. Naturally, all of the parking spaces were taken in front of the bakery. She sighed and looped around again. She'd pulled into a nearby parking spot when the train whistle blew. She glanced at the clock. Ten a.m. Perfect. She was right on time.

She got out of the SUV and glanced around at the empty storefronts. The windows were dusty, and the for-sale signs were sun-bleached. But beneath it all, she could easily imagine that once upon a time this town had been a hubbub of activity. And it would be again if she had anything to say about it.

As she grew closer to the bakery, the aroma of fresh dough and sugary goodness filled the air. Then again, agreeing to meet here for coffee might not have been one of her better decisions, but Piper did make some of the best coffee she'd ever tasted.

Alexis opened the glass door and noticed Piper busy at the counter, helping some customers. They waved to each other before Alexis glanced around for Mr. Santos. She'd never met the man before, so this would be a little tricky. There was a cowboy at one table, leafing through the *Whistle Stop Telegraph*, a weekly paper. Today must be its publishing day, as she'd found a copy outside her motel door that morning. She looked forward to glancing through it when she returned to her room.

The next table had a man in a pressed blue dress shirt with a bolo tie. Clean-shaven and with every dark strand of hair in place, he looked ready to do business. His gaze caught hers, and he smiled as he got to his feet. "Ms. Greer?"

"Yes." She moved to his table and shook the tall man's hand. "Thanks so much for meeting me."

"No problem. Please call me Ray."

"And call me Alexis." They both sat down. She lowered her voice. "I really appreciate you squeezing me into your busy schedule. This project is extremely important."

Piper approached their table. "Would either of you care for some coffee?"

They were both agreeable to coffee and a couple of blueberry muffins fresh from the oven. This place was impossible to enter without sampling something delectable. It was a good thing Alexis intended to keep up with her running.

Ray leaned back. "I was pleased to get your call. I'm looking forward to working with you. I have some ideas to run past you."

Alexis smiled. She liked a man who didn't beat around the bush. She had the feeling they'd work well together. "I like what I've seen so far of the Southwest."

"Is this your first time out West?"

"Yes. But it won't be my last." Turning the conversation back to business, she said, "When we move ahead with the construction, I'd like to disturb as little of the landscape as possible."

The Realtor ran his hand over his chin. "I like your attitude. Not enough people worry about preserving the natural landscape."

Piper dropped off their order and quietly slipped away.

Alexis stirred sweetener into her coffee. "I want this resort to look like a genuine part of the Southwest, including its surroundings."

Mr. Santos nodded. "I've identified a few properties on the market with ready access to a highway and enough acreage to accommodate a resort."

"Sounds good. Tell me more."

Ray withdrew a map from his briefcase. "These properties I'm about to show you don't have a ghost town, but that doesn't mean you can't erect a replica."

"No." She shook her head. "That won't work. We want a place rich in history and structures that have withstood the test of time."

"I hear you, but these properties I'm pointing out are a great steal. It might be worth sacrificing the genuine ghost town—"

"The ghost town is non-negotiable." She had no interest in anything fake. HSG's investors would never go for it. "We plan to use the authenticity and history of the town as the main thrust of our PR campaign."

"If I may be so bold as to ask, what's the problem with the Haggerty property?" Mr. Santos crossed his arms.

"Nothing as far as the land itself and the location, but the owner is hesitant to sell."

Mr. Santos nodded. "Then let me show you what I've uncovered since our phone conversation. Ghost towns in New Mexico are quite limited, so I took the liberty of expanding my search to include Arizona."

They spent the better part of the next hour enjoying two more coffees while pouring over maps of both states. By the end of their meeting, Alexis felt reassured that she'd chosen the right man for the job. This project would go through somehow.

♥♥♥

Cord strode into the house, slamming the door behind him. There was no way he was going to conduct business with a land developer—no matter how good she looked—coming...and going.

He halted his line of thought. He couldn't believe he'd let himself become attracted to another woman whose only interest in him was how much his land was worth. A sour taste filled his mouth. Hadn't Susan already taught him that lesson the hard way?

No way was he going to let Lexi's sweet smile and mesmerizing eyes sway him. She was trouble—in capital letters. His best course of action would be to avoid her. After all, even if he could trust her, he didn't want his land falling into the hands of a developer.

From what he'd been able to learn, developers were scouring the Western states buying up large tracts of land. They'd then subdivide the property into five-or-ten-acre home sites. And with all those homes would come businesses, like grocery stores and gas stations and strip malls. He hated the thought of having all of that noise and traffic butted up against his property. But if he didn't sell, how in the world could he make the balloon payment on his mortgage to save the ranch—his home?

Cord glanced around the spacious rooms of the prominent ranch house that his grandfather had built with his own two hands. Queasiness churned in the pit of Cord's stomach at the thought of losing everything he knew—the one place where he felt comfortable in his skin—where his difficulty with reading wasn't noticed by others, making him less in their eyes.

But there was something missing. In the wake of Susan's departure, he'd been thrilled to have the place to himself. He enjoyed coming home after a long, hard day and not having someone constantly nag him about all he wasn't doing or providing. For a while, a peacefulness had reined throughout the house, but lately the quietness had lost its luster. But that didn't mean he wanted to part with his home. Not a chance.

Spurred on by his need to find an alternative to the foreclosure—one that had nothing to do with Alexis Greer—Cord called the bank again. This time he reached a woman who agreed to pull his file and discuss his loan. After ten minutes of hearing the same old spiel, he gripped the phone tighter. "Listen to me. I just need a little more time."

"With no proof that an extension will provide the necessary funds to pay off the balance on your loan, you are prolonging the inevitable," the woman said without an ounce of emotion, as though she'd become indifferent to smashing people's dreams.

The loan officer continued to tick off the various reasons why pushing his balloon payment back was not feasible for the bank. Cord scrambled for any excuse to keep the bank from foreclosing. He'd already tried obtaining another loan from just about every bank he could think of, but they'd all turned him down.

With each passing moment, the band of stress ratcheted tighter around his ribs. He was about to lose not only Haggerty but also the Brazen H. His chest tightened. His home, the cattle, the horses and even his ranch hands—his only friends—would be gone.

They'd all be lost to him.

That just couldn't happen.

"We'll start foreclosure proceedings in the morning," the woman said matter-of-factly. "Unless you can come up with the full payment or you can produce a buyer willing to sign an intent-to-purchase agreement for the two hundred acres."

Cord rubbed his damp palms over his jeans. There had to be something, anything, to stave off the foreclosure. His gut knotted up. He had nowhere else to go. No other skills with which to earn a living. He was a rancher. He wouldn't change. He couldn't change.

"I have an interested buyer," he blurted out.

An awkward pause ensued.

"Why didn't you mention this earlier?" The skepticism rang out loud and clear.

Drumming his fingers on the large oak desk in his study, he thought of Lexi's offer—the one that left a sour taste in his mouth. Not wanting to give the banker too many details, he said, "I don't know anything about the buyer. My real estate agent just informed me last night. I'm waiting to hear back from him."

"Your agent is…" The sound of shuffling paper filled the silent void. "Ah, here it is, Mr. Forbes. If I were to call him, would he be able to verify what you've told me?"

Cord's jaw clenched until his muscles throbbed. He hated how this woman talked down to him. With great difficulty, he swallowed his indignation.

"Yes, he'll verify it. Does this buy me some time?"

"I'll need to speak to Mr. Forbes."

The woman summarized what they'd already discussed. Cord's thoughts strayed back to another businesswoman—the one with a sweet tooth. He couldn't help but wonder if Lexi would be as difficult to deal with as the woman on the phone. Although after haggling with Lexi over some silly candy bar and then finding out she liked to play hide and seek with the truth, he decided she'd definitely be worse.

Cord gave his word to the banker to be in touch as soon as he got more information about the interested party and hung up. The weight of his hasty agreement weighed on his shoulders like a gigantic boulder, threatening to crush him. How could he have promised the bank a buyer—a buyer whose blue eyes weaved a charming spell over him—a buyer who wanted to destroy his little piece of heaven on earth?

CHAPTER FIVE

The following morning, after assuring her father that she would e-mail him pictures of the ghost town in a day or two, Alexis dressed in a new topaz sundress that stopped a couple of inches above her knees. On her feet, she slipped on a new pair of tooled cowgirl boots. She worried the inside of her lip while trying to decide if she should wear such a casual outfit to conduct business. However, with her luggage still lost, her only options consisted of her dirty suit or the new things she'd picked up at Miss Mabel's Dress Shop and Sam's Hitchin' Post.

She wondered what Cord would think of her makeover. She wasn't so sure what she made of it herself. As she applied a light layer of foundation, she imagined herself as a cowgirl, riding horseback and rounding up a herd of cows. She laughed at the image—executive, up-town-girl goes country chic.

A month ago, the idea simply would not have crossed her mind, but after being here in the Southwest, where the sun warmed her face and the wind combed through her hair, she found herself drawn to this place like a hummingbird to sweet, red nectar.

Oh, who was she kidding? She'd never be a cowgirl. Her life was in a high-rise in downtown Manhattan. She had to think of her father. He'd spent years putting her interests ahead of his own, trying to be the best single parent. He'd planned out her future probably before she'd even been born. Now it was time for her to live up to his expectations by walking the walk and talking the talk.

Her father deserved no less than for her to look after him—starting with finalizing this deal for the land to build their latest resort—the key to saving her father's life's work. She just needed to get through to Cord. Why did he have to be so stubborn? Why couldn't he see reason?

Alexis ran the brush over her hair. Pushing Cord may have worked to gain his chocolate bar, but something told her it wouldn't work in buying his land—especially when he learned she had no intention of buying anything unless the ghost town was part of the package. She should make some sort of friendly gesture to regain her footing with him, but nothing over the top. It had to be something subtle but thoughtful.

She pulled her shoulders back and gave her reflection a nod of approval before heading for the door. The brilliant sunshine blinded her at the exact moment a light bulb went on in her mind. She shielded her eyes with her hand, gaining clarity on her surroundings. In that moment, a plan formed in her mind—a way to sweeten Cord's sour disposition. Chocolate. After all, she owed him some. He surely wouldn't turn away her peace offering.

The Hitchin' Post was only a few blocks down from her motel. In fact, with a limited number of stores, shopping in Whistle Stop could easily be accomplished on foot. However, when the resort was built, the town would flourish with supermarkets, department stores and a business district. The thought of being responsible for recharging the town's economy put the pep back in her step.

But as she stood in the motel's parking lot and looked around, she noted the simplistic charm of Whistle Stop, which would be lost as it modernized.

She could only hope some things about the town didn't change. She liked the friendly smiles and greetings of the citizens and their quaint shops. It gave the place an old-time flavor—an irreplaceable quality.

There had to be a way to balance the revitalization the resort would bring with the down-home ambience. And best of all, the resort would give families the ability to find work without having to move away from home. Not to mention money to fix up the town square. Now to convince Cord that this deal would be a win for everyone—him included.

"Alexis!"

She immediately recognized Mrs. Sanchez's voice calling from behind her. Would it be so wrong to pretend she hadn't heard her? The woman ran the motel's front desk and was nice enough, but she could certainly be long-winded.

"Alexis, wait!"

The manners her father instilled in Alexis as a young child insisted that she turn around. "Good morning, Mrs. Sanchez. Beautiful morning, huh?"

The woman hustled over to her. "Oh. Yes, it is. Just beautiful." She pressed a hand to her chest as though she were out of breath. "I'm so glad I caught up with you."

"Is something wrong?"

"Uh, no. Nothing's wrong. I just thought you might need some directions. We don't want you getting lost."

"Thanks, but I'm good."

Mrs. Sanchez stood before her in a bright green cotton dress with bright yellow flowers dotting it. "Rushing off to the Brazen H?"

Alexis froze. How in the world did she know that? Alexis was certain she hadn't told this woman any of her business, having gotten the feeling from the start that Mrs. Sanchez was "too" interested in her. So where did the woman gather her information?

"Don't look surprised," Mrs. Sanchez said. "Whistle Stop is just a bitty town. Not much happens around here that people don't know about."

Alexis swallowed hard, gripped her car keys and took a step toward her vehicle. "I really do need to go."

"That's why I'm here. You should know..." The woman paused, looking perplexed. "Oh, never mind. It's really none of my business."

Alexis was tempted to let the conversation end there and get on her way, but curiosity gnawed at her. The woman seemed to be a fount of information. What was Mrs. Sanchez dying to tell her?

"If I should know something, I'd appreciate if you'd tell me."

Mrs. Sanchez's gaze met hers. "Well, if you insist."

The woman was simply amazing with how she could twist a situation, but something told Alexis that she didn't mean any harm. In fact, if Alexis were to hazard a guess, she'd say the woman was lonely. One lonely person could easily spot another. Wait, was *she* lonely?

No, she was much too busy to be lonely. But ever since Steven had played on her emotions to get ahead at HSG before taking a job on the West Coast without even consulting her—his fiancée, the woman who was supposed to be part of his future—she'd kept to herself more than normal. She didn't exactly trust herself any longer when it came to judging the character of a person. If Mrs. Sanchez had something to say about Cord, Alexis wanted to hear it.

"Please tell me." Alexis implored the woman with her eyes.

"Well...with you being new to town, you should know that it'd be in your best interests to stay clear of the Brazen H. Cord likes to keep to himself...and it's for the best."

Well, talk about your cryptic messages. Curiosity ate at her to know more. After all, if she had to do business with this man, she needed to know more about him.

"Why is that?"

Mrs. Sanchez shook her head and waved her hand in an innocent way. "I'm not a gossiper. I probably already said more than I should have, but someone needed to warn you to keep your distance from that one. He has a temper. No matter how good-looking he is, he's nothing but trouble."

The woman's warning echoed in Alexis's mind as she stopped briefly at the Hitchin' Post on her way out of town. Was Mrs. Sanchez right? Somehow, the woman's description of Cord didn't fit with what she'd witnessed of him. She continued mulling it over as she maneuvered her rental vehicle along the two-lane highway. Soon, the telephone poles and the occasional gravel driveways were the only evidence of development. The farther she drove, the greater the distance between any signs of civilization and the closer she came to facing down the cowboy—the man who could make her life easy or hard. She got the distinct impression he never did things the easy way.

But could Cord spell trouble for her? She hadn't witnessed any hint of a mean streak in him. Sure, he could be stubborn, but he could also be kind. She recalled the way his hand had wrapped around hers. His gentle touch had soothed her raw nerves as she got to know Midnight Star. A man with the ability to put both human and animal at ease was not a troublesome person—more like misunderstood. Obviously, Mrs. Sanchez had latched on to some bad information.

Cord was a good guy, but there was obviously a lot more to him than anyone knew. What was he holding back? And why did the town have the wrong idea about him?

♥♥♥

Cord led Blaze, a chestnut mare, to the barn. He'd spent the early part of the morning out on the range, inspecting the new stretch of fencing being installed on the eastern border. Now that he had an interested buyer, blocking off the designated sale property had become a priority.

After he'd tended to Blaze and set the horse free in the corral, he started for the house. His thoughts circled back around to the blonde who'd been dogging his thoughts all morning. He didn't like that she'd befriended him without bothering to disclose the fact that she was a developer. He took the porch steps two at a time. Still, he should have handled the news better, but he couldn't shake the feeling that she was trying to pull something over on him, just like his ex had.

He'd been young and naïve when he'd met Susan. Looking back now, he hardly recognized the person he used to be. He'd done a lot of growing up since then. He wouldn't be deceived again. But he also couldn't afford to run off the one person who was offering him an out with the bank. He promised himself that if Lexi kept her word and returned, he'd hear her out.

At the doorway, he paused. He stared up the lane that led to the main road, willing her to turn into his drive. Yet there were no swirls of dust. No crunch of gravel. Absolutely no sign of her.

Maybe he should make his way into town. The thought made his body tense. He envisioned the puzzled stares and the hand-over-mouth whispers. No. He wasn't going. He moseyed into Whistle Stop only when he absolutely had to for business. Ever since Hurricane Susan, it was easier to keep to himself. Besides, if Lexi was serious about purchasing the land, she'd be back.

His lips pressed together in a firm line as his jaw tightened, and he subdued his lingering urge to see her. Maybe in this one instance he should make an exception and drive into town. After all, his entire future was on the line. What were a few more people gawking at him, trying to figure out if Susan's lies were true or not? He expelled a frustrated sigh and stomped inside, yanking off his T-shirt in the entryway. Nothing about this situation was going to be easy.

Some twenty-odd minutes later, he exited the house in a fresh pair of jeans and a clean shirt. He ran a hand over his damp hair before settling his hat snugly on his head. With his decision made, his boots thumped against each wooden porch step. His chest tightened. What in the world was he going to say to Lexi?

The hum of an engine and the crunch of stones being ground into the dirt drew his attention. Through the cloud of dust, he recognized Lexi's tan SUV. He caught himself sighing in relief. This wasn't going to be as hard as he'd imagined.

The vehicle pulled to a stop in front of the steps. Lexi jumped out and peered up at him through her dark sunglasses. "Hi. Are you on your way out?"

His gaze skimmed over the beautiful slip of a dress that revealed her bare shoulders. She looked different— way different. This casual outfit made her appear more approachable, more attainable. He swallowed the newly formed lump in his throat, but when he went to speak, the words utterly failed him. His gaze skimmed over the dipping neckline that showed off her creamy white cleavage.

Not wanting to be accused of staring, he forced his gaze back to her sunglasses. On second thought, her boring business suit wasn't so bad after all. At least with it he was able to keep his thoughts straight. With her dressed in this flirty little outfit, business was the last thing on his mind.

"Cord, are you listening?"

"Uh...no, I mean, I'm not going anywhere. We can talk."

"Are you sure?"

He nodded. "I was actually on my way into town...to find you."

Her eyes widened. "Me." Her pink lips lifted at the corners, making him wish their circumstances were different. "Does this mean you've changed your mind and are ready to sell me the land?"

"Possibly."

"Great. Now before I forget, I have something for you." Lexi reached into her pocket. When she withdrew her hand, her fingers obscured the object. "Here."

She reached out to him. Her fingers brushed over his. The heat of her touch caused his breath to catch in his throat. His fingers instinctively closed over hers. Her gaze met his and locked. His heart pounded in his chest. He assured himself that this strong reaction was due to his long dry spell when it came to female companionship. Yet, he couldn't break the connection. His thumb stroked the silkiness of her wrist.

All too soon, she pulled away, jarring him back to reality. *Keep it together, Cord. She's just passing through town. She'll be gone soon.*

"Aren't you even going to see what it is?"

He gazed down at the familiar brown wrapper. He couldn't remember the last time someone had made the effort to give him a present—even something as small as a bit of candy. The gesture warmed a spot in his chest.

"What's this for?" His voice came out thicker than normal.

"Consider it a peace offering." Her lips lifted into a cautious smile.

"A peace offering?"

"I was hoping we could start over."

Guilt gnawed at him. He had been a bit abrupt with her. But even now his gut was telling him that she was holding back something big. He needed to move cautiously with her. Still, he needed to make an effort to smooth things out between them if they were going to talk business.

Still, apologizing wasn't something he did often. His palms grew damp. He'd rather eat his hat than grovel, but his entire future rested on him making peace with her.

He sucked in a deep breath and exhaled. *Okay. Here it goes.*

"I'm sorry for yesterday." He forced his gaze to meet hers. "I'd like to start over—"

"I'm glad to hear you say that." She smiled, easing his tense muscles. "Guess I didn't need to come bearing gifts after all."

He waved the chocolate bar in front of her. "Already changing your mind about parting with this?"

"Nope." She sent him an ornery grin, reached inside her small black purse, and pulled out another candy bar. "I got myself one, too. So you're safe to eat yours."

He couldn't help but chuckle. The tension in his shoulders eased. He felt lighter than he had in months.

"Now that you're smiling," she dropped the chocolate back into her purse, "how about we talk a little business?"

Though he'd meant his apology, questions continued to poke and prod him. He'd learned to trust his instincts when he was young, and they had rarely let him down. Right now, they were sounding off loud and clear. He didn't trust Lexi, no matter how inviting her smile might be.

"Even though you've traded in your suit for something more…casual, you're still the diligent businesswoman at heart. Before we talk business, I have a couple of questions. Like, why fly all the way across the country to build a bunch of five-and-ten-acre ranches?" The way she glanced away, refusing to meet his gaze, reinforced his suspicion of her. "Or is there more to this deal than you've let on?"

Her forehead creased as though she were giving her answer considerable thought. Why would an honest response take so much effort? With each passing moment of silence, his gut tightened.

"I need to be straight with you." Lexi's steady gaze met his. "I'm hoping you'll be able to listen with an open mind."

An open mind? His insides churned. Wherever she was leading him, he didn't want to go. He was just beginning to appreciate the thought that a ranching community would try to maintain as much of the natural landscape as possible. But suddenly he got the feeling that wasn't what she intended to do with the land.

The tip of her tongue moistened her lips. "The truth is...in order for me to be able to make you a formal offer on the land, I need something from you."

"Stop with the theatrics and spit it out. What do you want?"

"Haggerty."

The word exploded in his mind, scattering his thoughts in a million directions. She wanted his town—his heritage. She'd had this one goal all along—to buy the ghost town. His initial reaction was to tell her she didn't have an icicle's chance in hell of getting it, but logic kept him quiet.

He remembered Mr. Forbes assuring him that the error on the sales listing had been worked out, but clearly that wasn't the case. Whether Cord liked it or not, she was his only chance to save this ranch. This time he needed to handle things differently from yesterday.

She stood unmoving, waiting for his response. The confidence in her stance—her unflinching eyes—said she thought she had him cornered. Not a good place to be. The one thing she must not have taken into consideration, though, was when an animal was cornered, was when they were the most dangerous. They had nothing to lose.

Cord crossed his arms and rocked back on the heels of his boots. "I was right about you. All of this friendliness was just a ploy. You wanted to sweet-talk me into a deal."

Lexi's face lit up with color. "Do you honestly think I'm so desperate to finalize this sale that I'd lead you on? Sure, we may have laughed a little, but it was all innocent and went both ways. It isn't like we've started negotiations—"

"You let me go on believing that you wanted the two hundred acres for a small ranching community. You made it sound like all I had to do was sign on the dotted line. You never even hinted that your offer came with strings attached."

Her mouth gaped open, but she snapped it shut.

"How long are you going to wait to tell me your real intentions for the land?"

"I'm not required to tell you." Her fine brows drew together as she frowned at him. "HSG waits for the ideal moment before revealing our plans for any land we acquire."

He pointed an accusing finger at her. "You admit it. You and your company are deceptive."

She shook her head, brushing her short blond hair over her shoulders. "No, we're not. I'm not. I would have explained everything yesterday, but you started throwing around accusations. You weren't in any frame of mind to take a proposal seriously."

His jaw tightened. She was right. He had let his temper get the best of him, but he wouldn't make that same mistake today. There had to be a way to get her to agree to buy the two hundred acres without the ghost town.

Giving up Haggerty wouldn't just be about losing a huge part of his heritage—he'd also lose a lot of valuable grazing land. His ranch would shrink considerably—his only source of income. A vise-like grip tightened around his rib cage. And then a thought came to mind—maybe he could work out something with her so he could retain grazing rights.

"I'm listening," he said, straining to keep his voice neutral, hoping they could reach some sort of compromise. "Tell me what you have in mind for Haggerty."

"While I'm not obligated to tell you, I will because I know how important the land is to you." Lexi tilted up her chin as her unwavering gaze met his. "HSG is in the business of building exclusive resorts. We believe the genuine ghost town will be a great marketing tool."

He stepped back, shaking his head in disbelief. "You want to turn my ancestors' land into some kind of amusement attraction?"

"I'm sure this idea will take some getting used to—" Her cell phone buzzed, and she took a moment to silence it. "That was a reminder that I have a meeting to attend."

"About my family's land, I presume."

She nodded. "I have to go. Don't make any rash decisions. I will contact you later to discuss this further."

Cord drew back his shoulders. "You're really serious about building a resort here? In the middle of nowhere?"

"Think of it as a win-win situation. You get to keep your ranch. And Whistle Stop gets a big boom in its economy." She started for her vehicle.

"And you get to build your money-making resort on my family's land."

She paused and turned back. "I understand you'll need some time to think things through. Right now, I'm due at a meeting with some county and state officials. It's probably going to take most of the day. I just stopped by because I wanted to straighten out this misunderstanding over the land. I'm sorry if I gave you the wrong impression."

At last, an apology. "Fine. I'll think it over, but I'm not promising anything."

She smiled, and her face lit up. "Fair enough. Before we talk again, I'd like to see the land in person."

"I don't think so." He hadn't even agreed to the sale. He needed time to think through it all.

"Photographs just aren't the same. Especially when it comes to the ghost town." She slid on sunglasses, hiding her expressive eyes. "How about I meet you here? Say, eight o'clock tomorrow morning? You can give me a personal tour of the ghost town."

Traipsing around the countryside with a land developer who held the power to save his little piece of the world was one thing, but spending the day with a woman who warmed his blood with just a smile was quite another. And this out-of-town, hotshot businesswoman was definitely the wrong female to let his guard down around.

"I've got to work in the morning."

"Then how about after lunch?"

"More work then, too."

"Fine. I'll go by myself."

"If you do, it'll be trespassing. And you should consider that an inexperienced person going out into the desert alone is a recipe for disaster. The desert can be harsh and unforgiving."

Her phone buzzed again. "I'm going to be late." She pulled out some folded papers and handed them to him. "Read these over and come up with a reasonable price for the ghost town. We can sort out the details later."

He glanced down at the papers, not relishing the time and effort it'd take him to read them. "I haven't agreed to any of this—"

"Not yet."

CHAPTER SIX

The jangle of the phone stirred Cord from his deliberations. He didn't move. With his dinner long cold, he continued staring out the kitchen window. The sun's lingering golden rays washed over the vast land he loved, like a final kiss.

All day while he'd tended the livestock and then updated the ranch's financial spreadsheets, he'd struggled to think up a way to stave off the bank—a way that did not include selling out to the determined lady developer with those hauntingly beautiful blue eyes. All he'd gained for his efforts was an incessant pounding in his temples.

At last, silence descended over the room, but before he could breathe a sigh of relief, the blasted telephone started up again. He smacked the glass tabletop and shoved his chair back, ignoring the protesting screech against the tile floor. Time to rid himself of this persistent caller.

He grabbed the receiver but before he could utter a word, he head, "Cord, it's Peter Forbes. I'm not disturbing you, am I?"

"Actually, I was just sitting down—"

"This won't take long," the man rambled on. "I thought I might hear from you today."

"Why? Is there another offer on the land?" His hand clenched the phone. He willed his real estate agent to say yes.

"No."

Cord's pent-up breath blew out in a sigh. "Then why would we talk?"

"The woman, Alexis Greer, she stopped by the office today. She wanted some more information about the land—"

"Did you make it clear to her that it's just the two hundred acres that are for sale?"

"Actually, she was telling me about her plans for Haggerty. In fact, she showed me the plans—you know, for the resort. They're quite impressive."

Was Lexi starting some sort of crusade to turn the town against him? His ex-wife had tried swaying him with public pressure—twisting his arm to sell the ranch. She'd painted such an awful picture of him that it'd been hard to brush off the whispers and stares when he ventured into town for supplies. He wouldn't stand for Lexi making matters worse for him.

After a moment of silence, Mr. Forbes cleared his throat and hurried on. "Have you taken time to consider her proposal? She has some good ideas that would bring some much needed tourist dollars to town. If it all worked out, it'd solve everyone's problems."

Everyone's problems but his. Cord's jaw tensed, holding back a burning retort.

"Think about it." Mr. Forbes cleared his throat. "This resort would give people job opportunities, and the economy would grow. And best of all, your ranch would be free of debt."

How was Cord supposed to argue with logic like that? No matter what he said, he'd sound like the bad guy. No one understood his desperate need to cling to the land where he was a confident rancher—where he didn't have to work to hide his dyslexia on a regular basis. On the Brazen H, he could just be himself.

Cord paced back and forth across the tiled floor. "She'll have to build the resort somewhere else. I can't sell her Haggerty."

"Before you turn her down, you might want to hear what she's proposing. The town really needs the jobs. It would keep the young people from leaving town in search of work. People would be excited—"

"Public pressure won't sway me."

Why was Mr. Forbes trying to make him responsible for the town's welfare? It wasn't like he was the town's mayor. He wouldn't stand a chance of even being elected dogcatcher. Not that he let it bother him. He got by just fine keeping to himself.

Then a legitimate thought occurred to him. "Did you ever stop to consider the resort's employees might not be locals? They could hire anyone, people from as far away as...New York."

"Guess you have a point." A defeated tone filled the man's voice. "Perhaps you should find out more about this resort before you sell to her. You'll talk to her, right? For the town's sake?"

A protest hung in the back of Cord's throat, but instead he said, "I'll listen to what she has to say, but that's all I'm promising."

"You know by bringing jobs to Whistle Stop, it might undo some of the hard feelings people have been harboring for so long."

"Their attitudes are their problem. Not mine." Cord ended the call.

He refused to be held responsible for solving Whistle Stop's struggling economy. He was already failing at the responsibility he'd inherited—saving Haggerty. And time was running out until foreclosure.

His thoughts turned back to Lexi. She had more spunk than he'd originally given her credit for. He regretted that they were on opposite sides of this fight, because he found her gorgeous, strong-willed, and fiercely   independent.   Quite   an   intoxicating combination.

And if he wasn't careful, she could end up walking away with his legacy.

♥♥♥

After an early morning phone call about her missing luggage, Alexis made her way to the front desk. Mrs. Sanchez glanced up from reading a glossy magazine. Her heavily made-up eyes gazed over the black rims of her reading glasses as she smiled.

"Good morning. My, don't you look like you're ready for an adventure?"

"Your suggestion of where to find some clothes to tide me over until my luggage shows up was very helpful. Thank you."

"Any time, dear." Mrs. Sanchez laid the magazine on the counter. "You'll find that Whistle Stop doesn't have all the amenities of New York City, but it makes up for it with a friendly community spirit."

"I've noticed. Everyone has been so nice and helpful. I could get used to this." And she meant every word of it.

Mrs. Sanchez's eyes widened. "Are you considering buying the Lawson land?"

Alexis hesitated. Mrs. Sanchez was friendly, but she was also very astute. Alexis didn't want to give away her plans before she was ready. But she wasn't about to outright lie—that wasn't her style.

"Actually, I am considering it. From what I've seen so far, the Southwest is beautiful."

Mrs. Sanchez beamed as though Alexis had directly complimented her. "It really does have its charms. And we'd love to have you as a resident of Whistle Stop. I'll have to introduce you to the girls in town. Let's see, there's Ana, the girl who owns the Green Chile Cantina. She's about your age." Mrs. Sanchez placed a red-painted fingernail against her chin as she got lost in thought.

"Thanks. But you don't have to bother." Alexis didn't want the whole town to get the wrong impression.

"Why in the world not?" The woman gave her the strangest look. "If you're shy, don't worry. Everyone will make you feel welcome—"

"No, it's not that. It's just that—well, nothing is definite."

"Oh. I understand. I won't say a word until the deal is official. The holdup, it's Cord, isn't it? Is he being disagreeable?"

Now she was the one who was confused. "What?"

Mrs. Sanchez frowned. "He's the reason you haven't bought the land."

What exactly did this woman know? Something told Alexis that it was more than she was letting on. She was certain that Cord wouldn't have said anything to her, but that didn't mean Cord's Realtor hadn't let something slip after she'd run her idea for the resort past him to get an idea if the town would support her plan. Mr. Forbes definitely thought that would be the case. She sure hoped he was right.

"Cord and I are talking, but nothing is definite."

Mrs. Sanchez leaned back on the stool that sat behind the counter. Her eyes glittered as though she were about to burst if she didn't share a secret. "I have it from a very good source that he isn't the easiest man to deal with. It's been said that he's unreasonable and has a temper with a short fuse."

"Cord? Really?" Alexis felt compelled to come to the man's defense. Just because he didn't want to sell his land to a developer didn't mean he was a bad man. "That's surprising. I've found him to be quite the opposite."

"Really?" Mrs. Sanchez leaned forward on the counter as though they were about to share a confidence, even though they were the only two in the office. "He's not mean or rude?"

"He's been a perfect gentleman to me. In fact, he's been quite friendly." She thought of the way he'd taken the time to show her his horse and to get her something to drink. "Whoever told you that about Cord was wrong."

"Perhaps." Mrs. Sanchez's forehead wrinkled as though she carefully considered Alexis's words. "Perhaps. So you like him?"

Something told Alexis no matter what she said now, this conversation would be around town in no time. But if she could help Cord, why not do it? It wasn't like she'd be here much longer.

"I think he's a very nice man who enjoys his privacy."

"Interesting." Looking into the woman's eyes, Alexis could practically see the wheels of her mind spinning. "Very interesting."

"It can be easy to misjudge a person. Maybe people should give him another chance."

Mrs. Sanchez's penciled brows rose. "You two must be hitting it off. Hopefully, he won't hold out on selling you the land. Seems as though this might just be the perfect match."

Alexis wasn't sure how to take her last comment. But the little voice in her head told her to just let it go. This conversation had the potential to go in the completely wrong direction. And the last thing she needed was Mrs. Sanchez playing matchmaker. After all, Alexis might find Cord amazingly attractive, but they were business adversaries. Anything beyond business negotiations was off-limits.

Anxious to wrap up this conversation, Alexis said, "I just stopped by to let you know that I spoke with the airline, and they should be dropping off my suitcase later today."

"Thank goodness they found it. I'll make sure and put it in your room when it arrives. Can I do anything else for you?"

She smiled, liking Mrs. Sanchez. The woman was the curious sort, but she had a good heart. "Actually, there is one other thing. Do you know where I can find the mayor?"

"Why certainly, dear. In fact, why don't I take you to see Mayor Ortiz?"

Alexis hadn't planned to talk to him just yet. She'd intended to make Haggerty her first stop of the day. She was eager to see her very first genuine ghost town. And now that she'd bought the right clothing and necessary supplies with the help of Sam at the Hitchin' Post, she was ready to go.

"Thanks, but I know you have work to do here." Though Alexis didn't have a clue what that work might consist of since she appeared to be the motel's only guest. "If you can just point me in the right direction, I'll find my way."

"Nonsense. I could use a mid-morning coffee."

Alexis couldn't think of a tactful way to tell the woman that she didn't want her overhearing her conversation with the mayor. And since the woman hadn't volunteered the mayor's location, Alexis didn't have much choice but to smile and follow her. As Mrs. Sanchez rounded the counter, Alexis took in her black dress with big fuchsia flowers. The woman was nothing if not flamboyant. She flipped a sign on the door so that it read: Be Back Soon.

As they walked along the sidewalk, everyone smiled and greeted them. A few times, Mrs. Sanchez stopped to hear a bit of news. Other times, she'd pause to share what she'd learned with others. Texting and instant messaging had nothing over these ladies. They were quite efficient and definitely stayed on top of everything that happened in town.

"It's a shame there's so many empty storefronts," Alexis said as they walked along Grande Avenue.

"Whistle Stop wasn't always like this. When I was a kid, this town was booming. There was a copper mine that kept the town thriving. When it closed up, people started to move away."

"That happens a lot with small towns. They lose their main employer and die out."

"It'd be great to see it grow again. I just wish Mayor Ortiz hadn't given up on the town. That man and his cronies that sit on the town council seem to have made peace with just letting Whistle Stop languish a slow death." Mrs. Sanchez shook as though she'd just had a sudden chill. "It just gives me the willies thinking of the town I grew up in turning into a ghost town like Haggerty."

Alexis didn't like the idea either. "I wouldn't give up yet. From what I've seen so far, this town has a lot of heart. It just needs a push in the right direction."

Mrs. Sanchez slanted her a suspicious gaze. "Do you have something in mind?"

Great. She'd said too much, and now she had to backpedal out of it. "No, nothing specific. It just sounds like whatever the town council has tried so far hasn't worked, and they'll have to try something different."

"Hmpf...that would mean they'd have to get off their duffs and get back to work." Mrs. Sanchez leaned closer. "This is all just between us girls. I wouldn't want it getting around."

"Of course not." Alexis bit back a laugh at the hypocrisy. "I won't say a word."

"What business did you say you're in?"

All Alexis wanted now was for the sidewalk to open up and swallow her. She could see why Mrs. Sanchez seemed to know everything that was going on in

Whistle Stop. She was exceedingly good at pulling information out of people. And now what did she tell the woman? The truth?

"Good morning." An older gentleman strolled up the walk in the opposite direction.

"We were just looking for you, Mayor."

Thank goodness for the interruption. Now it was time to get to work. Alexis just hoped her plan would work. Because she wasn't getting far with Cord.

"You were looking for me?" The man with thick, wavy silver hair and a friendly smile stopped in front of them. "I'm such a lucky man to have two lovely ladies looking for me. What can I do for you both?"

"Let me introduce Alexis Greer. She's visiting us from New York City. And she's interested in the Lawson land." Mrs. Sanchez lowered her voice. "I'm guessing that Cord isn't being reasonable and she may need your help."

"Is that so?" The man's blue eyes turned to Alexis with much interest. "I'm always happy to help out. I was just stopping by Tilly's Café for a cup of coffee. Would you care to join me?"

"I'd love to." Alexis was never one to pass up coffee. And since her meeting with the county and state officials had gone quite well, it was time to get the local community on board with her plans. "I'd like to discuss the future of Whistle Stop with you."

The mayor's bushy brows rose. "You will have my full attention." He pulled open the turquoise-painted, intricately carved door for her. "Shall we go inside?"

Alexis thanked the man as she passed by him. She noticed that Mrs. Sanchez was hot on her heels. This meant everything said in the meeting would spread around Whistle Stop faster than an express train. She would have to be extremely tactful.

Although if she worked this meeting just right, it might be what her plan needed to be a success. Alexis smiled. Her father wasn't the only one who could think fast to salvage a deal.

CHAPTER SEVEN

Cord gripped a large coffee mug in his hand as he stepped onto the porch. It was mid-morning, but he still couldn't seem to wake up. Nor could he sleep for worrying. He rested the cup of steamy and strong black brew on the white wood railing before stretching his tight muscles. There had to be a solution, a way to pay off the loan without selling out.

He yanked the papers Lexi had left him from his back pocket and unfolded them. At first glance, the words looked like gibberish. A groan started to form deep in his throat. He swallowed it down. He could do this. He just needed to take his time and focus like his mother had taught him all of those years ago when she'd patiently helped him with his studies.

With considerable effort, he saw the print on the page form words. He'd been struggling with this his whole life. He'd always been the last to finish school assignments, and the other kids had made fun of him for reading slowly or mispronouncing a word. Against his mother's wishes, he'd finally dropped out to help his father around the ranch—the only person to truly understand what Cord had to deal with day in and out. His father had the same disorder and insisted reading wasn't all it was cracked up to be.

Cord's mother had vehemently disagreed with her husband and refused to let Cord give up. Each evening after chores were done, she'd work with him to learn how to cope with his severe dyslexia. Thanks to her love and determination, he'd earned his GED and could read when necessary. It was necessary now.

He'd made it through the first paragraph of Lexi's legal document when the drone of an engine caught his attention. Expecting to find Lexi, he got to his feet. He straightened to his full height and pulled his shoulders back, ready to do business. It was time they got a few things straightened out. His gaze focused on an old but familiar pickup, definitely not Lexi's late-model SUV. His shoulders sagged. What in the world had gotten into him? Since when did he sit around waiting for a woman?

Manny, his foreman, pulled to a stop in front of the porch, turned down a Johnny Cash tune and leaned an elbow out the window. "Hey, boss. I thought you were checking on the herd."

"Getting some coffee first." Cord rested his elbows on the rail. "The new guy, Jesse, how's he doing?"

Manny's tanned face crinkled with confusion. "Thought you'd be asking about the new woman in town."

His neck tensed. "Why? What should I know?"

"She stopped me when I was at the end of the drive, grabbing the mail." Manny held out a hefty stack of bills. "She wanted some information."

"Get to the point." Cord stomped down the steps and accepted the various envelopes. "What did she want?"

"Directions to Haggerty."

Alarm flooded Cord's system, sending his pulse racing and chasing away any lingering tiredness. "I take it she's going alone?"

Manny pulled off his straw cowboy hat and ran a red bandanna over his forehead. "Sure seemed like it. I told her not to go, that it was dangerous, but she ignored me."

"That woman's nothing but trouble." Cord's fingers clenched, crinkling the mail.

Did she expect to reach Haggerty on her own? The ghost town sat in the middle of a desert mesa. There were no roads leading the way and certainly no signs to guide her. His gut knotted. If she ran out of gas or, worse, got lost, the consequences could be dire.

"Well, boss," Manny settled his hat back on his head, "what're you gonna do?"

"Me? Why should I do anything? If that woman is brazen enough to trespass and go hiking alone in the middle of nowhere, she has no one to blame for what happens but herself."

His speech sounded good, but it did nothing to calm the unease he had over her safety. He'd warned her not to go out there alone. Manny had told her not to go. Why should he have to forfeit his morning to go rescue her from her own stupidity?

Manny sighed and shook his head. "I just keep thinkin' 'bout those inexperienced hikers that nearly died last summer out in Red Devil Canyon."

His foreman had a valid point, but Cord wasn't her designated babysitter. She was a big girl. "I'm not responsible for her."

Manny didn't say a word. He just adjusted his hat and averted his gaze.

The nagging worry that something bad could happen to her ate at Cord's gut. Even a frustrating, pushy businesswoman didn't deserve to be lost in the desert. "How long ago did you see her?"

"Just a few minutes ago. She can't have gotten far."

Cord turned to head up the steps.

"You goin' after her?" Manny called out.

Cord nodded but kept moving.

"You want me to go with you?"

Cord paused and turned. "You can help me out by handling any problems that crop up here."

Manny gave him a two-finger salute. "Will do, boss."

Cord checked his wristwatch. Not quite nine. "I'll be back by lunch, at the latest."

"Good luck."

Lexi was the one who needed the luck. His back teeth ground together as he thought of the naïve woman out there on her own. Out in the harsh terrain, Mother Nature didn't take pity on anyone, especially the inexperienced.

♥♥♥

Where was it?

Alexis pulled her SUV to a stop at the edge of a dry gulch and ran the back of her arm across her forehead. The ghost town shouldn't be much farther. She'd been following a map and directions jotted out by one of Cord's men, but this obstacle wasn't mentioned on either document.

She got out and examined the drop-off. It didn't look so bad up close. If she went real slow, she shouldn't have a problem. Acres and acres of desert grass stretched out for miles in every direction. Sagebrush dotted it in a haphazard fashion. Cracks in the hardened soil crisscrossed and snaked their way into the distance. It'd definitely been awhile since this place had seen rain. She glanced up at the big blue sky, unable to find one single cloud anywhere in the heavens.

Suddenly, she knew what she'd forgotten— sunscreen. Too late to go back for it now. At least she'd remembered to throw on a lightweight long-sleeved top. It'd give her a little protection on her arms. Her jeans and boots would take care of her lower limbs. That left her face and neck exposed. She'd take her chances.

The only thing that would make the trip any better was if she could share this magnificent view with someone. Cord's handsome face sprang to mind. Why she thought of him was beyond her. He'd no sooner join her for this adventure than he would trade in his faded jeans for a business suit.

Ready to move on, she glanced around one more time and spotted a dark speck far off in the distance. The breeze kicked up, swirling a cloud of dirt and obscuring her vision. She turned her head and shielded her mouth and nose with her shirt sleeve.

The wind eased up, allowing her to turn and scan the terrain. This time the speck was more of a dot and seemed to be heading for her. A vehicle? Out here?

She waited. Curious.

In no time, a pickup pulled to a stop next to her. Cord jumped out. His brows were drawn together into a formidable line. His dark eyes left no doubt about his agitation. If she hadn't known better, she would have said he'd followed her out here because he was worried about her.

"Are you out of your mind?" His voice rumbled.

She straightened her shoulders. "Hello to you, too."

"What are you doing out here alone? If something had happened, no one would have known where to find you."

Had she been right? Was he truly worried about her? Impossible. Right now, he looked like he was about to throttle her. "I wasn't aware you cared so much."

"I don't." Anger flared in his eyes. "When we get back to town, I intend to have you arrested for trespassing."

Her mouth gaped. "You wouldn't."

"How much do you want to wager?"

"This isn't funny." She glared at him.

"You're right, it isn't. You intentionally broke the law. Once I turn you in, the case will be open and shut."

Worried he just might be serious, she flashed him her biggest and brightest smile, hoping it would thaw his frosty attitude. "Come on. Just forget you found me. I'll have a quick look-see and leave. No harm, no foul."

"I don't think so. Last summer, a couple of tourists decided to hike around a remote canyon south of here. I'm sure they thought nothing would happen either." He drew in an uneven breath. "Then one fell and the other hiker went for help, but he got lost. I was one of the volunteers on the search party that spent hours looking for them."

"What happened?"

"They survived, but it could have easily gone the other way."

She refused to be deterred. "Does this stern warning mean you'll accompany me?"

"It means I'll show you the way back to town— straight to the sheriff's office."

She crossed her arms, feet planted in the dirt. "I've come this far, and I'm not turning back until I've seen Haggerty."

Cord's lips pressed together in a firm line as his gaze narrowed. "It'd serve you right if I tossed you over my shoulder and threw you in the back of my pickup."

His words conjured up images. His hands on her. Their bodies rubbing against each other. His breath mingled with hers. His lips hovered over hers.

"What are you smiling about?"

His voice snapped her out of her daydream. She hadn't realized her thoughts had been translated onto her face. She'd have to be more careful in the future— especially around this sexy cowboy.

"Not a thing." She settled her hands on her hips. "Now wouldn't it be easier to satisfy my curiosity?"

"I'm quickly learning that nothing about you is easy." His unrelenting stare held hers as though he contemplated his options. "Why in the world would I help you after you've started a public campaign against me?"

"I did what?"

He shook his head. "Don't try the innocent act. I know for a fact you've been going around telling the whole town that I'm standing between them and economic prosperity."

She saw a flicker of pain in his dark eyes, but in a blink, it was gone. Had she imagined it? No. Impossible. But then again, could it have something to do with the warnings she'd received about him? Did he have any idea what some of them were saying behind his back? She sure hoped not. He might be a bit blustery at times, but she'd seen the other side of him— the kind, gentle side. She longed to see more of that.

She tilted her chin upward. "I may have spoken to some people about my proposal, but by no means did I speak with the whole town."

His weight shifted from one foot to the other. "You obviously don't know much about small towns. You only have to tell one person or be overheard and the gossip mill is fired up."

Tired of being on the defensive, she decided to turn the conversation around. "And why should that bother you? Afraid of a little public pressure?"

His brows drew together as storm clouds gathered in his eyes. "If you want to do business with me, speak to me. Don't drag outsiders into it. Understand?"

And yet another man dictating terms to her. It jangled her nerves. "I'll do whatever I need to do to conclude my business here. The sooner you agree to sell Haggerty, the sooner I'll head back to New York and get out of your way."

"It might just be worth selling." Though he'd been muttering under his breath, she'd caught every syllable.

The thought that he wanted her gone that badly pricked a spot in her chest. She may be a businesswoman on the outside, but on the inside, where no one could see, she wanted to be liked just like any other woman. She'd been kicked aside and forgotten enough in her life. First by her mother and then her fiancé. The backs of her eyes stung. She blinked repeatedly.

Refusing to let him know his words had hurt her, she kept her voice even and calm. "Are you offering to give me the grand tour? Or shall I continue on my own?"

He eyed her up as though deciding if she were serious. "You certainly can't be trusted to be left alone."

"I'll take that as your offer to show me around."

He sighed. "I'll lead in my vehicle. You can follow in yours."

Alexis didn't care how she got to the ghost town as long as she had a chance to do some exploring and make certain it suited HSG's purposes. She also had to snap some pictures to send to her father. The unexpected bonus of having Cord as her guide would only add to the experience—if his mood lightened.

Maybe she had come on a little strong. Maybe she needed to back off a little. Showing him a little more sweetness might help. In fact, maybe this little sightseeing trip would be a chance to move past their business relationship to a more personal level.

"Ready to go?" She took a step toward her vehicle.

"I don't know what you think you're going to find there. This ghost town is most likely not what you're imagining. There aren't any saloons with ghosts hanging around the bar, ordering another round of tequila. No skeletons dancing atop the player piano."

She laughed. "So this isn't going to be a spin-off of some sitcom?"

The corners of his mouth lifted a little. "No, and don't expect some bearded prospector in overalls to pop out of the woodwork and lock you up."

"That's reassuring."

"We better get moving."

They climbed into their respective vehicles. Her foot hovered over the brake, tapping it now and then as the SUV dipped down the side of the arroyo. Stones ricocheted off the undercarriage as the vehicle crept forward. The uneven ground jostled her back and forth in her seat. The rift wasn't too wide, and soon they rolled up the other side.

Less than ten minutes later, a rocky outcrop jutting out from the earth came into view. Cord's brake lights flashed on. She pulled up beside his truck and got out.

"We're here." He waved his hand around. "This is Haggerty."

"It certainly is a long way off the beaten path." She gazed at the remnants of Haggerty, awed by its rustic charm. It was like stepping out of a time machine. If she closed her eyes, she could imagine the clomping sound of horse hooves and piano music from the saloon.

"More than a century ago, settlers moved here for the promise of a new start. While they waited for the railroad to be built, scarce amounts of supplies were brought in by wagon. When they relocated the proposed rail line, people followed the train to Whistle Stop. Eventually, my great-great-grandfather was left with nothing but dry scrub weed and an empty town."

"Sounds sad." Thinking of the neglected town square, she hoped Whistle Stop wasn't heading for the same fate.

"There's folklore linked to the town. Would you like to hear some of it?"

What she really wanted to learn more about was him and why he let the townsfolk believe he was some sort of monster, when in fact she'd found him utterly captivating, even if he could be quite stubborn. Instead of caving in to her mounting curiosity and plying him with a bunch of nosy questions, she said, "I'd love to hear some."

He led her a short distance to a wall of rock. The opening to the mine was boarded up with weathered wood planks. A big Keep Out sign was nailed in the center. "Legend says many years ago, a young couple desperately in love wanted to marry, but the bride's family didn't approve of the match—"

"This is great." Alexis smiled and pressed a hand to her chest. "Everyone loves a tragic love story. It'll tug at the hearts of female visitors."

Cord frowned. "I'm not telling you this for you to plan out some promotional campaign—"

"Oh. I know." She didn't want to start another heated discussion with him. "Please tell me more of the story."

He cast her a doubtful look. Did he have any clue that he looked more cute and ornery than intimidating? In fact, she found him more attractive than she should.

Not about to let her thoughts dwell on his mesmerizing eyes or the bit of scruff trailing down his chiseled jaw that led to his inviting lips, she said, "I'll be quiet. I promise."

He cleared his throat. "The young man moved here, planning to strike it big in the mines. He needed to prove his worthiness in order to marry his true love. Months went by, and at last he'd saved up enough money to send for her. The day before she arrived, a cave-in at the mine buried an entire crew of men, leaving behind heartbroken widows and fatherless children."

Something told Alexis this part of the story was true, that this town had lost miners—husbands—and fathers. Her heart ached for the townspeople. She knew all too well about loss.

Cord crossed his arms and rocked back on his heels. "When the young woman stepped off the stagecoach, she was devastated by the news. Having turned against her family's wishes, she couldn't return home. Alone in a new town with not much more than her wedding dress and a broken heart, she refused to give up hope that her true love would find his way back to her."

A faraway glint in Cord's eyes had her wondering if he, too, had had an unfortunate romance. And did it have anything to do with the town's animosity? The uncomfortable thought caught her off guard. She told herself Cord's personal life was none of her business. She needed to keep her thoughts on the business at hand, and right now that included a history lesson about Haggerty.

Alexis enjoyed listening to the soothing tones of Cord's voice. "Is there more?"

He nodded. "The young woman returned here every day, waiting for her betrothed to find his way back to her. It's believed that on a full moon, you can see her pacing in front of the mine entrance."

"Is the story true?"

"I'm not sure. But once I found a set of footprints outside the mine."

"Are you serious?"

His lips spread into a smile, and his dimples eased the worry lines etching his face. Her heart lurched into her throat. If she thought the brooding look on him was sexy, the smiling version of him was downright captivating. The gleam in his eyes and the shrug of his shoulders let her know he'd added the part about the footsteps to tease her.

With effort she drew her gaze from his handsome face to the mine entrance. "Have you ever thought of writing down the history of this place? Sounds like you'd have enough to fill a book."

He kicked at a rock. "Uh...no. No one would be interested."

"I am, and I'm sure there'd be others. It'd be a way for you to honor you ancestors."

His smile faded as his lips pressed together into an uncompromising line. What in the world had he taken offense to this time? She sure didn't understand him, no matter how hard she tried. "I'm not a writer."

"But if you wrote down what you know, someone else could reword it—"

"Don't do that."

"Do what?"

"Mess with things you don't understand."

"But you're the only one who knows all of the details about this ghost town, and the people—"

"You're not getting what I'm saying. I can't..." He turned and started to walk away.

She rushed to catch up to him. "Can't what?"

"Leave it be."

She placed a hand on his shoulder. She could feel the corded strength beneath her fingertips. "Tell me. I want to understand."

He stopped suddenly, and her hand fell away. He turned to her with those dark, unreadable eyes. "You wanted a tour, I'm giving it to you. Don't push your luck. We can still visit the sheriff's office."

Was he serious? It was highly doubtful. If he'd intended to have her charged with trespassing, he'd have done it by now. No, there was something he'd almost let slip—something important. But what? And why didn't he want her to know?

She stared at his back as he strode away. There was so much more to the reclusive cowboy than his need to cling to his heritage, and she intended to find out what he was hiding. Maybe if he let down his barriers just a little, others would see him through new eyes—like she saw him. She assured herself that she wasn't getting emotionally invested in him. She knew all too well not to let a person get too close. In the end, she'd be the one to get hurt. And she refused to let herself become vulnerable again—not even for a lonely cowboy.

Not wanting to be left behind, she rushed after him. Honoring his wishes, she changed the subject. "Do you really believe in ghosts or spirits or whatever you want to call them?"

"There's a lot of unknowns in this world. I try not to be closed-minded."

"Too bad more people aren't like you." She stopped to scan the perimeter. The sight of a graveyard in the distance drew her interest. "Let's walk over there."

She took off without bothering to check if Cord was behind her. Row upon row of tombstones faced her. Most of the markers were so old the weather had worn away the names, leaving her to wonder about the people laid to rest here.

Cord's voice came from behind her. "This land was a symbol of a new beginning for my great-great-grandfather. He sold his businesses in the East to move here. He worked night and day to carve out a life for himself."

"I can't imagine giving up everything you've worked for only to start over again from scratch."

"Not surprising," Cord mumbled.

"Hey, what's that supposed to mean?"

He slid his hands in his pockets. "Just doesn't surprise me that you wouldn't be willing to give up your five-star restaurants and boardrooms to follow your heart—"

"Hey!" She poked him in the chest. "You don't know anything about my heart or what I'm capable of."

Before she could poke him again, his strong fingers wrapped around her hand and held it captive against the pounding inside chest. "Whoa there. I didn't mean to upset you."

She should yank her hand away. She should tell him he had struck a very sensitive nerve. She should turn and walk away. Instead, she tilted her chin up and met his concerned gaze. Those warm chocolate eyes drew her in and held her transfixed.

Why in the world had she let his words affect her so deeply? He wasn't Steven, the man who'd accused her of not being happy for him after he'd used her father's name and connections to get a bigger title with a bigger company on the West Coast. When she'd asked him for time so that they could work through this huge change in their life, Steven had said all of the right things, while simultaneously doing all of the wrong things with another woman behind Alexis's back.

A guilty look crossed Cord's handsome face as his steady gaze continued to hold hers. "Sometimes I don't think before I speak."

"And sometimes I overreact." She hoped to put him at ease, even though her heart was racing.

His gaze dipped to her lips. She knew that look—the desire was evident. And this was all wrong. She'd just got done stitching her heart back together. She wasn't going to let herself get hurt again.

She pulled her hand from his, immediately missing his touch. It'd been so long since she'd let down her defenses and enjoyed the warmth and tenderness found in the mere act of holding hands. It surprised her how much she longed for a longer connection, a deeper connection.

Giving herself a mental shake, she walked around the graveyard, trying to center her turbulent thoughts. While most of the gravestones were worn smooth, two large markers stood out. "Are those graves new?"

"They belong to my parents." A slight hitch in his voice let her know how much he missed his family. "Mama wanted to be buried here with her ancestors, and Papa would have followed my mother to the ends of the earth."

The knowledge that his parents were laid to rest out here shocked her. No wonder he didn't want to sell the land. A knot of emotion tightened inside her as she struggled with a moment of indecision. If she pushed ahead with her plans, Cord would lose. And if she gave up, she would lose her one chance to put HSG back in the black without her father finding out how close the company had come to filing for bankruptcy. She was doomed no matter which way she turned.

"I'm sorry, Cord." She reached out and squeezed his hand.

A tremor of awareness coursed its way up her arm and finally settled in her chest. Her sympathies encompassed more than him losing his family. Because even though she now knew how important this land was to him, she couldn't walk away.

Cord's brown eyes warmed as he tightened his long fingers around hers. "Now, are you beginning to understand why I can't sell you Haggerty?"

"I had no idea there was a cemetery out here. No one mentioned it. I'll make certain they fence off this area so no one disturbs it. You have my word on it." It wasn't a sales pitch. She'd definitely make the fence a priority.

He jerked his hand away as though her touch had scalded him. "Even after telling you how important this ghost town is to my family, you're still insisting on including it as part of the deal?"

As much as she'd like to make Cord happy by walking away from this land deal, she couldn't. This sale was necessary—for both their sakes. The Southwest contained only a handful of ghost towns. Mr. Santos had a lead on one in Arizona that was about to be listed, but nothing was definite yet. Still, Alexis found herself hoping for an alternative solution.

"The plan for the resort won't work without it. We'll work something out to protect this area." She waved her hand around at the cemetery. "Don't worry. It'll be fine."

"No, it won't. You can't understand unless you've lost someone close to you."

His words ripped a scab off her old wound. The pain was quick and intense. She struggled to swallow down the unexpected wave of pain. "What makes you think you're the only one to feel pain and loss?"

His head rose, and his eyes narrowed as if he was trying to determine whether she was being truthful. "Who did you lose?"

"My mother."

The lines bracketing his mouth and eyes eased. "I'm sorry. It's tough when a parent dies."

He misunderstood her. Though she didn't want to delve further into this subject, she felt obligated to correct him. "She's not dead."

"But you said—"

Alexis took a deep breath, all the while chastising herself for opening up this subject. "I said I lost her. I guess it'd be more correct to say she walked out on me and my father."

What had gotten into her to go down this road? She didn't even discuss the woman with her father, which seemed to suit him just fine. The fact Alexis resembled the woman was enough of a challenge for her father without her bombarding him with questions.

Alexis gazed into Cord's eyes, finding understanding and support—two things that she found herself craving. Since when had they moved from a business relationship to something more, something she couldn't quite name?

Cord's unwavering stare compelled her to continue, to let him know that sometimes the death of a loved one wasn't the worst thing that could happen. "My mother was beautiful and spoiled. My father gave her the best of everything, but when she got bored of playing mother and wife, she ran off with an associate of my father's. She never looked back, unless you consider the legal battle she waged to try to strip my father of his company."

"Surely she saw you. You're her daughter. What about visitation?"

"She didn't want to be bothered. I tracked her down when I was a teenager, but she gave me a list of excuses why a visit wouldn't be convenient. She was preparing for her third marriage, and her future husband didn't like kids. You see, you aren't so bad off. At least your parents loved you and would be here if they could. My mother is alive and wants absolutely nothing to do with me."

His arms lifted as though he was going to hug her. She was surprised by the powerful wave of anticipation that washed over her at the thought of being held in his powerful arms. Something told her that once she was held securely in his embrace, nothing could or would hurt her—at last she'd be safe.

As though he'd sensed the scary direction of her thoughts, he stepped back. "I...ah... don't know what to say."

Disappointment flooded her body. "You could admit my idea for protecting the cemetery is reasonable and agree to the sale."

He cleared his throat. "I can't. I promised my grandfather I'd always protect Haggerty. It's all that's left of my heritage, of my family."

Their gazes locked. She found herself drawn in by his chocolaty depths. The more she worked past his prickly defenses, the more she liked him. She'd never imagined that they'd have so much in common. If this was another time, another place, they might be able to build on that connection—

She had to get a grip on her rambling thoughts. Cord wasn't any more interested in a relationship with her than she was with him. She had to stay focused on her plans for the resort and not on how much she enjoyed his touch. And now that she understood Cord's ties to the land, her initial excitement over the prospect of building the resort dimmed considerably.

When had Cord begun to matter so much to her?

CHAPTER EIGHT

Voices of the past murmured in the breeze. The whispers teased Alexis's imagination, conjuring images of what Haggerty might have been like more than a hundred years ago. Her fantasy contained a street full of powerful horses with nostrils flaring, the rattle of buckboard wagons, and the hum of conversation between muscled cowboys wearing dusty hats and chaps.

She cast Cord a sideways look. He was a modern-day cowboy, but something told her that he could have toughed it out with the best of them in the good old days. She, on the other hand, was quite happy with indoor plumbing and electricity. Very happy indeed.

They strolled down the dirt lane past the broken hitching posts and came to a stop in front of the crumbling remains of a building. The lines of Cord's tanned face had eased. Perhaps he'd be willing to share more about the town's history. She'd have all sorts of things to report back to her father to hopefully placate him for a while. And it would keep her mind from wandering into dangerous territory—thoughts of what it'd be like for Cord to pull her close and kiss her.

She walked closer to the barely-there structure. "Do you know what this used to be?"

"A church. My great-great-grandparents were married here."

He certainly hadn't exaggerated about his strong ties to the land. Her heart thudded against her ribs as she imagined being married out here in a flowing white dress while holding a fistful of wildflowers—and staring up at Cord's smiling face.

Wait. This wasn't helping her to focus her mind on business. What was the matter with her? It must be a side effect of the desert sun's strong rays. She ran the back of her hand over her warmed forehead. Her life was in New York—in the city—a place where this cowboy wouldn't fit in. And at this critical juncture with the business, there wasn't time for distractions— no matter how good they looked.

She stepped through the gaping hole in the sidewall. She crossed the dirt floor, stopping next to the crumbling wall that now stood only waist-high. After brushing aside some loose pebbles and a bit of disintegrated adobe, she tested its sturdiness. Surprised to find the wall solid, she leaned back and took stock of her surroundings.

On the far side, stones were still aligned for the fireplace, although time and weather had eroded most of the chimney. A sorrow came over her when she thought of all of the people, including Cord's ancestors, who'd sacrificed everything to conquer this land but had ended up losing their savings, their dreams, and some even their lives.

A movement caught her attention. She focused on the round stones by the fireplace. She squinted into the shady corner and spotted a coil of red rope. Strange— what would it be doing here? She stepped closer, only to find herself face-to-face with a snake.

She jumped back. A lungful of air rushed up her throat and erupted in a scream. Cord's large hand clamped over her mouth, cutting off the shriek. His other muscled arm wrapped securely around her middle. She pressed back against his solid chest. Her gaze never strayed from the snake.

"You're safe." He spoke softly next to her ear. "If I let go, will you promise no more screaming?"

She nodded, but she refused to take her gaze off the scaly reptile. Goose bumps raced down her arms. Had she forgotten to mention how much she really, really despised snakes?

Cord moved his hand from her mouth. His other arm lingered around her waist, and she didn't rush to pull away. Slowly, they backed away. Once safely by the doorway, she turned to find him smothering a chuckle, which necessitated a playful punch to his solid bicep. "This isn't funny. What if we'd been bit?"

"He isn't going to hurt us. There's a saying you should learn. 'Red and yellow kill a fellow, but red and black is a friend of Jack.'"

"What does it mean?"

"Remember how the snake's red and black stripes were side-by-side?" When she nodded, he added, "That particular snake isn't poisonous."

"Who's going to stand here long enough to check the coloring?" She grabbed his hand. His rough calluses rubbed over her palm as she pulled him back to the dirt road.

"Are you reconsidering putting a resort out here? Venomous or not, your guests might not take well to meeting up with all the critters slithering through the desert."

Amusement twinkled in his eyes as his lips lifted, showing the dimples in his cheeks. How could one man be so sexy and at the same time so frustratingly annoying?

"If you think this is going to change my mind, think again. No snake is going to scare me off."

"Really? Looks like it just did."

She glared at him. "I need a drink."

The smile lingered on his lips as she marched past him toward the vehicles. She grabbed a couple of water bottles from the cooler in the SUV and offered him one.

"You came well-equipped," he said, peering into her vehicle. "A flashlight. A medical kit. You must have bought out the Hitchin' Post. I bet you made Sam real happy."

"I like to be prepared." The snake may have caught her off guard, but when it came to business, she planned for the unexpected. "And Sam was quite helpful."

She took a long, slow drink, swirling the fluid around in her mouth before swallowing and soothing her scratchy throat. The water tasted so good, she took another large swallow before screwing the lid back on and tossing the bottle into the backseat.

Refreshed, she followed Cord around Haggerty as he indicated the buildings in various stages of destruction, beaten by weather and time. In some instances, the only evidence a structure had ever existed was the foundation popping out from the ground.

"At one point in time, this was the General Store and the Pony Express stop. The most popular place in town, next to the saloon." Cord paused in front of a dilapidated hitching post.

This setting definitely suited Cord. He'd make a sexy old-fashioned cowboy. In her mind, she added a holster with a pearl-handled revolver on each lean hip as a set of leather chaps trailed down to a pair of dusty boots with silver spurs on his heels.

She pictured him all dressed up and modeling on the resort's billboard. Once they fixed this place up to resemble its former rustic charm, it'd be the perfect backdrop for the ad campaign. She took a couple of steps back to take in the full scene.

"Hey. Be careful." Cord lurched forward, grabbing her arm and yanking her toward him.

What in the world? The unexpected collision of their bodies knocked the air from her lungs. She glanced up at his intense brown eyes. Her heart somersaulted.

"What'd you do that for?" Her gaze lowered to his lips, inches from her own.

"I didn't want you to fall."

Too late to worry about that.

He continued to hold her close. A fluttering sensation returned to her stomach. She didn't move, didn't turn away. She continued to stare at him, willing him to kiss her. It wasn't logical, but she didn't feel like being sensible at the moment. For once, she wanted to live in the moment.

Cord cleared his throat, breaking the spell. Realizing he was talking about something totally different, she swallowed hard. "What?"

"Turn around."

With him still holding her arm, she pivoted around and saw some rotted wood planks covering a big hole in the ground.

He released her. "The mine preceded the town, so make sure to keep your head down and stay alert for cave-ins. In an old mining town, you never walk backward, or you might end up falling down a mine shaft."

She worried her bottom lip as she looked upon Haggerty with a renewed respect for the dangers lurking in the shadows. Her investors and insurance company wouldn't be happy about this discovery. Still, HSG had overcome bigger obstacles. Her father's motto was, *If there's a will, there's a way.* She'd definitely find a way to make this work.

Alexis continued looking around until she found herself standing once again outside the mine entrance. If it weren't so dangerous, she'd love to sneak a peek inside the mine shaft. Her father had always teased that she was a daredevil, but climbing into a hole beneath the earth's surface with untold hazards was just plain stupid. Not to mention the thought of running into more snakes or bats. The thought had her quickly retreating.

"Tour's over," Cord called over his shoulder as he headed for the vehicles. "I've got work to do, and we have that stop to make at the sheriff's office."

She pursed her lips as her gaze strayed to his very fine backside. She grew frustrated with herself for noticing his finer assets when he was once again threatening to make trouble for her. He was just trying to get her worked up. He wanted a little fun at her expense. Except it wasn't going to work this time.

"We both know you aren't serious."

"Sure am. I don't want you getting any other foolish ideas about coming out here alone. Anything could happen to you, and no one would know."

She had to take twice as many steps to keep up with his long strides. "And if I promise not to come back alone, can't you promise to drop the trespassing thing once and for all?"

"Why should I? You've wasted a large chunk of my day already."

"You're really enjoying dangling the sheriff thing over my head, aren't you?"

He flashed a small grin. "Something like that. I'll make up my mind when we get back to town."

"Of course you will."

He grabbed a couple of bottles of water from his truck and tossed her one. "Here."

He was right. She was letting him get her riled up over nothing. He wasn't going to press charges. Thank goodness. She could just imagine the headline: HSG President Arrested For Trespassing. New York City could be a very small place at times—almost as small as Whistle Stop.

She twisted the top off the bottle and took a long swallow. Time to change subjects. "I love this place," she mused. "I can now see the appeal of being a landowner. And having all of this to explore."

"You don't own any land?"

She shook her head. "Just a condo in New York. Although I'm home so little since my father had his latest heart attack that I barely remember my own address."

The concern reflected in Cord's eyes made her realize her slip of the tongue. She wanted to kick herself for not being more careful around him. Cord made it easy for her to let down her guard and be herself. Still, she and her father had agreed to keep his health condition under wraps for business reasons.

"Sorry to hear about your father. Will he be okay?"

She nodded. With the proverbial beans spilled, she didn't have anything to lose by confiding in him. She'd longed to talk to someone about her concerns. Back in New York she had a couple of girlfriends from college with whom she still kept in contact, but she rarely confided in them. She'd learned at an early age that most things were better kept to yourself or they'd come back and bite you. But she got the distinct feeling that her secret would be safe with Cord. And he appeared to be a good listener, as long as she avoided the subject of buying Haggerty.

"During my father's last attack, his heart was damaged. The doctors have warned that he can no longer work the long hours his job demands. Nor can he deal with the stress. The thing is, I can't convince him it's time to retire."

Cord's eyes filled with understanding. "Is that why this deal is so important to you? Because it's important to your father?"

"Yes. He raised me as a single parent, but that didn't stop him from working morning till night. As far back as I can remember, I did my homework at the table in his conference room. In fact, I swear I spent more time at HSG than I did at our town house. His administrative assistant became a surrogate aunt to me."

"Doesn't sound like an easy childhood."

"My father did his best," she said defensively. "For the longest time, I believed he put in all of those long hours and avoided a personal life because he was a workaholic."

"I take it with you being on the other side of the desk that you're seeing things differently."

She nodded. "This job will swallow you whole if you aren't careful."

"Has it swallowed you yet?"

"Not quite."

"That's good. Just be careful it doesn't. There's so much more to life than work."

She eyed up Cord, a down-to-earth man. She considered revealing how she had an escape plan should she ever need one—her trust fund. The account held sufficient funds for her to start over anywhere—not that she'd ever bail on her father.

What would this rancher think of her if he knew she was a trust fund kid? He'd probably get an even worse impression of her. Spoiled. Snobby. Those were just a couple of adjectives that came to mind. She wanted Cord to like and respect her, so she kept quiet. Besides, it wasn't as if it was a slush fund for parties and vacations. She'd specifically earmarked its use for emergencies only.

"Enough about me." She turned to him. "What do you enjoy when you aren't working?"

He rubbed a hand over his stubbled jaw. "I like to end the day kicked back on my front porch. There's beauty in a sunset and grace in the silhouette of a horse racing along the horizon." He hesitated as though embarrassed to be letting on that he wasn't a roughened cowboy, but rather a man who could appreciate the simple things in life.

"Those do sound beautiful. If I'm lucky, maybe I'll get to witness them while I'm here."

"The beauty of the land is all around you. Take a look. I mean, really see the beauty in the simplest parts of nature. You'll be amazed by the secrets of this land." He pointed to a little red flower in the distance. "Even in this harsh terrain, this plant refuses to be defeated."

Just like him, she thought, standing tall against all adversity.

"You know, I was warned about you."

"Maybe you should heed the warnings."

His facial expression didn't give any hint of his feelings. It was almost as if he wasn't surprised. Why would that be? Why would he let the townspeople of Whistle Stop assume he was some unfriendly hermit, when in fact he could be quite friendly?

Cord averted his gaze. "Now that you've seen Haggerty, is it what you were imagining?"

She wanted to ask more about the residents of Whistle Stop, but she decided not to press him for answers. "I think it's the most amazing place I've ever been. I can see why you're so protective of this place."

His gaze jerked back to her. "You really mean that? You think this place is special?"

"I do." Her pulse started to race as he continued staring at her. "This place is loaded with a rugged charm and rare beauty."

He lifted his bottle to drink. When a trickle of water trailed down his chin, she longed to reach out and run her finger over his damp skin, over the place where his vein pulsed. She wondered how he'd react if she gave in to the impulse.

"There's a far more beautiful sight." His voice was deeper than normal. The sweet words drizzled over her like thick, rich caramel.

"Where would that be?"

Their gazes connected and held. "The woman standing right in front of me."

Her gaze searched his. Could he read the desire in her eyes? Did he know how much she'd been longing to feel his lips pressed to hers? The heat was definitely affecting her now. There was no other acceptable explanation for her overwhelming yearning to have him kiss her.

When his hand claimed her hip, her heart soared. With a tug, he pulled her closer, and her body willingly obliged. This shouldn't be happening. It wasn't right. They were opponents. But, somehow, out here in the desert miles from civilization, reality no longer seemed quite so important.

Her gaze slipped to his lips. The breath hitched in her throat, and his head dipped toward her. This was it. The moment of no return. Her eyelids drifted closed. His mouth grazed hers, and her resistance melted away. For the moment, a truce let their differences fade into the background, and they melted together. His tongue gently probed her lips, parting them with ease. Their tongues moved in unison, as in a well-rehearsed dance.

When Cord sucked on her lower lip and ran the tip of his tongue over it, her fingers tightened on his shoulders. Shivers of need zinged through her, bringing her body to life. She should have pulled away, but she couldn't—not yet. His lips were as sweet as a Choconut Bar—no, definitely sweeter— and she was on a sugar high. Her very being craved more of his kisses—of him.

Much too soon, he pulled back.

Knowing he wasn't coming back for more, she let her eyes flutter open. Reality careened in on her, knocking her back to earth. She knew better than to put herself out there—she'd only end up getting hurt. But in this one particular instance, it'd been worth it. She licked her lips, savoring the memory. All the while, she knew it could never happen again.

She mustered up every bit of self-control and moved away. "We can't let that happen again."

His eyes flashed with surprise then grew dark. "You're right." He turned toward his truck. "Time to head back."

Alexis watched his retreating back. She didn't want things to end like this. "Cord, wait."

Without a backward glance, he climbed inside and fired up the engine before stomping on the gas, spraying the area with dirt. Obviously, she wasn't the only one unsettled by that mind-blowing kiss. But could they move past it?

Her fingers pressed to her tingling lips. She reminded herself that a kiss was just a kiss. Something she'd done in the past. She was making too much of it. Wasn't she?

She climbed into the SUV, still wondering what had gotten into her to let down her defenses with Cord. There wasn't a chance it could lead anywhere. They were adversaries over a very important deal. And when he realized that she was right about knowing what was best for both of them, his wounded male ego wouldn't be able to deal with it. She'd forever be the woman who stole away his land—his heritage.

With a resigned sigh, she glanced down to fasten her seat belt and noticed something sticking up between the passenger seat and the center console. Her fingers worked into the narrow space and yanked out her camera. It must have gotten jostled off the seat.

How could she have forgotten her camera? It had to have been Cord's sudden appearance and him bandying about threats to have her arrested that had her forgetting the main reason she'd come out here. She needed photos to send to her father. She could imagine him checking his e-mail every hour on the hour waiting for them. She didn't have a choice. She had to get pictures. It was her job.

Until she'd set foot in Whistle Stop, she'd been fine with putting her life on hold to work her way up through the ranks at HSG. But it hadn't worked out like she'd hoped. At one point she'd thought being in charge—being president of HSG—would make her happy, but it hadn't. There were too many people to please and no way of pleasing everyone. With so many hoops to jump through, there was never any time left to smell the roses.

She didn't know if it was the sense of community she'd witnessed in this small desert town or spending time with Cord, but the nagging sense of wanting more than a successful career grew each day she was here.

A trail of dust behind Cord's truck beckoned to her, but she continued to hesitate. She'd be fine here on her own. He had already given her a stern lecture about the hazards of this place.

In all honesty, it shouldn't be too hard to follow his tire tracks back to the main road. After all, it seemed like it was pretty much a straight shot.

She wouldn't even be sitting here contemplating all of this if he hadn't planted those worst-case scenarios in her mind. She was certain he'd been exaggerating—trying to keep her off his precious land. Well, she wasn't falling for his scare tactics. She'd be fine on her own. She clutched the little camera and headed back to Haggerty. Cord's stern warnings echoed in her mind. She stared down at the clay, watching every step she took.

She snapped pictures of the General Store, the telegraph office and the opening of the mine. She even made a point to trek over to the graveyard. This place was special with a reverent air about it. Knowing that Cord's family was buried here, she intended to ensure it remained as is by thoroughly documenting its current state.

While standing there taking photos, she decided the chain-link fence she'd originally envisioned wouldn't do this place justice. A high stone wall would be more in line with the landscape and would ensure privacy. She wondered what it'd take to convince Cord that she would do her best to secure the graveyard.

Her footsteps picked up the pace as she headed back to the center of the ghost town. A few more photos and she'd be on way her—most likely to the sheriff's office, after the way Cord tore out of there. Oh well, she'd deal with him later. Right now, she had to get the rest of the pictures she'd promised her father.

She paused by the remains of the church where Cord's ancestors had been married. She carefully checked for the snake. Not spotting it, she stepped just inside the opening.

A nostalgic feeling came over her as she snapped pictures. Her imagination conjured up images of life back in the old days. She leaned back against one of the adobe walls, resting her hand on the sun-warmed clay. What would it be like to have someone pledge their undying love and then to grow old together? A wistful sigh passed her lips.

Something tickled the back of her hand. She wiggled her fingers, causing the sensation to cease. Lost in her fantasy, she pictured the women in their prairie skirts and the men with their chaps and side arms.

The image of Cord intruded into her daydream, ruggedly handsome, all done up like an old-fashioned cowboy. She imagined he'd followed her back here. A smile tugged at her lips as she savored the thought of him making a play for her, his fingers grazing over the back of her hand as his mouth nuzzled a sensitive spot on her neck.

Once again, she noticed the tickling on her hand, and as much as she wanted it to be Cord's fingers caressing her, she knew it couldn't be. He was long gone, and by the sour look on his face, he wouldn't be back any time soon. So if he wasn't touching her, then that meant…Oh no! Could it be another snake?

She tensed. Her chest tightened. She glanced down. There sat a tan insect bigger than a half dollar with numerous legs.

A scorpion.

Its long tail lifted and curled, ready to strike her.

Panic crowded in, smothering her common sense.

A scream ripped from her lungs.

CHAPTER NINE

Cord pressed his boot down hard on the accelerator and clutched the steering wheel as the truck bounced over the rough terrain, jostling him in the seat. He seriously reconsidered his threat to have Lexi charged with trespassing. It'd certainly teach her a lesson and keep her at arm's length, just in case he lost his mind again and decided to kiss her.

He sighed. The last thing he wanted to do was deal with the sheriff. He hadn't been friends with Will since a fight in third grade. After all of this time, Cord couldn't even remember what their disagreement had been about except that it had something to do with playing baseball. Things had been quiet between them for the longest time, until Cord's ex-wife had stirred up that hornets nest of lies. Ever since then, Will had been giving him strange looks. Cord always shrugged it off. If the man wanted to think ill of him, there was nothing Cord could say to change his mind.

Cord shifted his gaze to the rearview mirror. He squinted to see through the cloud of dust. Not making out Lexi's vehicle, he eased up on the gas pedal. As the air cleared, it only confirmed his worst thought—Lexi was missing.

Where had she disappeared to? His fingers tightened around the steering wheel. That kiss had so unnerved him that he hadn't made sure she'd pulled out at the same time. He'd only had one thought—putting distance between them.

Back at Haggerty, when she'd revealed her love of the land, he felt like he'd finally found the right woman. He'd caved in to his desires. For one idyllic moment, he'd dismissed the stark facts of his reality—his shortcomings—and he'd let down his guard. He wouldn't let it happen again. He remembered vividly how much it hurt when the dream faded.

Down deep, he knew he was the main reason his marriage had failed. His difficulty with reading left him wanting to stick close to home. His ex-wife, Susan, had been a dreamer. She'd wanted to see the world, but when he'd refused, their troubles had begun in earnest. She hadn't understood him and how inadequate he felt when he was outside of his element.

He refused to let that happen again. If he should ever marry again, it would be different. It'd be with a woman content with life on the Brazen H—someone who would accept him the way he was. That definitely left the up-and-coming president of HSG off of the list.

Cord lifted his boot from the accelerator, waiting for Lexi to catch up. His gaze remained glued to the mirror. The seconds ticked away, but still nothing. A bad feeling churned in his gut. He imagined her with a flat tire out there in the barren land. What were the chances she knew how to switch out a tire? He had no choice but to head back.

He stomped the gas pedal and spun the steering wheel hard to the left. The more ground he covered with no sign of her, the more his sense of urgency increased. Something was wrong. He got these intuitions only when it came to the weather or the livestock—never with another human. However, none of it changed the fact he knew in his gut Lexi was in trouble.

His truck skidded to a stop next to her SUV. He jumped out and ran over to her vehicle. Empty. Had she gone back to the ghost town? For what?

A shrill scream sliced through the air, raising the hairs on the back of his neck.

Lexi!

His heart slammed into his ribs. He set out at a dead run.

Please don't let me find her crumpled form at the bottom of a mine shaft.

The horrific thought sent his legs pumping harder, faster. His lungs burned, but he kept moving. He had to get to her. She had to be all right. *Please God, let her be safe.*

He stopped on what had once been Main Street. One deep breath after the other, he sucked in oxygen. His eyes continually scanned for any sign of her.

"Lexi! Where are you?"

Blood pulsed in his temples. If she had fallen into a mine shaft, the chances of hearing her weren't good. She'd be deep underground. He refused to accept the possibility.

He paused, thinking he'd heard something. "Lexi, I can't hear you."

"Cord," a thready voice reached out to him. "Cord, over here."

He made his way up the street, scanning to the left and then the right. At last, he spotted her sitting on the ground in the opening of the church. Thank God. As he drew nearer, her red, blotchy complexion became apparent.

"What's wrong?" He crouched down beside her. His hand cupped her warm cheek, while his thumb stroked her smooth skin. "Why are you sitting here in the dirt?"

"A scorpion stung me."

She trembled like a leaf in a windstorm. He pulled her to him. His own heart pounded from the scare she'd given him.

"Calm down. You're okay now," he murmured, trying to keep her from having a panic attack. "Show me where."

She held out her jittery hand. No doctor's diagnosis was necessary to tell him that the swollen red patch was a sign of a reaction to the venom.

"What did it look like?"

"It was ugly. And it was tan."

Her description didn't tell him much. He'd like to see the culprit for himself. "Where were you when it stung you?"

"Back there." She pointed over her shoulder. "I was leaning back, and it crawled on my hand."

He walked over and scanned the designated area. He knew from growing up here that there was more than one species—one more venomous than the others. A thorough scan of the area turned up nothing. The little devil must have scampered off into a crevice.

He returned and helped her stand. "We need to get you to a doctor."

"Should I be worried?"

He smiled, hoping if he portrayed a calm composure she'd do the same. "Trust me, you'll be fine."

"Don't scorpion bites kill people?"

"Only in the rarest of cases. You might get a little sick, but that's all. This never would have happened if you'd listened to me." He didn't want to lecture her now, but if his words kept her from panicking, so much the better.

"I'm hurt, and all you can do is say, 'I told you so'?"

He wrapped a secure arm around her waist to guide her back to his vehicle. "You're lucky you didn't end up at the bottom of a mine shaft."

She glared at him. "I'm not dumb. I listened to everything you said. You just didn't warn me to be careful where I put my hands."

Her last statement sent his mind whirling off in a totally inappropriate direction. When she was better, he knew exactly where he wanted her hands. First, though, he had to get her to the doctor.

"The problem with you is, you'd do anything to get out of trouble," he teased, trying to keep her talking.

Her eyes flared with anger. "Meaning what? I got stung by the scorpion so you wouldn't have me arrested?"

"Calm down. I was only teasing."

"Well, it's not funny."

"Point taken. It's just that I knew you were in trouble."

"You did?" Surprise rang out in her voice.

Now why in the world had he gone and told her about his intuition, or whatever you wanted to call it? She'd think he was crazy, or worse, she'd start thinking they had some kind of deep connection. Neither of which was true.

"I figured that if you hung around here by yourself, sooner or later you'd get yourself in trouble."

"I forgot to take pictures of Haggerty for my father."

They stopped next to his pickup, and he opened the door for her. "Hop in."

"But my vehicle—"

"Will be fine right here. I'll send a couple of ranch hands out to pick it up later."

The red splotches on her face hadn't faded, and the swelling of her hand was getting worse. No way was he letting her behind the wheel.

Holding her arm to her chest, she climbed in without any further argument. That in and of itself set off alarms in his head. He jumped in the driver's side, fired up the engine, and tramped the gas.

"Can you turn up the air conditioning?" She leaned her head back against the headrest.

Damn. He'd meant to have the air fixed at the beginning of summer, but he'd put it off for one reason or another. "Can't. It's busted."

"You should have said something before. We could have taken my SUV. Turn around."

"No. We've wasted enough time." He wasn't up on his first aid, but it was obvious she was having some sort of reaction to the venom. "We're going straight to the doctor's. You'll be fine. Think about a swimming pool or Antarctica or something cold."

"Boy, you're a lot of help." Her frustrated voice faded.

His foot rested heavily on the accelerator, letting up only when the ground got too rough and Lexi groaned from being jostled. At last, they reached the paved road. He floored the gas, ignoring the posted speed limit. *Please, God, make her better, and I'll do whatever it takes.*

Minutes later, they rolled into Whistle Stop. With no open spots in front of Doc Willard's, he ended up double-parking. He jumped out and rushed over to open her door. She was drenched in sweat and clutching the wrist of her enflamed hand.

He didn't waste time with words. He scooped her up. Lexi's cheek pressed against his shoulder. The alarming heat of her skin penetrated his shirt. His arms tightened protectively around her.

He strode into the office. A familiar face turned his way, Tony Granger. They'd been friends the whole way through school. Tony had always been a good guy in Cord's book, and that was saying a lot. They nodded at each other in greeting, and then Tony's gaze drifted to Lexi.

With a hand on his young nephew's shoulder, he stepped back from the receptionist's window. "Go ahead. We're just here for Johnny's annual physical."

"Thanks."

Cord rapped his knuckles on the glass partition.

Mrs. Willard ambled over. A smile pulled at her bright red-painted lips. "Goodness gracious, Cord. You never come here. What—"

The words trailed off as her gaze took in Lexi resting against his chest. The woman wheeled around and rushed to open the door leading to the exam rooms.

"What happened to her?"

"A scorpion stung her. Think the doc better have a look at her right away."

"Poor thing." Mrs. Willard held the door for him. "Bring her this way."

She guided him down the hallway past a couple of closed doors. She pointed to the room at the end of the corridor. "Let her rest in there. I'll get Doc."

She hustled off in the opposite direction, while he carried Lexi inside and set her down on the paper-lined exam table.

Seconds later, footsteps echoed in the hallway, and then Doc Willard stepped into the room. "I hear you've brought me a new patient."

Cord turned to the gray-haired man in his usual white coat—the same man who'd delivered him and patched up all of his childhood scrapes. He was one of the few people in town who'd never judged him or his short-lived marriage.

"Doc, this is Lexi Greer. We were out visiting Haggerty, and she had a run-in with a scorpion."

The doctor's gaze moved from him to her and back again. "Okay. I can take it from here. Why don't you go wait in the waiting room? We'll be a few minutes."

Leave? An unfamiliar sensation came over him—protectiveness. Cord turned to Lexi for direction. He wasn't anxious to clear out, but he'd do whatever would make her the most comfortable.

"Go ahead," she said.

He slipped out of the room, closing the door behind him. The weight of responsibility hung round his neck, pulling down on him. He never should have given in to her plea to traipse around Haggerty. He'd known nothing good would come of it. And he'd been right.

Once in the waiting room, he started to pace. He didn't know why he'd let himself get so worried. He'd seen a lot worse after spending his whole life on a ranch. So why did Lexi's incident strike him so profoundly? It wasn't like she meant anything to him.

A little boy, not much more than a toddler, waved a toy airplane above his head. He spun around and bumped into Cord. With lightning-fast reflexes, Cord bent over to steady the child.

"Hey there, buddy, be careful." Cord's vision moved to the toy. "That's a really cool plane."

The boy shot him a wide-eyed stare before running to his mother and clinging to her jean-clad leg. Cord smiled, hoping the boy would do the same—he didn't. Cord hated the thought of a little kid fearing him. He didn't think of himself as being big and scary. He sure hoped it wasn't the impression he gave other people— especially not Lexi.

Was she scared of him?

He hadn't exactly gone out of his way to show her his nice side. He expelled a frustrated sigh and ran a hand over the back of his neck. He'd have to work on being nicer to her. Just because he didn't want her building a resort on his land didn't mean he had to come across as an ogre.

He glanced around, finding all of the chairs in the small waiting room filled. When his gaze landed on Tony, his friend slid over on the bench, making room for him.

"Thanks." Cord sat down, even though he'd prefer to be pacing. His knee bobbed up and down.

"So that's the lady the whole town is buzzing about?" Tony nodded toward the exam rooms. "The one who wants to buy your ranch?"

"Just part of it. And yeah, that's her. She had a run-in with a scorpion and lost."

"Cool." A school-age boy's eyes opened up. "Is she gonna be okay?"

"Sure, she is." Tony spoke up before Cord could think of an appropriate answer. "Johnny, why don't you go check out the books over there? I thought I saw one about horses."

Johnny's uncertain gaze moved between the two men. "Okay."

When Johnny was across the room, looking at the bookshelf, Tony leaned back and crossed his arms. "This parenting stuff sure is tough to adjust to, especially when I'm just the uncle trying to fill the roles of both Mom and Dad."

"You look like you're doing a good job." Not that Cord had any basis for his observation, since he had zero experience with little people.

"I'm trying. I just never know if I'm doing anything right."

"I don't know if anyone knows what they are doing. They just give it their best try. And fake the rest."

Tony's brows rose. "You think?"

Cord nodded.

"Hey, I just got a new stallion." Tony smiled. "You should stop by sometime and check him out. He might be as big as that one you've got. What's his name?"

"Midnight Star. I bet they'd certainly put on a fine race."

"Is that a challenge?" Tony's eyes lit up.

"I'll have to see your horse first. I'll stop by when I get a chance." This wasn't the first time Tony had invited him over, and Cord had always meant it when he'd said he'd stop over sometime, but sometime never seemed to roll around. Cord was stuck in a rut, so used to keeping to himself. It was hard to change.

The blare of a car horn drew his attention. He glanced out the window, finding his truck was blocking traffic. He was hesitant to leave in case he was needed, but what would they need him for? His biggest contribution would be holding Lexi's hand, and obviously, she could do fine on her own. He shoved his Stetson on his head and strode up to the reception window.

Mrs. Willard slid open the clear glass partition. "What a horrible thing to happen to that poor girl. Don't you worry now. Doc will get her fixed up. You'll see."

"I'm going to step out for a moment and move my truck. It's blocking traffic. I'll be right back."

She nodded. "If anyone is looking for you, I'll let them know."

He thanked her and stepped outside. He was actually happy to have something to do other than get lost in his troubled thoughts. They always came back to Lexi. Her sickly complexion haunted him.

He drew his thoughts up short. What was wrong with him? He didn't even worry like this when his favorite horse had colic. After all, this woman was a stranger to him. Well, maybe they weren't exactly strangers any longer. They'd shared a lot during their visit to Haggerty. He'd noticed that opening up about her parents had been extremely hard for her. The fact that she'd taken him into her confidence gave him an unfamiliar sensation in his chest.

And then there'd been that kiss.

It hadn't been just any kiss. When her sweet lips moved beneath his, he'd wanted to stay in that moment and forget the reality of their situation. She made him want to believe in rainbows and fairytales.

He drew his meandering thoughts up short. There was no room in his life to get caught up in fantasies—no matter how pretty they are. He couldn't let her get under his skin like Susan had—he couldn't let Lexi sweet-talk him into selling her the land.

Which sounded all fine and good, but he just couldn't readily dismiss how nice she'd been to him—genuinely nice. Sure, she wanted his land, but she didn't have to bother listening to him and trying to understand his deep connection to the land. And he couldn't—wouldn't—forget her kindness.

When he returned from moving the truck, Mrs. Willard called out, "Cord, you can go on back."

"Thanks." He wasted no time heading to the exam room.

The door was cracked open. Not wanting to intrude, he rapped his knuckles on the doorframe.

"Come in," Doc called out.

Cord stepped inside to find Lexi sitting up, holding an ice pack to her hand. Her face remained a bit flushed, but her cheeks were no longer fiery red. His gaze moved from her to the doctor.

"How is she?"

"I'd like to admit her to the hospital overnight—"

"What? How bad is she?"

"Relax, Cord. If you'd let me finish, I was going to say I'd put her in for observation—as a precaution."

"Do you really think that's necessary?" Cord asked, hoping the doctor was just being overly cautious.

Doc Willard noted something on her chart and then turned to gaze at him over his reading glasses. "I'd feel better if someone kept an eye on her to make sure her symptoms don't get any worse. Besides the allergic reaction, I also think she's suffering from too much sun exposure. The New Mexico sun can be hard on people who aren't used to it. You should know that."

Why did Cord get the feeling that people thought there was more to their relationship than buyer and seller? Maybe because there had been that amazingly scorching-hot kiss—but, wait, no one knew about it.

"Quit talking about me like I'm not here," Lexi interjected. "I'll be fine. The ice is helping."

Doc made another note in the file. "I gave her a shot that should help. She can have acetaminophen for the pain, but I want her to avoid ibuprofen and aspirin."

Cord nodded. "I'll drive her to the hospital."

"I'm not going." She glared at Cord. "I'll be fine. Won't I, Dr. Willard?"

The doc frowned. "I'd really feel better if you had some fluids and round-the-clock monitoring."

"I promise that if I have any problems, I'll call you," she said.

"You'll have to get plenty of rest and keep ice on that sting."

"I will." She flashed him a weak smile. "Now can I go?"

"Not so fast," Doc said. "If you aren't going to the hospital, I want someone with you overnight to make sure you don't experience any complications."

Cord swallowed hard, knowing the responsibility fell to him. She had been hurt on his land, and his promise to do his part to ensure her health haunted him. But when he'd made the promise to God, he hadn't envisioned sharing a roof with her.

"I'll do it, Doc," Cord said, ignoring his reservations. "She can come home with me."

Lexi scooted off the table and stood between them. "Would you two quit making decisions for me? I can take care of myself."

Cord eyed up her ice pack. "We can see how well that turned out for you."

Her eyes narrowed into a you're-going-to-pay-for-that-one look. He didn't care, just as long as she was safe. It was only one night. He was fairly certain they could survive each other's company that long.

"Just let me have the care instructions," Cord said, "and we'll get out of your way."

"My missus will have them up front when you check out. Make sure you're alert for any signs of blurred vision or difficulty swallowing or breathing."

Cord nodded while Lexi's lips pursed together.

In the hallway, she said, "I'm not going home with you."

"You will unless you want me to drive you directly to the hospital. Take your pick."

"I'm going back to my motel room. Alone." Her words lacked conviction. The bravado seemed to zap her strength as she started to slump, deflated like a leaky balloon.

Cord slipped an arm around her, liking the feel of her body against his. "We'll see about that."

He escorted her to the waiting area and led her to a chair, while he took care of the paperwork. Mrs. Willard handed over the patient instructions and rattled off the highlights. He gazed down at the tiny print. The letters blurred together. The muscles in his neck tightened. He folded the paper in half to read later.

After he promised to bring her back for a checkup the next day, he turned and found Lexi slouched in the chair. She reminded him of a beautiful flower that had started to droop. She definitely needed someone to watch over her until she regained her strength—no matter what she said.

He'd never played nursemaid to a human before. But there was a first time for everything. He'd hazard a guess that his horses made much better patients than this stubborn, opinionated woman. Oh boy, he was up to his Stetson in trouble.

CHAPTER TEN

*T*his *can't be happening.*

Alexis sat rigidly in the passenger seat of Cord's truck. She leaned her head back, wondering how in the world she'd gained Cord as some sort of guardian. This was the same man who hadn't been able to get away from her fast enough. Sometimes the world worked in mysterious ways. And this time the universe seemed to be having a good laugh at her expense.

Cord maneuvered the truck into traffic. "Would you like me to stop and get you something to eat? Name your craving, and I'll do my best to get it."

She crossed her arms. "I'm not hungry."

"You will be, once that medicine kicks in."

"Right now, I'd like to get some fresh clothes. Would you mind stopping at the motel?"

He pulled up to a stop sign and glanced her way. "You promise to keep your word and come home with me?"

A little voice in the back of her mind warned that it was not a good idea—in fact, it constituted an awful idea. "I'll be fine at the motel. You don't need to bother. I promise to call you if I have any problems—"

"That wasn't our agreement. I gave my word to Doc Willard that I'd take care of you, and I'm not going back on my word, even if it's uncomfortable for the both of us."

"Is your word like some sort of cowboy code?"

"Something like that."

The last thing in the world she wanted to do was spend time alone with him. That kiss kept haunting her. It'd been oh-so-much better than she'd ever imagined. Just the memory of it made her insides shiver with excitement. Of course, she knew that some of that came from them reaching a deeper connection as they'd strolled down the dusty main street in Haggerty. Cord had given her a glimpse of the man inside the coat of armor.

Her head started to ache. She leaned it back against the seat and refused to rub her temples, not wanting to give Cord another reason to play caregiver. But maybe it wouldn't be so bad to have a sexy cowboy at her beck and call.

And if truth be told, she was curious to learn more about him. Not that she was interested in him—that kiss had been a one-time thing. Most likely, it had been the result of too much sun. Even the doctor had confirmed she was suffering from sun exposure. Rather, her interest was business-related. The more she learned about Cord, the easier it'd be to strike an irresistible deal.

Deciding she could move past the kiss, just like he'd obviously done, she said, "Fine. I'll go to the ranch with you. But first I'd like to stop at the motel."

"That's doable. I just have to get us turned around." He slowed the truck and checked traffic.

In no time, he parked in front of her motel room. Without a word, he leaped out and rushed to open her door. He was forever the gentleman, which made her wonder about his offer to care for her. Was it out of concern? Or was it some sort of obligation?

He stood there, blocking her exit. "I can get whatever you need if you'll just tell me where it is."

She shook her head, chasing away the thought of him sorting through her lacy undies. "Thanks. But I'm not helpless."

He shrugged before offering her a hand to help her out of the truck. He didn't say anything, but his brows were knitted together in a definite frown.

"Don't worry. I'll be fine."

He followed her to the motel door when her cell phone began playing *Beethoven's Fifth*. She stopped and turned to Cord. "It's my father, and I really need to make sure he's okay. Would you mind waiting in the truck for me?"

"Don't take long. And let me know if you need any help." Surprisingly, he didn't put up a fight and quietly turned back toward the truck.

She grabbed the phone and pressed it to her ear. "Hi, Father. I didn't expect to hear from you again so soon. Is something wrong?"

"Yes."

Her hand tightened around the phone at the sound of his clipped tone. "What is it? Do you need to call the doctor?"

"No. I told you the ticker is just fine. It's the land deal. I don't understand what's taking you so long to get those papers signed. We've received the surveyor's report and the geological reports. In fact, we've gotten all of the paperwork except for a signed sales agreement."

Alexis unlocked the motel door. "I told you I'm working on it—"

"Don't feed me any more lines. I'm not some flunky. I'm your father—your boss."

"Yes, sir." Her body tensed.

"Now, out with it." Agitation laced every syllable. "What's the problem? Is the seller holding out for more money?"

She bit down on her lower lip. What in the world was she supposed to tell him? What had she been doing? The steamy kiss beneath the desert sun came to mind. Just as quickly as the memory came to her, she dismissed it.

"Spit out the truth, girl," he said, as though he were privy to her thoughts. "Lies won't help either of us."

She glanced up, finding Cord standing next to the pickup, speaking with Mrs. Sanchez. Glad he was distracted, she stepped into her room. She left the door open so there wouldn't be any need for Cord to come checking on her, thinking she'd changed her mind about going to the ranch with him. The last thing she needed was for him to overhear her conversation with her father. Or for her father to overhear Cord fussing over her. She had enough problems already.

"I don't have the papers signed because the seller has a deep sentimental attachment to the ghost town."

"Why should we care? Are you going soft? Or does this Mr. Lawson have you thinking about things other than work—"

"Father," she said indignantly. Her cheeks flamed with heat as her father's words hit far too close to the truth. "I can't twist his arm to sign."

Not feeling too swift, Alexis sat down on the edge of the bed. The throbbing in her temples increased. She didn't know if it was due to her run-in with the scorpion or the stress of dealing with her father. But if he would just back off and let her handle things, she'd finalize the deal and save the company. One way or another.

"Alexis, I don't understand. If Mr. Lawson is so gung ho about keeping his land, why'd he go and put it up for sale?"

"It was a mistake by the realty office." Her voice grew softer as the fight went out of her. All she wanted now was some peace and quiet. "The ghost town was never supposed to be listed."

"Alexis, are you all right?"

No way was she telling her father about her encounter with a scorpion, or the fact she was spending the night with Cord—erm…staying at his house.

"Yes, I'm fine. I just got distracted."

"You're sure?"

"Yes." She hoped her voice sounded reassuring.

Her father hesitated, as though trying to decide if he believed her. "Okay. Now how are you going to convince this sentimental cowboy to sell?"

"I overheard him say that he doesn't have the money to make the balloon payment on his mortgage. If he doesn't sell, the bank will foreclose on his entire ranch."

"So what's your next step?"

"Convince Cord that retaining part of the Brazen H is better than none of it."

"And if that doesn't work?"

"I got a phone call from the Realtor in Albuquerque. He's located a ghost town in Arizona that's about to hit the market. I should know more soon."

"That isn't going to work. We'd have to start back at the beginning with this project."

He had a point. It would take longer to move their plans for the resort to Arizona, but it'd be worth it if she could find a way to help Cord. "I'm doing what I can."

"I've heard from the investors, and they're getting nervous. We have to move on this before we lose their support. Give me the name of the Realtor."

"Why?" She didn't trust her father to take care of himself. He always had to be involved—even when he was under doctor's orders to rest.

"Alexis, don't be difficult. I just have a few questions for him." He expelled a resigned sigh. "I promise not to interfere with your deal."

What could it hurt? Maybe if her father felt included, he'd quit worrying so much. She read off the Realtor's information.

"With Arizona being a long shot, I expect you to push Mr. Lawson," her father said. "Make sure he understands our offer is his only viable option."

"I'm working on it, but I don't think strong-arming Cord is the right approach."

"Sounds like you've gotten close to this man. I've never known you to get personally invested in a project. Is there something going on between you two?"

Did the outlandish desire to follow up that most amazing kiss with another one—a far more intense one—constitute a relationship? Not that she'd ever let that happen. Once her business in Whistle Stop was concluded, she'd be on the first plane back to New York. "Nothing's going on."

"You're sure about that?"

"I've been here long enough to get to know some of the town's people, including Cord, and I've come to understand how much the land means to him."

Her father grunted. "While you're getting all friendly with that cowboy, don't forget that our project is on the line."

She stifled a groan. She realized the severity of the situation more than he did, but she also believed Cord deserved to keep his family's land intact. She didn't bother trying to explain any of this to her father. He wouldn't understand.

"Quit stressing," she said. "I have everything under control."

"I can fly out—"

"No. Stay there and go to your physical therapy."

"I still think there's something you're not telling me. What is it?"

She ignored his question. "There is one more thing. After we complete this deal, how about you sell HSG and retire? There are a couple of companies interested in acquiring it."

"This isn't the time to discuss such things. You have more important matters to attend to," he grumbled.

More stalling tactics. "Father—"

"Fine." He sighed. "I don't want to argue about this over the phone. We'll discuss me cutting back on my hours after you've returned to New York."

"I'll take that as a promise."

New York hadn't crossed her mind until now. Other than her adoring father, she hadn't left behind anyone to miss her, not even so much as a cat or a dog. The fact her parent would be the only one to notice if she didn't return to the city was a sad commentary on her life. She'd have to change that when she returned, but she wasn't quite sure how to go about it.

With high hopes for the Arizona property, she grabbed her laptop, hoping Cord had Internet access at the ranch. She wanted to go back over the information the Realtor had e-mailed her about the prospective property's specifics. She yawned. She was anxious to find an alternative site, but she wasn't foolish enough to rush in without checking the specs. Another yawn soon followed. Still, she couldn't douse the rising hope that this would be the answer to their problems. And maybe she'd consider all of it after she closed her eyes for a bit.

The ride to the Brazen H was quiet and short. She wondered if Cord was starting to regret his insistence that she stay with him. It'd serve him right for being so stubborn. She could have taken care of herself, but it was nice to have someone worry about her—even if it was out of some sense of obligation.

Now, as Alexis stood in Cord's living room, she immediately noticed how everything was in its place. Interesting. For some reason, she'd thought a bachelor would be messy and his house would be chaotic. Cord surprised her—and not for the first time.

While he was still outside having a word with his foreman, Alexis glanced around at the cream paint covering the walls and the tan draperies that hung on either side of the large bay window. She noticed how the room lacked any books. Upon closer inspection, she found it devoid of magazines or even a newspaper. *How strange.* She'd always found that she could tell so much by a person's reading habits, but Cord still remained an intriguing mystery.

A small collection of antique black-and-white photos drew her interest. She couldn't resist walking over to have a closer look. A tall, light-skinned man posed in front of a rustic wood building. She squinted to read the name on the post office. Haggerty, New Mexico. In the picture, the man's hand rested above his gun belt as he leaned casually against a rough-hewn pillar near the open doorway. His eyes gleamed with pride while a full beard partially obscured his smug smile. Everything about his appearance said he'd conquered the world.

Just then Cord strolled into the house. "Sorry about that. We were discussing moving the herd to a new field."

"No problem. I was just looking at your photos. Is this the man who founded the ghost town?" She glanced over at Cord, who took a seat on the couch.

"Yes, that's James Haggerty." Pride rang out in Cord's voice. "The boy in the photo is my great-grandfather."

Another photo of the same man hung to the left. This time a beautiful Hispanic woman dressed formally in a hat and fancy dress accompanied him. A little boy stood between them. Their smiles reflected in their eyes. What had they sacrificed to settle this land? Between what she'd learned from Cord about Haggerty's history and now putting a face to the land made Alexis begin to regret her plans, but it was too late to back out now. She'd already put her plan in motion to rally the town's support for the resort. And it would help so many residents of Whistle Stop—it'd also help Cord.

She glanced back and forth between Cord and the photograph. "Definitely a family resemblance."

Cord didn't respond. He sat across the room from her, looking stiff and uncomfortable. Their gazes connected and held longer than necessary. Her heart thump-thumped harder, faster. Her mouth grew dry. She continued to stare at him as the tip of her tongue swiped over her lips.

"You need more ice for your hand." Cord jumped to his feet. "They gave me a few of those plastic cooling packs so that you would always have an icy one. I'll go get it."

He practically tripped over his own feet making a hasty exit. Had he felt it, too? That magnetic pull that had drawn them together out in the desert was still there—no matter how much she wanted to deny it. But she had no intention of acting on it—not a chance. No matter how tempting the idea.

CHAPTER ELEVEN

Having a woman—not just any woman, but one he'd passionately kissed—staying in his house was enough to drive Cord to distraction. He wasted the entire afternoon paying two measly bills. With the likelihood of transposing the numbers, he made a habit of taking his time and triple-checking his work. The rest of the time, he'd been tiptoeing down the hall to check on Lexi. He couldn't believe he'd been reduced to creeping around his own house. Once he'd even caught himself gazing at her longer than necessary to ascertain she was breathing comfortably.

Even now, he envisioned a cozy dinner and lighthearted banter. Later, they'd share a bit of coffee out on the porch. He'd follow that up with a kiss...or two. He sighed. Of course, none of that was going to happen. She was here with him because she had to be, not because she wanted to be. She'd made that all too clear when she'd rejected his kiss.

He stood next to the center island in the kitchen and glanced up at the clock on the wall for the third time in the past five minutes. Six o'clock straight up. Time to eat.

He prepared a couple of steaks to add to the foil-wrapped potatoes already on the grill. When he came back inside, there was still no sign of Lexi. Thinking that she might want more than meat and potatoes, he tossed together a salad.

He should probably go wake her. Then again, maybe she'd be better off sleeping. He pulled out her care instructions and in the silence began deciphering the words one at a time. He was a slow reader, but with determination, he could make it through to the end.

"Would that happen to be the instructions from the doctor?" Lexi came up behind him.

Too late to hide the paper. "Ah, yes. Here you go."

"That's okay. Can you just read the part about what symptoms to watch for?"

"Is something wrong?" He was poised to drop everything to drive her to the hospital.

"Um...no. I'm just being cautious is all."

He looked at her as she made her way to the sink. His gaze settled on the gentle sway of her hips. He swallowed hard before forcing his attention back to the care instructions. He hadn't gotten to the symptoms section. His chest tightened as the letters formed a jumbled mess. His throat clogged. There was no way he'd read it out loud to her. He'd sound like...like a complete and utter jerk, or worse. He might have opened up a bit to her while they were at Haggerty, but he was not sharing this part of his life. Absolutely not.

"You can read it." He pushed the paper toward her as she lifted a glass of water to her lips.

Before she could even take a sip, she lowered the glass. "If you don't want me here, I'll leave."

He shook his head. "It's not that. In fact, it's the opposite. It...it's nice to have some company."

The corners of her mouth lifted, and she stepped up to him. "Really?" Her voice purred with delight. "Well, thanks for having me. Sorry I wasn't so agreeable earlier. I wasn't feeling very well."

"But you're feeling better now?"

"Much better. That nap was just what I needed."

His needs ran in a completely different direction. His gaze dipped to her lips. They were still damp from the cold water. He should turn away and keep busy, but his body seemed to have a will of its own as he leaned down and brushed his mouth over hers. Sweet and delectable, just like he remembered. He also remembered that he was doing the exact thing he'd told himself not to do. She was his opposition. But more than that, she was way out of his league.

However, she didn't reject his advance. In fact, she didn't say one thing about his moment of spontaneity. That was a good thing. Wasn't it? Or was she just too startled to speak?

He pulled away. "I have to get the steaks off the grill."

He hustled out the back door. He should tell her the truth—he couldn't read. At least, not like others. Then she'd see him clearly. At last this crazy attraction thing would stop. But his male ego refused to be lessened in her eyes. For some reason, her opinion meant a lot to him. If he could just hide his deficiencies for a little longer, she'd be gone.

Just for once it was nice having someone around who hadn't known him all of his life. She didn't know about the merciless teasing because he couldn't read as fast as the other kids. She didn't know how he still struggled. Instead, Lexi saw him as a man—a landowner—someone with whom to do business. And he liked it. He really liked it. Most of all, he really liked her and her spunk. He didn't want any of that to change.

He'd just returned from the grill with a platter holding two medium T-bones and the potatoes when he glanced up in time to catch Lexi in mid-stretch. The curves of her body strained against her turquoise top while a sliver of her bare stomach peeked out from beneath the hem of her shirt. He practically dropped their dinner right there on the floor. He swallowed hard as he continued to stare.

Her amused gaze caught his eye, and he turned away. "I didn't know what you like to eat, so I grilled up a couple of steaks. If that's okay with you, we can eat just as soon as I set the table and pour us some iced tea."

"Sounds good. Is it really after six? I didn't mean to sleep all afternoon."

The memory of her stretched out on the bed did nothing to help him regain his composure. His appetite for steak vanished. He craved something else— someone with rumpled hair and bare feet. His gaze strayed to Lexi. Wasn't it just like a man to hunger for a woman he could never possess? He inwardly groaned.

With the table set and the drinks poured, he grabbed a couple of acetaminophen caplets and handed them to her. "Here. It's past time for you to take these."

She accepted the pills and chased them down with some tap water. "Since I'm feeling better, how about after dinner you give me a ride back to the motel?"

He knew her suggestion would be best for his sanity, but he'd given his word to watch over her tonight, and that's exactly what he intended to do. "You're stuck with me for twenty-four hours. I'll give you a ride back to the Doc's tomorrow for your follow-up appointment. If he okays it, you can go back to the motel then, but not before. Now, let's eat."

"And that's your final word?"

"It is."

She rolled her eyes and shook her head.

After she washed up, she joined him at the table. They filled up their plates with steak and the salad he'd tossed with red wine vinaigrette.

They quietly ate until the silence started to bother him. "Did you tell your father about your encounter with the scorpion?"

"No. I didn't want to worry him. He's already more stressed than he needs to be."

This was where Cord was supposed to interject something to keep the conversation going. But what? He had zero experience playing host or striking up an engaging conversation.

He settled for the first thought that came to his mind. "Your steak…is it cooked the way you like? I could put it back on the grill."

She glanced down at her plate as though she'd momentarily forgotten about the food. "It's great. Thank you for making it. I feel bad for making you go out of your way."

He shrugged. "I don't get many guests. I'd forgotten how nice it is to share a meal with someone."

Now why in the world had he gone and said that? But then Lexi smiled at him. A genuine smile. One of those that lit up her whole face and warmed a spot in his chest.

"This is so much better than eating alone at my desk while poring over reports." She took a bite of steak.

He couldn't imagine someone so young and beautiful spending all of her time working. He'd have thought her social calendar would be booked. "Maybe you should cut back on your hours at the office. I'm sure there has to be a lot to do in New York City." Not that he'd know. He'd never ventured beyond the New Mexico border. Everything he needed was right here. "What sort of things do you like to do?"

"You mean, aside from work?" She sat back as though giving his question serious consideration. "I like to read cozy mysteries. I started a really good one months ago, but I haven't had time to get back to it."

"You know what they say about all work and no play…"

"I do. But I have priorities."

"That doesn't mean you can't take a moment to enjoy yourself." He couldn't believe what he was saying. Why should he care how she chose to spend her time? It was absolutely none of his business.

"Maybe you could show me more of your ranch. I really enjoyed seeing Haggerty. And I'd really enjoy riding one of your horses."

He bit back an eager invitation. This was so unlike him. Even with his ex, he hadn't been interested in her so quickly. Susan had been the one to initiate things. And look where that had gotten him. Still, he couldn't be rude. His mother had raised him better than that. And Lexi deserved only the best.

"If there's time before you leave, we could take a ride to a remote spot that you might enjoy."

"Great. I'm looking forward to it."

He glanced up, surprised by her eagerness. Maybe they didn't have to be adversaries. Maybe they could agree to disagree about what was best for the land and be friendly with each other. He didn't have many friends, aside from the ranch hands. Something told him Lexi would be a good friend.

She added some butter to her potato. "Do you have any relatives in Whistle Stop?"

He shook his head. "Not anymore."

She looked as though she were about to ask something else, but instead she mashed the butter into the potato before taking a bite.

Eager to make the most of the opportunity to connect with her, he said, "The land and the animals keep me grounded."

"What about friends?" She laid down her fork and stared at him.

"Obviously, you must have heard some of the gossip about me that's going around town." She nodded, and he continued, "Then there's nothing more for me to add."

Her concerned gaze met his. "Sure there is. If you know what they're saying, why don't you stop it?"

"I can't fight the truth." So much for his fantasy about being a "real man" in Lexi's eyes.

"You call that bunch of rehashed garbage the truth? I haven't known you very long, but I know you aren't like the man they described to me in town. And I told Mrs. Sanchez that—"

"You did what?" He didn't need anyone sticking up for him.

"I told her that you've been nothing but kind and considerate."

He had? That's really how she saw him? The funny feeling in his chest left him feeling off-kilter. What was he supposed to say now?

"Don't look so shocked. You can be quite the gentleman when you set your mind to it."

No one had ever said such kind things to him. Unable to look her in the eyes, he gazed down at his plate. "You shouldn't have wasted your time. They already have their minds made up about me."

"Mrs. Sanchez seemed quite interested in my opinion of you. Perhaps you should give them a second chance, and maybe they'll give you one, too."

Uncomfortable with this line of conversation, he decided to turn it around. "You made quite an impression on Mr. Forbes. He thinks your resort would be good for the local economy. He insisted I learn more about your plans. So now it's your turn. Tell me more about this resort you're all gung ho to build."

"I have some information in my room that you're welcome to read." Her chair scraped over the tile floor.

He held out his hand to stop her from getting up. "I don't want to read some sales pitch. I just want you to be bluntly honest with me. What kind of resort would you build?"

"A Wild West-themed one."

Hence, the need for the ghost town. "Why in the world would you build a vacation destination in the middle of nowhere?"

"That's one of the land's many charms. It'll provide privacy to the resort's guests."

"Why would they need privacy?" A dull ache in his gut told him he wasn't going to like the answer.

"I suppose at this point it won't hurt to tell you that this will be an exclusive resort. The clientele will be high-profile people who want a vacation without having to worry about the paparazzi snapping pictures for those grocery store tabloids."

"And the ghost town?"

"We'll provide it as an attraction for the guests to explore."

Speechless, he stared at her. She wanted to take the land his family had eked out a living on and turn it into some sort of amusement for the rich and famous. His gut twisted.

He stood and grabbed his half-empty plate. He strode to the sink and deposited it. What had happened to his plans for some fun banter and kissing? His jaw tightened. This wasn't anywhere close to the ending he'd dreamed up.

"Hey, where are you going?" she called to him.

"I have to clean up the kitchen."

"You didn't finish eating. And you didn't share your thoughts about the resort."

He kept his back to her. His hands clenched the edge of the counter. "That's not a good idea. I don't think you want to hear what I think."

"Sure I do."

He shook his head. "Go rest while I clean up."

He needed the time alone to wrap his head around what she'd told him. Even though she appeared to be a desirable lady with lots of love for her father, Cord couldn't get past his horror of her wanting to do something so trivial with the land—his land. When he was out there on the range, he could be comfortable with himself. He wasn't constantly reminded of his shortcomings.

What he had now was all he would ever own. By giving up a large chunk of his family's land, his acreage would drastically shrink—his ability to make a living off the land would be severely compromised. Less land would mean a smaller herd of cattle, which would mean significantly less income. He'd have to let go of some of his ranch hands—men who counted on him for a paycheck. The thought washed away the sweetness from his iced tea, leaving behind only bitterness.

"I don't want to rest," Lexi insisted. "I want to talk—about the resort. Admit it, the plan has a lot of potential. Not only will it save the Brazen H from foreclosure, but it'll bring a lot of business back to Whistle Stop."

He turned to her. "Why did you have to pick my family's land? This is a large desert area. There's lots of other remote property. Why do you have to destroy my heritage to make a profit?"

Tense lines etched her beautiful face as her painted nails tucked a strand of hair behind her ear. "Our investors want something new and invigorating. Your land offers a host of unique resort activities from rock-climbing to hiking to exploring a genuine ghost town. In addition, the area allows for an airstrip for private planes, as well as commuter flights out of the Albuquerque airport."

In any other circumstance, he'd have applauded her for devising a resort unique from the ski and golf resorts such as the ones up north in Red River and Angel Fire. If only she hadn't set her sights on his land.

"What would you say if I told you my investors want to preserve as much of the ghost town as possible?"

"I'd say I'm still opposed to you buying the land." He just couldn't bring himself to tell her the whole truth—that cowboying was all he was cut out to do.

"Is it really your heritage that you're fighting for?" Her narrow gaze poked at him.

He glanced away. "What else would it be?"

"I just thought...oh, never mind." She shook her head in frustration. "Let me help you with the dinner dishes—"

"I've got it. Just go." Realizing the gruffness of his voice, he attempted a friendlier tone. "Go get some rest. I'm fine here."

She walked away, leaving an overwhelming loneliness to sweep over him. They'd reached a stalemate, and both had too much riding on the deal to back down. And once again, he was alone. The story of his life.

The whole time he scrubbed at the dishes with unnecessary vigor, he rolled around everything he'd learned that evening. He tried to ignore how much he'd enjoyed sharing a meal with her and the way she'd smiled at him. Instead, he focused on her intention to make his family's land a playground for those with enough money to visit an exclusive resort. How in the world was he going to stop her? And keep his home— his refuge?

CHAPTER TWELVE

What in the world had she been thinking?

Obviously, she hadn't been, at least not clearly. Alexis paced around the living room. The evening had started so well. Cord could be kind and considerate. And that kiss, where had it come from? And what in the world had it meant?

Maybe her rising desire to kiss him back—her curiosity to see where things would go if they'd quit dancing around each other—had her retreating behind the safety of her business persona. She just couldn't let him get too close. She knew all too well what happened when she got too close to people—they let her down.

First, her mother abandoning her and then her fiancé using her as a stepping stone to further his career. She highly doubted that Steven had ever cared about her. He'd cared only about what doors she could open for him. Once she'd accomplished that, he'd forgotten her like yesterday's sports page.

But that didn't mean she had to wage war every time she was alone with Cord. It wasn't like either of them was going to let things go beyond a kiss. And right about now, she was certain he wasn't any too eager for a repeat—not after she'd detailed her plans for Haggerty.

Still, she should apologize for ruining his dinner. She'd step into the kitchen, say her piece and slip away. She leveled her shoulders, mentally rehearsed her apology, and started for the kitchen. She'd just about reached the door when it swung open. She stumbled back to avoid getting hit by it.

Cord's eyes opened wide when he noticed her. "Sorry. I didn't know you were there."

"I...um...it's okay." Her stomach quivered with nerves.

"Do you need something?"

She backtracked into the living room while searching for the right words. Why was she making such a big deal of this? She crossed her arms and turned to him. "Actually, there is something I want—"

"You're cold. I'll start a fire. The evenings get rather chilly now that it's getting late in the year."

Cord's back was to her as he stepped up to the stone fireplace. Normally, she'd wait until he straightened and faced her, but perhaps this would be easier. She settled on the couch. Her gaze never left him as the well-defined muscles of his arms flexed while he placed logs on the grate.

Why did everything have to be so complicated? In another set of circumstances, she'd be snug in his very capable arms, and they'd be repeating that delicious kiss over and over again. She stifled a frustrated groan. She had to stop these thoughts. Absolutely nothing was going to happen while she was here alone with this sexy cowboy. Absolutely nothing.

"There's a throw on the back of the couch that you can use until the fire warms the room." Cord struck a match.

It wasn't the throw she wanted wrapped around her. Realizing her fantasy wasn't going to become reality, she doused the heated thoughts.

She still owed him an apology. Best to get it over with so that they could move on. "I'm sorry about how dinner ended. I didn't mean to ruin it, especially after you've gone out of your way for me."

"You didn't ruin anything. I shouldn't have let it get to me—you know, your plans for the land. I know you have good intentions. Maybe we can just agree to disagree about that issue."

"I think that might be doable…at least for tonight." He impressed her with his ability to be a gentleman about the incident. "By the way, the meal, it was a really good. You're excellent in the kitchen."

His brows rose. "You're just saying that—"

"No, I'm not. You can cook for me any time you want." There was a part of her that hoped he would invite her to dinner again. Not that it was realistic, but a girl was allowed to indulge in a fantasy every now and then.

"I'll just let you rest." He started to walk away.

"Don't go." She couldn't decide which was more distracting—drinking in his sexy image with her eyes or fantasizing about him when he was out of sight. "Why don't you sit down?" She drew up her knees, making room for him next to her on the couch.

She didn't know why she'd made the move, considering there were two overstuffed chairs and another couch in the spacious living room, but he accepted her gesture. In the background, the fire hissed and popped. With the setting sun casting long shadows over the room, she realized just how cozy a setting they'd created. If she were to straighten her legs, they'd end up in Cord's lap. She closed her eyes, imagining his long, skillful fingers working their magic over her toes, her feet, and up her legs. Mmm…

"Are you all right?"

The sound of Cord's voice had her eyes snapping open and heat stinging her cheeks. "I'm fine."

"Are you sure? It isn't quite time for more acetaminophen, but I can check with Doc Willard to see if you can have it a little early, or maybe he can give you something stronger if you need it—"

"No. Don't." She reached out, squeezing his arm in an attempt to reassure him. But the contact sent shivers of awareness cascading up her arm and down her spine. "I don't need anything. My hand is getting better."

"Are you sure?" He sent her a disbelieving look.

"Positive." She held up her injured limb and flexed her fingers as proof. Her joints were still a bit stiff, but she was certain it was just a matter of time until she was completely better. "In fact, I'm so good you could take me back to the motel—"

"Don't start again. You're staying. Got it?"

"My, you're bossy." She smiled, letting him know that she was teasing him. Her good hand was still on his arm, and she had absolutely no desire to move it. "You're a great guy...even if you are a bit stubborn at times. I'm surprised someone hasn't snatched you up."

He pulled away. "I was married. She decided that I wasn't such a great catch and threw me back."

Alexis knew it was none of her business, but she couldn't help herself. "Were you married long?"

"Almost five years. Now she's off pursuing her dreams." His tone held a note of discord.

"I couldn't imagine giving up a home like this and such a great guy."

He got to his feet, strode over to the large picture window, and stared into the night. "You don't know what you're saying. This place couldn't compare to the excitement of New York City. You wouldn't like it here. You'd grow bored and restless."

Alexis got to her feet. Her bare feet moved soundlessly over the wood floor. She joined him by the window, noticing the last shades of the fading sun on the distant horizon. Her gaze moved to him, and her voice came out soft and sultry. "I'm sure I could find something to keep my attention."

"You shouldn't do that."

"Do what?"

"Flirt with me."

Was it still considered flirting if she meant every word? "Why not? What if I'm serious?"

Was that a groan she heard? A smile tugged at her lips. Common sense warned her to leave well enough alone, but she couldn't recall the last time she'd enjoyed herself this much.

His dark eyes met hers. "Lexi, you don't know what you're asking."

"I take it you don't date much?"

He shook his head. His gaze dipped to her lips. Her stomach somersaulted. He was going to kiss her again. Her heart fluttered, and the little voice in her head that talked reason drifted away.

"It must get pretty lonely being out here all by yourself." Her voice was soft. "Maybe you should consider getting yourself a dog. I hear they're good for companionship."

His gaze lifted, meeting hers. Unmistakable desire flashed in them. "I have a better idea."

She knew what he had in mind, because she had the same thought. "What might that be?"

"It might be better if I show you." He stepped closer, pulling her into his arms. There was a moment of hesitation, as though he were waiting for her to pull away.

She wasn't going anywhere. There was something special about this cowboy—something that drew her in. The place where his fingers rested against her hips grew warm, as though his fingerprints were now tattooed upon her skin.

He was going to kiss her, and mentally she willed him on. That kiss in the desert and the brief one in the kitchen had been a prelude to this moment—the main event. Her hands slid up over his muscled chest, appreciating the firm contours. Her hands wrapped around his neck. His gaze held hers. She wasn't about to turn away now. She was a woman who knew what she wanted—she wanted him with every fiber of her being.

Yet she could feel the stiffness of his muscles. There was a war raging within him. Longing to tip the odds in her favor, she leaned up on her tiptoes and pressed her lips to his. He didn't move at first. Nor did she pull away. He wanted her, that much she was certain.

She moved her lips slowly and tantalizingly over his. And then she heard something. The sound grew louder until she realized it was a moan, and it was coming from Cord. She'd have smiled in triumph, but she had other, more important things to do with her lips—much more important things.

He deepened the kiss, and she eagerly met him move for move. She reveled in her ability to seduce this solitary cowboy. But it was more than that. There was a vulnerability to him—scars that ran deep. She didn't know exactly what they were, but she wanted to assure him that he was worthy of being loved.

His hands slid up her back. Her heart pounded, and their kiss took on a passion all its own. He wasn't the only one who was lonely—who needed to feel a deep connection. It wasn't until that moment that she realized she'd been burying all of her pain of rejection behind a mountain of work. She'd closed herself off from the world in hopes of heeling. And now, in Cord's arms, she felt alive again.

Maybe together, they could help each other.

As though reading her thoughts, Cord pulled her snug against him. Her stomach fluttered with anticipation. His lips moved hungrily over hers as his fingers slid up her neck and combed through her hair. For one night, their troubles would disappear. Here on the Brazen H, they'd find happiness and release in each other's arms.

Cord stopped kissing her. His breathing was deep and uneven as he rested his forehead against hers. "Are you sure about this? About us?"

For a moment, she hesitated. She was here to work—to save her father's company and quite possibly his life—not to indulge in a moment of passion. But who would know? She certainly didn't plan to tell anyone. And she had no doubt that Cord would keep this night under wraps.

"I'm sure."

That's all it took for Cord to scoop her up into his arms and start down the hallway. Her arms naturally wound around his neck. She trailed kisses up his neck, enjoying the salty tang of his smooth skin and the way she could make his breathing unsteady.

He moaned and tightened his grip on her. "You're driving me crazy."

"And I've only just begun."

"I'll remember you said that." His voice was deep and gravelly.

She smiled. "I'm sure you will."

He paused outside the door to the master bedroom. "Last chance to change your—"

She smothered his words with a kiss that would leave no doubt in his mind of her intentions. He kicked the door open as the chime of the telephone shattered the silence. In the doorway, Cord hesitated.

"It's okay." She purred in his ear. "I'll wait."

He cursed under his breath and lowered her feet to the ground. "I'll be right back."

Cord surprised her when he strode back to the living room instead of taking the call in his bedroom. Maybe he didn't want to talk in front of her. Maybe he thought it might be something about the sale of the land. The thought of a potential buyer had Alexis eager to follow him just to assure herself that she didn't have any competition—for the land, that is. But she wasn't about to lower herself to eavesdropping.

"Lexi, phone's for you," Cord called out.

Was it her imagination or did he sound unhappy? Was it the timing of the call? Or the caller themselves? The questions circled round and round in her mind as she returned to the living room and took the phone from Cord, who didn't even bother to meet her questioning gaze.

Disappointment washed over her as Cord strode down the hall. As sure as she was standing alone in his living room, the promise of an amazing evening had been dashed. And though she should be relieved that she'd be saved from making another mistake and getting in too deep, all she could think was, *Why? What changed Cord's mood so drastically?*

She lifted the phone to her ear. "Hello."

"Ms. Greer, this is Mayor Ortiz. How are you? I heard about your unfortunate incident."

There was a distinguishable thud of Cord's bedroom door closing—further confirmation that their romantic evening was over before it'd even begun. Reality had shattered their happy illusion. A frown pulled at her lips.

"Ms. Greer, are you still there?"

"Uh, yes. Sorry. I'm fine."

"Are you sure? If you'd rather come stay with my family, my wife would love to have you. Or if you'd be more comfortable, I'm sure Mrs. Sanchez would love the company."

"Why would I do that? Cord has been the perfect host."

"He has?" There was a note of surprise and utter disbelief in the mayor's voice. "I mean, I'm sure he has. Is there anything else you need?"

You mean other than the ability to go back in time and take the phone off the hook?

"No. Nothing that I can think of. Cord has taken care of everything." Almost... "I just feel bad for imposing on him."

"I...I'm sure he's enjoying your company."

At this particular moment, she wouldn't want to wager any money on that one.

Before she could think of something to say, the mayor continued, "The other reason I called is to let you know that I've spoken with the other council members. They are receptive to your idea and would like to hear more. Could you present your ideas at the next town meeting?"

"Certainly." At least something was going right for her. "When is it?"

"Next Tuesday evening. I'm looking forward to it."

The mayor rushed off the phone while Alexis reconciled herself to the fact that she needed to modify her presentation to include ways the resort would be beneficial to Whistle Stop.

Her mind was buzzing with ideas. It was just as well, because Cord's closed bedroom door spoke volumes. He no longer wanted her. They were adversaries, and he was not going to be happy when the entire town was involved in their negotiations. Guilt gnawed at her. Public pressure was not a new concept for pushing through a struggling sale, so why was she letting it bother her now?

She didn't want to examine her evolving feelings for Cord. She was afraid of what she might find if she did. Because she'd promised herself she wouldn't risk her heart—it wasn't worth the pain of rejection. Because in the end, those she loved abandoned her. For one reason or another, she wasn't worth their effort.

And Cord obviously wasn't going to be any different.

♥♥♥

Late the next morning, as promised, Cord drove Lexi into Whistle Stop. He'd been avoiding her ever since the phone call. He didn't need to ask why the mayor had called. He knew the call was about more than Lexi's health—it was about the proposed resort. It was a project that could potentially help the town's sagging bottom line.

What had gotten into him to forget all of this and get swept up in the moment? He usually kept his wits about him, but there was something special about Lexi and her very tempting kisses that had him willing to take a risk. He couldn't let that happen again. That's why he'd been up and out the door before sunup. He'd avoided her until it was time to drive her into town for her doctor's appointment.

And now silence hung heavily in the truck. He didn't know if she was quiet because she regretted their intimate moment or if it had something to do with her plans for his land. Whatever it was, Cord was certain of two things: One, he wasn't going to like it. And two, it wasn't going to change his mind.

When they walked into the doctor's office, the waiting room was empty. They'd barely sat down when Mrs. Willard smiled and waved Lexi back to an exam room.

Lexi paused in the doorway and glanced back at him. "Aren't you coming?"

"Me?" He couldn't believe she'd want him around.

She nodded and sent him a hesitant smile. The fact she wanted him by her side meant a lot to him. He followed her down the hallway. Maybe he'd been all wrong about everything. Maybe she was quiet because she was worried about her hand. And maybe the mayor had called only out of concern for her health—as he should have.

As she sat on the papered exam table, Cord couldn't help but notice how she appeared vulnerable. "I don't like doctors' offices," she whispered. "They make me nervous."

"You don't have to worry. I'm sure everything will be just fine."

She held out her hand and examined it. "I hope you're right. If I'd listened to you in the first place, I wouldn't be here."

"But you'd have missed seeing an authentic ghost town."

"True."

"Not to mention hearing the ghost story."

"I really liked the story." Her eyes lit up. "I could just imagine that distraught young woman pacing back and forth in front of the mine entrance, waiting for her true love. But it's such a sad story. Can you imagine being so close to having a life with your soul mate and then having it snatched away?"

What in the world was he supposed to say to that? He wasn't even sure there was such a thing as soul mates. The happily-ever-after thing certainly hadn't worked out for him.

Doc Willard strode into the room, wearing his white coat and his reading glasses propped high on his balding head. "Good morning. How are you feeling?"

"Much better." Lexi's face reverted back to a worried frown.

After an exam and some questions, Doc smiled. "You can relax. You're on the mend." He turned to Cord. "And I hereby release you from nursing duty."

With a couple of warnings, Doc sent them on their way. Cord knew it was ridiculous, but he was going to miss having Lexi around the house. He'd forgotten how nice it was to share a meal with someone and to make small talk.

Acting on impulse, Cord held the front door for Lexi. "How about an early lunch?"

"I'd like that." She stepped out onto the sidewalk.

Before he could say more, he heard his name being called. "Cord! Cord!"

It was a familiar female voice. He wanted to keep going—in the opposite direction—but Lexi stopped and glanced around. He stifled a frustrated groan and turned.

Mimi Ortiz smiled broadly and waved as she tried to walk quickly in pink heels that matched the purse dangling from her arm and the tiny flowers on her snug sundress. "Oh, I was worried you hadn't heard me."

"Hello, Mimi. You look nice today." She had an insatiable ego, and he knew it was easier to feed it than to have her work for the compliment.

"Oh, thank you. This old thing is nothing special." She smiled broadly, failing miserably at being modest. "I can't believe I ran into you. You don't come into town nearly enough."

"Only when I have business to tend to."

That's when Mimi's gaze strayed to Lexi. "I see." Mimi's smile dimmed considerably. "Hi." She held out her hand to Lexi, who hesitantly shook it. "I'm Mimi Ortiz. The mayor of Whistle Stop is my father."

A light of recognition shone in Lexi's eyes. "It's nice to meet you."

"And you're that lady who wants to buy Cord's land."

"Um…yes. I'm Alexis Greer."

"I know." Mimi's tone was short and clipped. "Daddy mentioned you—"

"We've got to go." Cord wrapped his fingers around Lexi's arm and guided her away from Mimi toward the truck. He sensed that this conversation was about to take a bad turn, and he wasn't about to play referee.

"What'd you do that for?" Lexi asked once they were seated in the truck.

"Let's just say I was doing you a favor. Mimi isn't all sweet and innocent—"

"And you were afraid that I couldn't handle her."

"No." He was quite certain Lexi could handle herself. He admired that about her. "The truth is, I do have someplace to be."

"Oh. So I guess lunch is off."

"Not at all. As long as you don't mind waiting for me."

"Will it take long?"

"Nope."

"Then you have yourself a date."

An awkward silence ensued as he guided the truck across town to the Green Chile Cantina. He assured himself this offer for lunch didn't constitute a true date. His invitation had been an impulse—nothing more. After all, they both had to eat, so why not do it together? And he did have something to ask her— something important.

He pulled to a stop in front of the adobe building. "This place has the best food in the state."

"I've had all of my meals at Tilly's Café. It'll be nice to try something different." She reached for the door handle. "I'll see you soon, and maybe you can tell me some more about Mimi. She seems…interesting." With her laptop in hand, Lexi climbed out of the truck and headed for the Cantina.

The very last thing he wanted to discuss was Mimi. He didn't want to explain how he'd briefly dated her before he'd met Susan. No way. Things with Lexi were already complicated enough. And right now, he had one last chance of stalling the foreclosure, of clinging to the only world he'd ever known.

CHAPTER THIRTEEN

Why in the world had she referred to this as a *date*?

Alexis paused in the restaurant's entryway and sighed. She'd noticed how her slip of the tongue had made Cord stiffen. There couldn't be any more slipups. She had to stay focused. Her chance to carve out a delicious memory in Cord's arms had passed her by. She told herself it was for the best, but she still wasn't convinced. There was something different, something special about him. And she wanted to help him save his home, if only he'd listen to her and really hear what she was saying.

Inside the spacious dining room a large ceramic Native American Indian chief solemnly greeted her. While she waited to be seated, she glanced around, taking in the details of the quaint restaurant. Her gaze scanned the dining room with its red tile floor and white walls. Though the furniture was basic and a bit on the old side, the colorful red chile ristras, brightly painted Southwestern folk art, and Native American paintings brought life to the place. The decorations were almost as colorful as the town in which the restaurant resided.

A petite, dark-haired woman showed her to a corner booth. "Hi. Have you been in here before?"

"No. But I've heard great things about the place. And I've been anxious to try your food."

The young woman smiled brightly. "It's nice to meet you. I'm Ana."

"Hi, Ana. I'm Alexis."

"So what brought you to our little corner of the world?"

"I have some business in town." She wasn't about to tell this woman about her plans for the resort. There would be time enough for that later, when she could properly present her ideas.

But this was an ideal time to learn more about Cord's corner of the world—more than the statistics and data she'd already collected. She wanted to know more about the people who lived here, what their lives were like. Sure it would help her pitch, but it was more than that. This town and its residents were growing on her. She truly wanted to do what she could to help revitalize Whistle Stop.

"Would you mind telling me a little about the area?"

Ana walked to the front door and grabbed a pamphlet. She returned to the table and set down the canary-yellow paper. "This lists most of the area's highlights. You'll love the homey feel of the town. Now, what can I get you?"

"How about some coffee to start with?" After the waitress moved toward the kitchen, Alexis flipped through the pamphlet. There were numerous community activities listed for Whistle Stop, such as the dart league and the quilting guild and many events.

When the waitress dropped off the steaming cup along with a basket of chips and some salsa, then moved to a nearby table to refill the salt and pepper shakers, Alexis said, "Thanks for the information about the area. It's surprising how much a small town can offer. The Whistle Stop Labor Day Picnic sounds like a big deal."

"It's more important around here than Cinco de Mayo or the Fourth of July." Ana screwed the cap on a refilled saltshaker. "There's a rodeo, a best-shot competition, and lots of kids games."

"No sporting events? Or concerts?"

"In this area, rodeo and shooting are considered sporting events."

She could easily imagine Cord taking part in both events. Too bad Labor Day had already passed. She'd love to see him bull riding...on second thought, it sounded too dangerous.

"Did you grow up here?" Alexis asked, taking a liking to the woman who appeared to be about her age.

"Born and bred." Ana turned her attention to screwing the lid back on a peppershaker. "And you're from New York."

"Good guess." She didn't think she had much of an accent.

"No guessing involved. Mr. Forbes has been talking about a woman who's in town to build some fancy resort. I put two and two together."

So much for keeping her project low-key. She took a tortilla chip still warm from the deep fryer and scooped up some of the chunky salsa. "This is exceptionally good."

"Thanks. It's homemade from an old family recipe."

"I'm impressed. It's the best I've ever had." Alexis took another bite. "So what's a person to do around here for evening entertainment?"

"The cinema's new releases run a couple months behind the rest of the world."

"I'm not much into movies."

"There are a couple of saloons scattered around town, but nothing to rival Albuquerque's night life. You could try bingo at the town hall on Wednesdays. But go early to get a seat. A large number of Whistle Stop's residents play."

"Really? I've never played, but I just might give it a try."

"Meet me here on Wednesday at six, and we can go together."

Alexis smiled. "Sounds good—"

"What sounds good?" Cord asked, approaching the table.

Ana's gaze moved from Cord to Alexis. "I'll stop back to get your order."

After Ana moved on, Alexis turned to her lunch date—erm, her, uh...*to Cord*. "She was just telling me a little about Whistle Stop and what there is to do around here."

He hung his hat on a post at the end of the booth, combed his fingers through his unruly hair, and slid into the seat. "You made friends with Ana already?"

"Would there be a problem if I had?"

"Not at all. I just didn't think you'd be making friends since you'll be leaving town soon."

His comment struck her as odd. What exactly was he saying? Was he trying to usher her out of his life? The thought saddened her. Surely she hadn't understood him correctly. "But you and I are friends, aren't we?"

His gaze met hers. "I don't know what we are." He fidgeted with the menu. "It's complicated."

She couldn't argue. When it came to Cord, there were no easy answers. Perhaps they were better off not trying to define their relationship.

Thinking Ana looked to be about Cord's age, Alexis asked, "How well do you know Ana?"

His brows rose. "We were in the same grade in school. She was always nice to me."

Always nice to him...Definitely not a normal thing to say about a friend. Was he implying that other kids weren't so nice? One by one, pieces of Cord's life started to fall into place. She'd bet he'd learned at an early age to keep to himself. And the ranch probably provided a buffer between him and the rest of the world. Her heart went out to him.

When she found herself staring into his eyes for much too long, she turned away. Her gaze stumbled across something on the floor. "What's that? A penny?"

He glanced down at the floor. "Yep."

"Aren't you going to pick it up?"

"Nope. Don't need a dirty old penny."

She hustled out of the booth and picked up the coin. "Find a penny, pick it up. All day long, you'll have good luck."

He chuckled. "You sound like a little kid."

Heat warmed her cheeks. "Maybe, but guess who's going to have a good day and who isn't?"

"We'll see about that." He pulled a folded document from his back pocket. He laid it on the table and smoothed the creases with his palm. "I just picked this up at the Realtor's office, and it needs your signature."

"Dare I ask what it is?"

"It's an intent-to-purchase form, giving the bank holding my mortgage proof of your interest in buying the couple hundred acres."

"I see."

So that's where he'd gone. He was doing everything in his power to save his home—except accepting that the resort was the answer to all of his problems.

He slid the letter and a pen across the table. "It just needs your signature."

"And if I don't sign it?"

His lips pressed into a firm line. "Why wouldn't you? It's a non-binding letter. Besides, it'll forestall the foreclosure."

"So far you've sworn you won't sell me Haggerty."

"But I will sell you the other land. Land you could build a home on. You could buy your own horses. Heck, you could buy a stableful if you wanted. Just sign the paper."

She wanted to help him, really, she did, but he'd presented her with a bargaining chip, and she intended to make the most of the opportunity. Now was her time to strike.

"I want something in return for signing this letter."

He paused and shot her a suspicious look. "You don't mean Haggerty, do you?"

She shook her head. This was much more personal. Alexis clasped her hands together and flashed Cord her brightest smile. She couldn't believe this prime opportunity had landed in her lap. This was way too good to pass up.

Frown lines bracketed his eyes and mouth as he slouched back against the booth. "What's your price?"

"Don't look so worried. This won't cost you a dime."

"Spit it out."

She placed her elbows on the table and leaned forward. "I want to go horseback riding."

Disbelief reflected in his eyes. "Let me get this straight. All I have to do is take you riding and you'll sign?"

She grinned before nodding. It was time she got over her riding accident…way past time. And with her hectic work schedule, this might be her only opportunity.

His facial muscles relaxed. "Okay, what's the catch?"

"I want to go tomorrow—after lunch." After her meeting with the railroad about its part in her pitch to Whistle Stop and before she lost her nerve.

He rubbed his chin. "I was planning to check the progress on the new fence line then, but I guess I can do it another time. Anything else?"

"I want to ride Midnight Star."

"I don't think so."

She crossed her arms. "Those are my terms. Accept them or take your paper back."

He sighed. "Are you always this difficult? No wonder you aren't married."

His words stabbed at a tender spot in her chest. She blinked away the stinging sensation at the backs of her eyes. She remembered how her ex-fiancé, Steven, had said something quite similar when she hadn't been willing to toss aside her career at HSG and leave her father to follow him across the country. Steven never understood her need to please her father or her inability to abandon him—for so many years, it'd been only the two of them.

"I'm sorry," Cord muttered.

Her chin jutted out. "My marital status has nothing to do with this. If you want the papers signed, you'll have to let me ride your horse."

"What about your hand?"

She held up her injury. "Good enough to hang on to some reins."

"You haven't been on a horse since your accident—that must have been some fall. Mind telling me about it?"

She worried her bottom lip. He'd get the wrong idea. He'd react like her father and insist she had no business riding a horse. She didn't want to hear it all those years ago, and she didn't want to hear it now. But with Cord staring at her with an expectant look on his face, what choice did she have? Besides, it wasn't a secret or anything.

"If you must know, I was competing at a district horse show when my horse unexpectedly stopped. I didn't."

"And…"

Why did he push? Was he still looking for an excuse to keep her from riding? If that was his intent, he wouldn't get her signature. Armed with that thought, she continued, "My arm ended up with a compound fracture, requiring surgery and months of physical therapy."

"Why haven't you ridden since?"

"My father canceled my association membership and sold my horse. He said he wouldn't pay for me to break my neck riding some fool horse."

The long-ago argument and her subsequent sobbing echoed in her mind like the continual wave sounds from a conch shell. She'd been devastated by the loss of something else she loved dearly—her Black Beauty.

"That had to be tough for a kid." Sincerity rang out in the somber tones of his voice. "I remember the first time I got bucked off. After my father knew I was okay, he laughed. A big old belly laugh. I refused to let the horse get the better of me and climbed right back on. I think that's the day I won my father's respect as a cowboy."

If she'd learned anything about Cord, it was that he definitely didn't give up. He kept trying until he got it right. Kind of like how he'd defend his family's land until the bitter end—she just hoped he didn't wait too long to make the right decision.

"So now you see why this ride is so important to me?"

His brown eyes warmed to a milk chocolate. "Yes, I do. I just don't think you're ready to ride Midnight Star."

Before Lexi could respond, Ana approached the table. "You two ready to order?"

They both ordered the same thing—huevos rancheros with a sunny-side-up egg and red sauce. Alexis's stomach rumbled at the thought of food. She hadn't bothered this morning with anything more than coffee. With Cord up and out of the house before she'd even opened her eyes, she hadn't seen any point in messing up the kitchen just for herself. Besides, breakfast was never a big deal for her. Toast and coffee usually covered it.

"You aren't going to change your mind, are you?" He leaned back in his seat, but his eyes never left her.

She shook her head.

"I should make you sign a paper saying I'm not responsible if you break your neck. How in the world I let you talk me into these things is beyond me. You know there's a possibility he won't let you ride him?"

"I understand. So do we have an agreement?"

"You're either one of the most daring women I've ever met or one of the most foolish."

She smiled while nerves churned in her stomach. "I'll go with daring."

"Now, will you sign?"

"Not until I get my ride."

He shook his head, but a smile lifted the corners of his lips. "Stubborn."

"And hungry." She returned his smile.

As if on cue, Ana returned with a fresh basket of chips and another bowl of the homemade salsa. Alexis's mouth watered. She reached for a handful of still-warm chips.

Lunch was delicious. And for once, Alexis didn't worry about the countless calories. There'd be plenty of time for dieting when she returned to New York and had to worry about fitting into one of her many business suits. But for now, she was enjoying her new casual wardrobe and the fact that she no longer stood out—she looked like she belonged in Whistle Stop.

Cord insisted on buying lunch, saying it was his idea so it was his treat. Alexis settled for leaving the tip. When they reached the door, it swung open, and a tall, rugged cowboy stood before her. They sure grew them big, strong, and handsome in these parts.

He tipped his cowboy hat at her and smiled. "Howdy. Are you feeling better?"

"Hi." How in the world did he know about her run-in with the scorpion? "Yes, I am. Thanks for asking."

The handsome cowboy held the door for them to exit. He and Cord exchanged a couple of pleasantries before continuing on their way.

Once the friendly cowboy was out of sight, Alexis turned to Cord. "Who was that? And how did he know about my incident?"

Cord smiled. "I told you, this is a small town—"

"And everybody knows everything that happens." She worried her bottom lip. "That means they all know I spent the night at your house."

"Yes, they probably do. But relax, they'll also know why you were there. And that man is an old friend. His name is Tony Granger. And he happened to be in Doc Willard's waiting room with his nephew when I took you in the first time."

"Oh." Now she felt silly for being paranoid. "He seems like a nice guy."

"He is. But life hasn't treated him fairly. When his brother and sister-in-law died in an accident, he became an overnight parent to his nephew. I get the feeling the adjustment has been far from easy for both of them."

"That's awful. Hopefully things will turn around for him and his nephew."

Cord shrugged. "I hope so—"

"Alexis! Alexis!" Mrs. Sanchez's voice had them both turning around. The woman rushed down the sidewalk in a burnt-orange and royal blue dress and big-rimmed sunglasses. Her face, as always, was made up with bright pink lipstick. And her dark hair was piled high on her head with a plastic clip.

"Hello, Mrs. Sanchez." Alexis smiled.

Cord mumbled a greeting before stuffing his hands in his pockets and shifting his weight from foot to foot.

Mrs. Sanchez fanned herself with a stack of colorful papers. "It's going to be another hot one."

"It sure is." Alexis glanced up at the clear blue sky. It was only going to get hotter out. "I'm thinking I might have to start drinking iced tea instead of coffee."

Mrs. Sanchez frowned and shook her head. "I could never do that, no matter how hot it gets out here." She stopped fanning herself and removed a baby-blue sheet of paper from her large stack. "You'll be wanting one of these."

Mrs. Sanchez handed her the paper and then handed one to Cord. "The mayor was so impressed with what you had to say the other day that he had flyers printed up announcing the town meeting. He's hoping to get everyone there. It's going to be exciting."

Alexis's gaze skidded to a halt as she took in the bold headline:

A New Vision for Whistle Stop

She gasped and glanced at Cord. His brows were drawn together in a formidable line. She should have mentioned this to him sooner. She shouldn't have let herself get distracted.

"I need to get going," Mrs. Sanchez said. "I told the mayor I'd help hand these out." She patted Alexis's arm. "You take care of yourself and let me know if you need anything."

Mrs. Sanchez entered the Cantina while Cord made his way toward his pickup. He didn't waste time saying good-bye to Alexis.

"Cord, wait! Let me explain." Somehow, she had to make this right with him. She couldn't have him going off thinking she'd somehow deceived him.

He stopped in his tracks. His shoulders were rigid, and he kept his back to her.

"Aren't you even going to face me?" She didn't want to talk to the back of his head. She wanted to look into his eyes and know that he'd truly heard what she was trying to tell him.

He turned. His face was creased with frown lines, and his mouth was set in a firm line. "I don't need a speech. It's obvious that everything I've told you about my family and the land has been a complete waste of time."

"That's not true. Let me explain—"

"Is there a problem here?" The authoritative voice had them both turning. A tall, well-built young sheriff stood on the sidewalk. He tilted his cowboy hat to her and then turned a cold, hard stare to Cord.

"Um...no. No problem." Alexis glanced at his nametag. "We're fine, Sheriff Carson." She flashed the sheriff her friendliest smile, wanting him to believe her and quickly move on. Cord was definitely not in the mood to make peace with the man who obviously had issues with him.

"Okay, ma'am." He shot Cord a warning look. "If you need anything at all, my office is over on the corner of Mesa and Main streets."

"Thanks."

They both stood there awkwardly until the sheriff strode out of earshot.

She turned back to Cord. "I take it you two aren't BFFs?"

"He isn't worth worrying about. I don't need people to like me."

"But don't you get lonely?" When Cord's brows gathered and his eyes darkened, she realized she should learn to keep her thoughts to herself.

"I'm fine on my own." His voice was loud, as though he had to speak up to be heard over the wall he'd built around himself. "Not that it's any of your business. You came here to do a job, and you aren't about to let anything stand in your way—"

"That's not true. But you have to understand that without my offer you're going to lose the land anyway.

Otherwise, you wouldn't need me to sign this." She held up the still-unsigned letter of intent.

"Save it." His hand crinkled the announcement of the town meeting into a tight ball. "Do you really expect me to believe you after you went behind my back to rally the town against me?" He threw the wad of paper toward a red garbage can and hit it squarely.

"It's not what I meant to do." The mumbled words drifted away in the wind as Cord jumped into his truck.

She wanted to argue with him, but he was right. She'd been doing what she'd been taught—applying pressure to bring about a quick and satisfactory resolution. But somewhere along the way, things had changed—she'd changed. For just a little bit, she'd been an honorary member of Whistle Stop. People had befriended her, and she liked it—and she liked Cord a whole lot. The thought of how quickly she'd come to care for him scared her.

She'd never intentionally do anything to hurt anyone in Whistle Stop. Right then and there, she promised herself that she'd do what she could to help Whistle Stop before she left town—regardless of whether Cord sold her the land for the resort or not.

CHAPTER FOURTEEN

Two very long, very quiet days had passed since Cord had last seen Lexi. He told himself that her absence didn't bother him—that her plotting against him was reason enough for them to keep their distance. So then why was there a giant knot in his gut? Worst of all, he'd stormed off before he'd gotten her to sign the letter of intent. And the phone call from the bank that morning inquiring about its whereabouts hadn't gone so well. He had to do something quick, but what?

"Hey, boss." Manny strode over to where Cord was refilling the oil in his pickup. "You ever thought about doing something besides hanging out around here?"

Manny was always trying to talk him into heading over to Cactus Mike's Saloon to join one of the dart tournaments. It was amazing that as many times as Cord had turned him down, the guy kept asking. "I'm not really up for darts."

"No, not darts. I was thinkin' you could join me at the fire department. They need more volunteers. And your friend Tony Granger was asking about you and whether you'd give it a try."

"I don't know." He had so many things on his mind right now, especially one beautiful blonde who kept complicating his life.

"Hey, boss, something bothering you?"

"No." Liar.

"Then you might want to stop filling your oil. It's going everywhere."

Cord's hand jerked the almost-empty quart of oil upright. He cursed under his breath, knowing what a smelly mess it'd be once he started up the engine. With a frustrated sigh, he closed the oil fill and used a rag to clean up as much of the spill as possible. If he was smart, he'd call it a day. It'd be safest for everyone.

"I don't blame you for being distracted, boss. Women are always messing with us guys."

Cord snapped the cap back on the oil bottle. "What are you talking about?"

Manny crossed his suntanned arms and rocked back on his dusty, worn boots. "When I was at the saloon, I heard about the special town meeting. They were saying how that snooty woman is trying to turn the town against you so that she can make a quick buck. If'n you want, I can talk to the guys. Maybe some will go to that meetin' and back you up."

"Don't bother." Cord closed the hood on the pickup. "I appreciate the offer. But I can handle this."

Manny shook his head. "I don't know. I think you're gonna be outnumbered."

Cord grabbed the empty quarts of oil and a jug of wiper fluid and headed for the garbage barrel on the side of the barn. He could hear the scuff of Manny's boots behind him. Cord didn't want to discuss his impossible situation, or anything that had to do with Lexi. He still hadn't been able to forget her lips or how close they'd come to fulfilling the promise in that kiss—if only that phone hadn't rung. His hand tightened on the trash in his hands.

"Don't worry." He was doing enough of that for the both of them. "I'll handle this."

"You got a plan, boss?" Manny yanked a can of chewing tobacco from his back pocket, gave it a shake, popped the lid off, and stuffed some in his mouth.

Cord didn't know how the man could stand that stuff. He turned his back on the bulge in Manny's lip. There were more important things to think about, like persuading Lexi to buy *only* the section of land he had listed for sale. She could use it for...for a vacation home. Why not? She obviously loved horses.

"Hey, boss."

Cord tossed the garbage in the can before turning to Manny. "I've got a plan."

"That's good, because here she comes."

The sound of tires crunching over gravel had him staring down the lane. Lexi pulled to a stop behind his pickup. A smile adorned her beautiful face as she joined him on the driveway. His gut tightened at the sight of her in a white cotton top and a short denim skirt. Her brief outfit showed off the beginnings of a golden tan.

He cleared his suddenly dry throat. "I didn't expect to see you. You're lucky you caught me. I'm about to head out on a horseback ride to a nearby canyon."

"Sounds like I have great timing."

The mischievousness reflected in her eyes shot an arrow of alarm into his chest. "Great timing for what?"

"That horseback ride you promised me. I'd love to see the canyon, if you're up to playing tour guide again."

Her interest in the land impressed him, but spending time with a woman who was set to turn the whole town against him was courting disaster. "I don't think that's a good idea."

"Come on. You know you love my company." The smile pulling at her lips made her blue eyes twinkle.

She reached out, grabbing his hand. He looked down at where they were linked. His thumb instinctively rubbed over her smooth skin. This wasn't right. She shouldn't set his heart racing with just a smile. She was the enemy.

His gaze moved to her eyes. Okay, maybe *enemy* was too strong a word. The real problem was that aside from their issue with the land, he liked her. He really liked her smile, her laugh, her chattiness. Oh boy, was he in big trouble. But as he stared into her eyes, his apprehension about her tagging along slowly ebbed into a whisper of warning in the back of his mind.

"If you give me this tour," she said, still keeping hold of him, "you won't have to worry about what I'm up to while you're gone."

"Why? Are you planning to do some more trespassing?" He cocked a brow at her. "Or are you working to turn more townspeople against me?"

She released her hold on him. "That isn't my intent."

"Really?" He crossed his arms and stared at her. "From where I'm standing, your little town meeting is intended to apply public pressure so I'll agree to the sale of my family's land for your resort."

Her face filled with color. "It may have started off that way, but..."

He wasn't about to let her off the hook. He needed to know what she wasn't saying. "But what?"

She glance away. "But things have changed since then."

"Mind elaborating?"

"Yes, I mind."

It was nagging at him. What had changed? Was it the kiss? Or should he say, *the kisses?* They promised so much and left him barely able to think of anything else. And spending more time with her wasn't going to help that situation. Of that he was certain.

He needed to remind her that the idea of them spending the day together was a bad one. "Your adventure to Haggerty didn't turn out so well. I'm surprised you would want to go exploring again so soon."

She planted her hands on her hips. "I'm not a quitter."

"No, you're not."

"As I recall, we have an agreement about the letter of intent," she said, gaining his full attention. "I'll sign it once you let me ride your horse."

His jaw tightened. He didn't like being obligated to anyone and he didn't go back on his word. What was it with this woman? She was more stubborn than the old bull he had in the north pasture. "You'll be bored. There's no ghost town to explore or folklore attached to it."

She shrugged but her gaze never left his. "I'm sure I'll find something to hold my interest."

His heart thumped. Was there an underlying meaning in her words? Did she want to go to be near him? His gaze lingered on her face before zeroing in on her lush lips. Maybe having her along wouldn't be so bad—as long as they stuck to a little innocent flirting.

She clasped her hands together. "Does the smile mean I can join you?" When he didn't say anything, she grinned and added, "I could always go by myself."

"Don't even think about it."

"Fine. I'll play nice."

Playing with Lexi filled his mind with all kinds of naughty scenarios. He'd start with exploring those tempting full lips, and then he'd find the ticklish spot on her neck... Each thought was steamier than the last. He swallowed. If he intended to spend the day with her, he'd best lasso his rambling thoughts. He couldn't let the memory of her sultry kisses erode his defenses. Or he might end up doing something he'd later regret.

"You can come, but what about your clothes?" He glanced down at her skirt and cowboy boots. "Do you have anything to change into?"

"You mean with me?"

He nodded.

"I only have what I'm wearing. But I can run back to the motel, if you'll wait."

Her pleading expression tugged at his misgivings. "No need." He tilted up his hat and rubbed his forehead. "I might have something to fit you."

Lexi fell in step beside him. He couldn't resist glancing her way. There was something special about her—and it went much deeper than her beautiful eyes, pert nose, and rosy lips. And it was impossible for him to stay upset with her for long. Since when had he become such a pushover?

When Lexi lifted her sunglasses to rest them on her head like a hairband, he noticed the gold emblem on the side. Designer glasses. They probably cost as much as his new boots, if not more. Then again, she was a big-city woman and he was just a cowboy. How could he ever hold her interest when he couldn't even read like a normal person? Cord shrugged off the inadequate feeling.

Lexi stopped dead in her tracks.

Cord turned back. "What's wrong?"

"Nothing. I'm waiting for you to move so I can go around the ladder."

His gaze moved from her slender form to the ladder leading to the loft. There was plenty of space to walk on either side of it, but she preferred to walk on his side. Who was he to complain?

He kept going until he reached Blaze's stall. The mare was out in the paddock, but the wheels in his mind shifted into high gear. Blaze was a gentle mare, even-tempered and practically read minds. She'd be perfect for Lexi, especially since it'd been years since she'd ridden a horse.

He imagined Lexi would probably put up a fuss if he were to switch the horse she rode, but dealing with her temper would be better than her getting tossed on her cute backside, or worse. After the scare at Haggerty, he wasn't up for another trip to the doctor's office.

Lexi followed him into the tack room, where he moved to the back and started clearing boxes off an old trunk. Lexi glanced around the room, examining this and that. It didn't bother him as it kept her from peering over his shoulder and asking questions.

"Do you have a hammer and some nails?"

"What?" Surely he hadn't heard her correctly. He spun around. "For what?"

"This old horseshoe on the wall."

It had hung there all his life. He didn't even know how it'd come to be there. "I don't understand."

She wiggled the old shoe back and forth until she was able to turn it upside down. "See? It should be hung with the U facing up."

"I'd probably be better off not knowing, but why?"

She sent him an incredulous look. "To catch all of the good luck, of course."

Of course. How could he have missed that? He shook his head in disbelief. The memory of the ladder came back to him. She had made sure not to walk *under* it. Could this refined New York businesswoman actually be superstitious?

He shuffled around until he located a hammer in an old toolbox and a couple of nails. He turned to her. When she reached for them, he pulled back. "Ms. Greer, I'd have never guessed you believe in superstitions."

She shrugged. "It's no big deal. Everyone does to some extent."

"I don't think so."

Her hands rested on her hips. "Oh, come on. Are you saying you've never made a wish on your birthday and tried to blow out all of the candles in one breath so it would come true? Or believed in a lucky charm? How about knocking on wood three times for luck?"

"Maybe when I was a kid, but certainly not now."

"Really. And would you disagree that bad luck comes in threes?"

She had him with that one. "My parents always said it, and over the years, I've seen it come true time and again."

"Gotcha." Lexi's tempting lips spread into an ear-to-ear grin. "Most people believe in superstitions to some extent."

"You seem to believe in them a little more than most. How come? Who taught you all of these superstitions?"

"Mrs. Baker." Lexi's voice held a nostalgic tone. "She was my father's assistant when I was a kid. She kept me out of mischief after school while my father worked."

"And she was a superstitious woman?"

"Very much so. I followed her everywhere and asked a million questions. She was a patient woman. I certainly don't believe everything she told me, but it doesn't hurt to take all of the luck I can get."

Sympathy welled up in him for the motherless girl who'd had to reach out to her father's assistant for a mother figure. How could a woman abandon her own child? The thought was inconceivable to him.

"You better get to work then." He held out the nails and hammer to her. "With time running out for me to save this ranch, I guess I better grab some of that luck."

"You don't need luck. You have me." She flashed him a warm smile that lit up her eyes.

He longed for her to literally mean she was his. Then he'd sweep her up into his arms and enjoy her sweet kisses. He'd make sure to make up for their lost moment the other night when they'd been interrupted. Boy, would he ever.

Cord undid the lock of the trunk and lifted the dusty lid. He hadn't looked in here since he'd packed what was left of Susan's things after she'd cleared out. After her sob story, the court had given him enough problems as far as the divorce was concerned, and he hadn't wanted to be accused of stealing. Then he'd forgotten about them.

He pulled out a pair of faded jeans. "Here, these might work. You can wear whatever you want."

"Thanks." Lexi stepped forward and started fingering through the contents. "Are you sure the owner isn't going to mind?"

"These things are long forgotten. I'll get rid of them one of these days. So help yourself."

"I'm not sure anything will fit, but I'll give them a try."

His thoughts strayed to his ex. She had been a bit more full-figured—but curves weren't everything. His ex certainly never made his heart pound like Lexi did when she brushed up against him—

Halting the direction of his thoughts, he moved to the doorway. "You can change here. You won't be disturbed. I'll go saddle the horses."

CHAPTER FIFTEEN

Maybe things were beginning to look up.

Alexis knelt in front of the old chest and gazed in at the assortment of women's clothing. Colorful tops, a stack of shorts, but only one pair of jeans. Who in the world had they belonged to? Alexis removed a white top. It consisted of a sleeveless corset that laced up the front. Interesting. Cord must like his women hot and daring. Alexis frowned. She was neither.

She folded the clothing and placed everything except the jeans back where she found it. With the faded denim in hand, she stood up. She held the jeans in front of her, finding a rip above the knee. She couldn't tell if it was from wear or if it was a fashion statement. And then there were streaks of paint, from sunny yellow to royal blue with a few other shades in between. The woman who once wore these must have been a painter, or her tastes ran on the unique side.

In Alexis's mind, she conjured up some pretty brunette, laughing and teasing Cord. If he still possessed a trunk full of her clothes, she must have meant a lot to him—the love of his life? A burning uneasiness churned in Alexis's belly—could it be jealousy?

Nonsense. What did she have to be jealous of? It wasn't like she had any claims on the man. Still, wearing another woman's clothes bothered her. She swallowed her ego and slipped on the mystery woman's jeans. The one thing to soothe her was the fact that they were a little big on her. It wasn't much, but it's all the comfort she could find in this most uncomfortable situation.

Not wanting to be reminded of the other woman—the one who'd obviously been an important part of Cord's life—Alexis sent the trunk lid slamming shut. She dusted off her hands and headed out of the tack room. Not quite ready to face Cord, she walked to her SUV to retrieve a bottle of sunscreen. With a healthy amount smoothed over her exposed areas, she ran her palms over the jeans to clean off the excess. She grabbed her cowboy hat from the front seat. With all of her new acquisitions, she'd need to buy another suitcase—a really big one.

All set for their outing, she turned toward the corral. With Cord nowhere in sight, she meandered over to where Midnight Star stood. When the horse heard her boots crunching over the gravel, he turned in her direction. His big, dark eyes studied her. As she drew closer to him, she realized he was much, much larger than she'd remembered. She swallowed hard.

"Hey, boy," she called out in a soothing voice. "Come here."

The horse studied her for a moment before approaching her. Alexis smiled. Okay. She'd definitely misjudged his size. Midnight Star had to be at least seventeen hands. Way too much of a horse for her to start out on.

"I can't stay." She stroked his neck. "I just wanted to say hi."

She should get moving, but she didn't want to leave—not yet. She didn't realize until that moment how much she'd missed being around horses. If only she hadn't fallen. If only her father hadn't sold her horse, her beautiful Black Beauty. The sudden wave of memories brought with it regret and a deep sadness of how she'd sacrificed the things she'd cared about to become the daughter she thought her father wanted her to be. And yet even with all of the sacrifices, she still kept coming up short in her father's eyes.

"I see the jeans fit." Cord strode into the corral with a horse all saddled up and ready to go.

"Uh...yes. They're a little big, but they'll do. Thank you."

"Good." He stopped on the opposite side of the fence and gave her a funny look. "Are you okay?"

"Sure. Why?"

"It's just that you keep flexing your hand. Is it bothering you again?"

"No. I'm fine. See?" She held up her arm and waved it around as she forced a smile. "Good as new."

She hadn't even realized she'd been clenching her hand. The scorpion sting was almost healed. She made a conscious effort to hold her arm at her side with her hand still. It must have been the memory of her accident that had sent phantom pains shooting through her arm. The compound fracture had been a painful experience, but she also realized that she was one of the lucky ones. Her injuries could have been so much worse.

Cord looked her over. "Are you still up for a ride?"

"Sure. I can't wait." She resisted the urge to worry her bottom lip as she glanced over at the intimidating size of Midnight Star. She'd really gotten herself into a fix this time.

Her stomach was a bundle of jittery nerves. How in the world had this sounded like such a good idea an hour ago? She climbed up over the fence surrounding the corral ready to tell Cord that she'd changed her mind about riding Midnight Star when he handed her the reins to the horse he'd just led from the barn. She sent him a puzzled look.

"This is Blaze. You'll be riding her today."

Not about to argue, she said, "Okay. If you think it's best." She breathed a sigh of relief. "Would you mind if I ride around a little in here while you get your horse saddled?"

If she was going to fall again, it might as well be here rather than out on the trail. *Way to go, Alexis. You're not even on the horse yet and you're planning to eat dirt.*

Cord gave her a hesitant look. "You know it's not too late to change your mind."

"I know. But I want to do this. I...I just need a moment."

Cord held Blaze in place while she climbed into the saddle. Her stomach shivered and her hands were clammy as they clutched the reins, but she was most definitely back in the saddle. *See? That wasn't so hard.*

She started to smile, but then Cord went to release his hold on Blaze. "Don't let go!"

He arched a brow. "You really are afraid, aren't you?"

"Do you have to rub it in? You have no idea how traumatic the accident was for a teenage girl, especially one with an overprotective father."

"Okay. Okay. I'm sorry." Lines bracketed his eyes and mouth. "How about I walk both of you around the corral so that you can get your bearings again?"

"You promise you won't let go?"

"Do I look like the type of guy who goes back on his word?"

She didn't know that honest men had a certain look, but she did know that Cord took his word very seriously. And good to his word, he led Blaze around the corral. Though her stomach was still uneasy by the time they returned to the starting point, she was feeling a bit more confident.

Cord moved to stand next to her. "Maybe we should skip the ride. We can do it another time."

"No. I want to do this." She was more determined than ever to regain this part of her life. Horses were something she'd been very passionate about, and she didn't want to walk away now. "I can do this."

"You're sure? Because if you aren't, it's okay. I swear I won't think any less of you."

The fact that he was that generous of spirit meant a lot to her. They'd gotten this ride off to a bad start, but she intended to remedy that from here forward.

"I really appreciate you doing this for me." She meant every word. "I was beginning to think that I'd never get on a horse again, and I'm so glad I was wrong. Thank you for helping me get over my nerves."

"I didn't do a thing." He said it as though he didn't deserve any of the credit. And that simply wasn't the truth. He was thoughtful and patient.

"Do you mind if I circle the corral again while you get your horse?"

He shrugged. "It's fine by me. Will you be all right by yourself?"

It was a good question, but if she didn't squelch the last of her fears now, she'd never know the utter bliss of riding horses again. And that simply couldn't happen.

"I'll be fine." She set off at walk. By the second round, she was smiling as Blaze trotted around the large oval.

In no time, they took off on their adventure. She tensed up again as they hit the trail, but Blaze responded to her commands almost before Alexis made them. It was as though the horse was psychic. For a while, they rode without saying a word. The silence didn't bother Alexis, as she was distracted by the beautiful landscape—surrounded by an enormous field of desert grass that swayed to and fro with the breeze. And now that her uneasiness about being astride a horse again had for the most part passed, she was having the time of her life. Of course, it didn't hurt that she had the world's sexiest cowboy next to her.

"This area is so different from the East Coast." She really enjoyed the beauty of the Southwest, from the wide-open spaces to Roca Mountain standing tall in the distance.

Cord cleared his throat. "I wouldn't be able to make the comparison since I've never stepped foot outside this state."

"Doesn't it bother you to miss an opportunity to explore the States—heck, the world?"

"New Mexico has everything I need. Can't imagine I've missed too much."

"If you ever make it to New York City, I'll give you the grand tour." She wished he'd take her up on the invitation, but in her gut, she knew he wouldn't leave his little piece of heaven for any reason—her included.

If it meant seeing more of Lexi, he was tempted. "I just might take you up on the offer."

She flashed him a bright smile. "Do you spend much time outdoors?"

His lips lifted at the corners and his eyes reflected his amusement. "I'm a rancher. What do you think?"

"Oops." She couldn't help but laugh at how that question must have sounded to him. "I meant, do you do much riding or hiking?"

His smile faded. "Not nearly as much as I'd like. But when I was a kid, my mother rarely knew where I was until dinnertime. When she'd ring that dinner bell, I'd come running."

"A dinner bell?"

"It used to hang by the steps on the porch. My mother got lots of use out of it."

Alexis grinned and shook her head.

"What's so amusing?"

"Just imagining you as a young Indiana Jones setting off on an adventure in the desert, seeking out treasure."

"Not treasure. More like horned toads and tarantulas."

"Yuck!"

This time he chuckled, and the hearty sound melted over her. This was the part of Cord that made her job here so hard. She really, really liked him. And everything about their relationship was one complication after another. *Don't go there. Just enjoy this time together.*

"My mother used the exact same word right before she ordered me outside with my newfound friends."

"Boys. You all seem to like anything creepy and crawly." She scrunched her face up into a disgusted look and gave a little shake.

His lips spread into a full smile. The simple gesture tugged at her heartstrings. She couldn't afford to lower her defenses with him. She was already more personally involved with him than she ought to be. If she weren't careful, he'd undo all of her carefully constructed barriers.

She had to steer the conversation in a less personal direction. "This definitely isn't an easy place to reach. Are we close to the ghost town?"

"Not really. Although this is still part of the Brazen H."

She'd seen the Brazen H marked out on a map, but she hadn't comprehended its true size until she'd visited the ghost town. The ever-increasing rocky terrain and towering cliff enthralled her.

What surprised her most was how much she enjoyed the tranquility. Out here, there was nothing but sunshine, fresh air, and peace. She didn't even have to reach for her cell phone to know there wasn't a signal out here, and strangely enough, that didn't bother her in the least.

This time it was Cord who broke the silence. "When my grandfather was alive, he'd take time to teach me all sorts of things about life and nature."

"Those must be very special memories."

"They are the reason I wish you'd give up on your plan to destroy my family's land."

She clamped off the groan in the back of her throat and swallowed hard. "I don't want to destroy anything. In fact, I'd like to preserve as much of the surrounding landscape as possible."

"Why can't you build your resort somewhere else?"

"I'm sorry, but I can't back out of this project."

"Can't or won't ?"

A washed-out spot where the path narrowed at the beginning of a canyon had them going single file. She doubted this backcountry could get any more primitive. She followed Cord wishing she could understand his reasoning for risking the entire ranch rather than accepting her offer and saving a little more than half of this paradise. As the path smoothed out, so did her thoughts. Getting into a confrontation with him now about the ghost town wouldn't do either one of them any good.

She urged her horse up alongside his. "I just meant we're running out of time to make this deal happen," she said softly, as though that would ease the impact. "Soon you're going to have to trust me to care for the land."

"And what if I don't trust you? What if your friendliness is nothing more than a sham to draw me in and get me to sign away my heritage?"

His words jabbed at her chest. She'd really hoped they'd moved beyond their mutual mistrust. Her fingers tightened on the reins. "Is that what you think of me?"

"I honestly don't know what I think anymore."

Somewhere along the way, she'd let herself foolishly think they had something genuine growing between them. She blinked repeatedly and focused on the rutted path. How could he think she'd stoop low enough to use their kisses, touches, and looks to work a business deal?

CHAPTER SIXTEEN

What in the world did he go and say that for?

Cord glanced at Lexi, who now refused even to look his way. His hands clenched into tight balls. The leather reins dug into his palms. He had absolutely no idea how to deal with women. None whatsoever.

Every muscle in his body grew rigid. He shouldn't take his frustration out on her for his inability to remain immune to her charms. But just for once, he wanted a woman to like him for his own qualities instead of his assets. Was that asking too much?

How long would Lexi wait before she once again broached the subject of buying Haggerty? Before she did, he intended to derail her by selling her on the idea of buying the couple hundred acres for a vacation home. He'd never been much of a salesman, but he'd give it his best shot.

He guided his horse over to a shady area, and Lexi followed. Once he had the horses squared away, he turned to her. "We walk from here."

Her head turned toward the steep wall of the canyon. "We're going up there?"

"Yep. Are you up for it?"

"Uh…sure." Her tone lacked sincerity.

"Don't worry. It looks worse than it is."

"I sure hope so," she mumbled.

"Here." He offered her a bottle of water. "You look like you need it."

"I have some bottled water in my backpack." She retrieved it from Blaze's saddle as well as a Choconut Bar. She waved it at Cord. "Want it?"

The sight of her freely handing over her favorite candy lightened his mood. "Do you go anywhere without one of those?"

She smiled, making him eager to believe there was something real growing between them. He wanted her—as much as he wanted to hold on to his family's land. Wait. What? When had this happened? When had she sneaked past all of his strategically placed defenses?

"A girl has to be prepared for anything." She smiled up at him, and that funny feeling started again in his chest.

It was true—she'd gotten to him. Still reeling from the revelation of how much she'd come to mean to him, he struggled to act normal. He couldn't let on that his world had suddenly tilted off-kilter. "And you figured that with a trusty Choconut Bar handy, you're ready to face any problem?"

A hesitant smile lifted her lips. "Something like that."

"But if I eat this, won't you get hungry?"

"I'm fine. I stopped by the Cantina this morning for some more of those huevos rancheros."

He smiled. That simple action eased his tension. "I told you they have the best food this side of the Mississippi. Put the candy in your bag. You'll want it when we get to the top."

She did as he suggested. It was good to know that she didn't always have to have her own way. Maybe there was a chance for them—oh, who was he kidding? Selling or not selling the land was a small part of their problems. They came from two totally different worlds.

He could never make her happy long-term—eventually, the novelty of having a cowboy escort her around would wear off. But no matter how he rationalized it, he still couldn't extinguish the desire to pull her back into his arms and show her what she was missing—what they were both missing.

As they started their ascent up the jagged cliff, Lexi asked, "Is there a name for this place?"

"I call it the Little Grand Canyon." He paused to glance back at her. "If we hike to the top, you won't be disappointed by the spectacular view."

Usually, he'd meander around exploring for wildlife, but not today. With Lexi being an inexperienced hiker, he planned to take the most direct path. He led them at a steady pace, while skirting the patches of desert grass and scraggly brush. His boots safely deflected the sticker burrs with tiny, painful barbs. The only sound was from the wind whipping through the canyon and the stones crunching beneath their feet.

He paused about halfway up the wall of rock. "Do you need a break?"

"I'm fine. You can keep going."

He didn't stop until they reached the overlook with a spectacular view of the narrow canyon. He moved to a large rock, his favorite place to sit and take in the scenery. He set his backpack next to a boulder as Lexi caught up to him. She dropped her supplies on the ground. Her face was splotchy, and she looked exhausted. Maybe he shouldn't have been so eager to share this spot with her.

He held out his hands. "Let me help you up on the rock."

Not giving her a chance to protest, his hands spanned her waist. His gaze dipped, taking in her full bottom lip. If he were to lean forward a few inches, he could snag a kiss—one of those mind-blowing kisses that haunted him at night. He swallowed. Caving in to his desires now wouldn't solve anything between them—it'd only complicate things further now that he had feelings for her.

With her settled on the rock, he turned his back. If he kept staring at her pink lips, he knew his resolve would crumble. Instead, he focused on the familiar beauty of the vast canyon. "You're the first person I've shared this spot with. I've been coming here since I was old enough to take the horses out on my own. I'd lie on this rock and daydream."

"You were lucky to have such an amazing childhood. I can definitely see what draws you to this spot. It's like sitting on top of the world. I wish I'd had a spot like this to unwind and do some thinking."

"You could have it now." He turned to her, wanting her to take him seriously because he'd never been more serious in his whole life—for a variety of reasons. "Buy the couple hundred acres I have up for sale and build yourself a house. Consider it a retreat from the craziness of New York. Better yet, move here permanently and…and breed horses. You have a way with them."

"Really? You think so?" He nodded but then doubt shadowed her eyes. "I'm no horse breeder or rancher. I wouldn't even know where to begin."

"Okay. Then start your own business—an Internet business. And when I finish up my chores for the day, I can head over to your place to share an evening meal." Now where had that idea come from? But the thought of being able to see Lexi whenever he wanted had a smile tugging at his lips.

"And who's going to be in charge of whipping up those supposed dinners?"

"Why?" How could he have forgotten that he was talking to a high-powered executive? Something told him that she didn't eat dinner at home very often. "You don't cook?"

She shook her head. "Not even a little."

She certainly wasn't making this sales pitch easy on him. "You could learn—"

"Save it. Me in the kitchen will never happen." She rolled her eyes and sighed. "I'd be an utter failure."

"Have you ever tried?"

She shook her head. "Are you saying this because you want me to move here or because you'll do anything to stop the resort from being built?"

"Would it be so bad if it were a bit of both?"

"But you can't make me into the woman you want me to be. I'm a businesswoman. I'm not a homemaker, not that there's anything wrong with it. It's just not the path my life has taken. I understand numbers and spreadsheets. I know nothing about recipes and measuring cups. Sometimes, I wish I was good at both. I always envy women who can balance everything life throws at them."

"I didn't say you have to be a homemaker," he ground out. "But how do you know what you want if you don't try it on to see how it fits?"

"You can't expect me to change into something that I'm not. It won't work."

This wasn't how he'd hoped the conversation would go, but what would it hurt to keep talking? "You know, exploring other interests doesn't mean you have to change."

She tilted her head to the side and looked at him. "If I were to consider your idea—and I'm not saying I am—but if I were, what do I do about HSG? My father and the investors are counting on me to bring home this deal and keep the company profitable."

"I don't have all of the answers." Cord refused to be sidetracked. HSG wasn't his responsibility. "If you were to buy the land for personal reasons, do you envision yourself living here or just flying back for the occasional vacation?"

"We're talking hypothetically?"

He nodded, eager to have her give his idea real consideration. The more she talked about it, the more tangible the possibility would become for her—at least, he hoped so.

"If I owned land here, I envision building a house and moving here."

He smiled, liking the way her mind worked. They were headed in the right direction. Now, how in the world would he persuade her to take such a massive leap?

"And since we're talking hypothetically," she gave him a pointed look, "I'd have Midnight Star on my ranch. He needs to be ridden and often."

Cord inwardly groaned. That horse wasn't the only thing that needed to be ridden and often. He swallowed hard.

He drew his thoughts up short. He needed to focus. The only way to keep Lexi close would be to figure out a way she could still work for HSG while taking up residence here in Whistle Stop. But was that even possible?

Still, she was really taken with Midnight Star. "So you're going to swap your business persona to become a horse thief. Looks like we'll be taking that trip to the sheriff's office after all."

Her eyes sparkled with amusement. "If you'll recall, I got out of it last time. I'm sure I'll find another way out, should the need arise."

He didn't doubt with her easy way with words and those pouty lips that she'd be able to get out of any little scrape, but he wasn't about to admit it. "The scorpion sting only works once. You'll have to find another compelling reason to wave that sympathy card if you want me to fall for it again."

Her chin jutted out. "Are you challenging me?"

He shrugged. "Guess you'll have to pull up stakes and move to Whistle Stop to find out."

"You know I hate to turn down a challenge. Be careful, or I just might, and then you'll be minus a horse."

Cord found himself wishing she was sincere, and it had nothing to do with saving Haggerty. He didn't like the thought of her returning to New York and never getting to see her again. He enjoyed their time together a lot—a whole lot. As for giving up Midnight Star, it'd be worth it if he gained Lexi for a next-door neighbor— oh, what a beautiful neighbor.

"Could you hand me some water?" She wiped a palm over her forehead.

"Sure. As long as you're willing to share the Choconut Bar."

"I suppose if I have to." She smiled, letting him know she was teasing him.

For a while, they shared the rock, the candy, and the water. The moment felt so right, even though he knew all of their talk was just that—talk. Frustration balled up in his gut. Lexi hadn't changed her mind about the land. And neither had he.

"Look at that!" Lexi's voice held a note of excitement.

He glanced her way to find her gazing up at the sky. With a hand shielding his eyes from the brilliant sunshine, he scanned the clear blue sky. And then he spotted the source of her excitement. Two brightly colored hot air balloons drifted lazily across the sky.

"I actually saw a balloon the other morning when I was out for a jog around town. I didn't know I'd be lucky enough to see more." She didn't turn away from the sight of the two balloons. One was blue and white. The other had orange, red, yellow, and blue stripes. "Did you ever see anything so beautiful?"

Actually, he had seen something much more beautiful—her. But he kept that piece of information to himself. It'd do him no good at this point to show his growing feelings for her. "There are actually quite a few hot air balloons around here. In fact, every year in October a balloon fiesta is held in Albuquerque. It's the biggest in the world. If you like balloons, you should definitely go. And make sure you don't miss the morning glow as the balloons light up. It's followed by the mass ascension of hundreds of balloons. It's like nothing you've ever seen before. Just remember to take a jacket. Those early morning hours can be cold in the desert."

"I just might do that." She bestowed a smile on him before turning back to the balloons. "It doesn't look like they're going to drift any closer, so I guess this is the best picture I'm going to get." She pulled her phone from her pocket and snapped some pictures. "Wait until I show my father these. He's going to love them."

"That's not the only amazing sight out here. See how the rocks appear brown now? Well, come sundown, they'll glow with a red hue—like jewels." He got to his feet. "In the evening, it's like having your very own private art gallery."

"Stunning." Her eyes never left his.

A flash of heat consumed him as she licked her dry lips. With no place to hide and no distractions, he couldn't dodge the desire that overtook his common sense. Drawn to her like a restless stallion to a perky mare, he couldn't turn away. Though this would only succeed in muddying his feelings further, he was willing to deal with the consequences. It'd be worth it to hold her and kiss her once more.

The differences between them slipped to the back of his mind. Before him sat a woman who'd given up everything to please her father. Maybe Cord just needed to remind her that there was more to life than work and duty.

His gaze shifted to her lush lips. His heart thumped, sending blood rushing to his extremities. Her blue eyes narrowed, and she licked her lips as though waiting for him to kiss her. He stepped toward her. She scooted forward on the rock. He stood between her legs. He gazed deep into her eyes, seeing the unmistakable flames of desire.

"I wish things were different." Her voice was soft, drawing him closer. "I'd love it if you and I could start over."

"Let's start over right here and now." His head dipped to hers. His lips brushed over hers, tentatively at first. He didn't want to scare her away.

His fingers slid up the velvetiness of her neck. His thumb brushed over her warmed cheek. She was the most amazing woman he'd ever known, and he never wanted to let her go. He deepened the kiss, and she responded. Her tongue met his.

Her hands slid up over his shoulders. His heart thump-thumped against his ribs. Her fingertips dipped beneath his shirt color. His head started to drown in the most delicious sensations. The one thing he did know was that, in this moment, he wanted this—being with Lexi—more than anything in his life.

And that wasn't going to happen.

He shouldn't be doing this. One or both of them would end up getting hurt. Before he could pull away, she leaned against him. Her soft curves pressed to his hard muscles. The pleasure center of his brain took the driver's seat. His hands slid down her back, and before he knew it, her legs were wrapped around his waist. Logic and reason fled his mind.

A deep, guttural moan filled his throat. He'd never wanted anyone this much. He wanted more of her kisses—more of her. He didn't know if he'd ever get enough of Lexi. Her shirt rose up, and his fingers spanned her tender flesh. He must have tickled her, because she jumped.

She moved her mouth from his. She rested her forehead against his as they both tried to calm their breathing. "We can't do this. Not here."

"You're right." Still, he wasn't ready to let her go. Not yet. "But you know you want more, don't you?" His fingers moved over her waist, and he felt the rush of goose bumps.

"Cord! You're impossible." She smiled, and it lip up her whole face.

He leaned in close and pressed his mouth to her neck, hoping to prove a point. His lips slowly trailed down to her collarbone. The rapid pulse of her artery let him know that she was enjoying this momentary lapse of judgment as much as he was. If only they were back at his place and not in the middle of this rugged terrain, he'd show her how good they could be together.

Lexi pulled back. "Cord, we have to stop."

With his mouth a fraction of an inch from hers, he asked, "Why?"

"Because neither of us is thinking clearly." She pulled away. "Even if I gave up my pursuit of purchasing the ghost town, we still couldn't be together. My business isn't here. It's in New York. Did you ever consider what I'm supposed to do if you and I start something? Do you expect me to abandon my father when he needs me most?"

Cord pressed his now-empty hands to his sides before kicking a stone, sending it rolling along the clay earth. "You can't deny that there's something going on between us. We owe it to each other to see where it leads."

"And what about everything else? Like the town meeting where we'll be on opposite sides?"

"I didn't say it'd be easy."

"Say we find a way to get past all of that. What happens when it's time for me to return to New York?"

His gaze met and held hers. Why was she making this so difficult? He'd never claimed to have all of the answers. But he was willing to search for them with her. "Who knows? You might be sick of me by then and be thrilled to leave here."

She frowned at him. "This isn't getting us anywhere. We should head back."

"Before we go, I want you to know I was serious about having you as my neighbor." He took her hand in his and stroked the pad of his thumb over her silky smooth skin. "Think of all the benefits there'd be by living so close."

Her pupils dilated as her gaze dipped. "You don't know how tempting your offer is…but I can't."

"Because of the resort?"

She nodded.

He pulled his head away. Frustration knotted up his gut. "Why are you so dead set on making this deal?"

She leaned back against the rock. "HSG was in the middle of some big negotiations when my father collapsed. Those deals went belly-up, and we lost a bundle. This project is our last chance to turn things around. My father doesn't know any of this yet. I've been covering everything up, hoping to nail down this Wild West resort before he returns to the office. If something were to happen to HSG, I don't know if his heart could handle the strain."

This revelation stunned Cord. From her confident attitude to her tailored suits and diamond stud earrings, she oozed success. Yet, her company's entire future rested on him and his land. His stomach churned.

"I'm sorry for your predicament, but my family's land can't be your only solution. Sell your investors on another site. Tell them anything to get that glitzy playground for the rich built somewhere else."

"I'm trying, but so far Haggerty is our only viable option."

Not knowing what else to say, he turned away. "You're right. We should start back."

He took off down the narrow path without waiting for her to answer. He led them along the narrow trail at a steady pace. A glance over his shoulder showed that she was right behind him. A half hour later, they returned to the horses. She sucked in one mouthful of oxygen after another. He regretted the pace he'd set. In his desire to burn off his frustration, he hadn't considered that she might not be used to this kind of exercise.

When she caught her breath, she said, "I didn't mean to upset you back there. I thought maybe if you understood the position I'm in—"

"You didn't upset me." He met her worried gaze. "I just can't give up that land."

"Even if it means you lose everything? Will sacrificing your home ease your conscience about not being able to protect Haggerty? Is it some sort of penance you feel you must pay?"

"I don't want to talk about it." His tone was short and clipped.

Her eyes widened, but she didn't say a word.

The fact that she'd gotten so close to the truth shook him. How had she figured him out in such a short amount of time? It was almost as if she could read his mind. He didn't know if this special sort of bond they shared made any of this better or worse. He was becoming increasingly confused with each passing moment.

She'd turned to her horse when Cord reached out, grabbing her hand and pulling her back to him. The pain in her eyes bore clear through to his soul with such force that it knocked the breath from his lungs.

Her lips pursed together as though she held back something. A silent moment passed before she uttered, "I didn't come out here to fight with you."

"What was the reason?"

"I wanted a chance to be with you and see this land through your eyes. Never mind, it doesn't matter now. You're too stubborn to listen to reason." With a huff, she turned back to Blaze.

Cord longed to believe her. The glimpse of her tender, caring side had only increased his attraction to her. Was she being honest with him? He'd been lied to before by a woman who'd professed to love him forever. He didn't exactly trust his own judgment these days when it came to women.

Was it possible Lexi was a dutiful daughter stuck in an impossible situation? Nothing more?

CHAPTER SEVENTEEN

Two days later, the shower pulsated off Alexis's sore muscles, muscles she'd abused by leaning over the little desk in her motel room for far, far too long. She'd endeavored to find a solution that would make everyone happy. The hot water soothed her stiffness. For all of her efforts, she still hadn't come up with an all-encompassing solution.

It didn't help that Cord's sexy image kept filling her mind. Every time she recalled the kiss they'd shared at the canyon and the way his fingers had brushed over her bare skin, it sent her heart racing. The steam from the shower swirled around as the memories of Cord crowded in. She groaned in frustration. Why did she have to meet him now when her life was so complicated?

She considered the idea of giving up the fight and letting herself fall head over heels for this rugged cowboy. Drawn to the thought like a cat to milk, she toyed with the thought of how to make it work. What would a cowboy do in a big city? Modeling work. He was cute enough. Most definitely. But a man used to working the land would be miserable in front of the camera. And how could she move to New Mexico and leave her sick father when he needed her most? The answer was, she couldn't—she wouldn't.

So what did that leave for her and Cord? A long-distance relationship? Alexis's nose scrunched up.

She'd been there and done that. The results had been disastrous for her heart. Even though Cord wasn't anything like Steven, she still wasn't going to set herself up to be hurt again. No matter how much she liked him—dare she admit it, cared for him—they didn't have a chance of making this thing between them work.

The chime of classical music sounded from her phone on the edge of the sink. She hurried to rinse off and get dressed. After running a brush through her wet hair, she called her father back.

"Hi. What do you need?"

"Did you get the sales agreement signed?"

Not a *Hi. How are you?* or even a *Good morning.* Instead, her father was already talking business. But then again, he had no idea how much this deal was costing her and how her heart was being torn in half. And there was no way she was going to explain it to him. She could only imagine how it'd make his blood pressure spike.

She sighed. "I'm getting ready right now to head out to the Brazen H."

"Quit stalling." His voice took on an agitated tone. "You should have had his signature days ago. What is going on out there?"

"I went horseback riding the other day," she said, still pleased with herself for getting back in the saddle.

"You what? You aren't out there for a vacation. And you certainly don't need to be taking foolish risks when there's a huge deal in the works. What's that man up to? Is he wining and dining you, hoping to get a better offer?"

"Cord isn't like that." She wasn't going to let her father tarnish her accomplishment. "Aren't you even pleased that I got back on a horse again?"

"Alexis, I never thought of you as a coward. You're a strong, intelligent woman who can do whatever you set your mind to, even if it includes horseback riding."

This was her opening, a chance to ask a question that had lain dormant for years. "Then why did you sell Black Beauty?"

"I don't want to discuss that horse. We settled this years ago."

"We never settled anything. You announced he was sold, but you refused to talk about it."

Her father sighed. "You aren't going to let this subject drop, are you? You have that determined tone to your voice."

"I need to know. I need to understand why you took away the horse I loved."

A strained silence ensued. "The day of your accident, I...I'd never been so scared in my life. You were still my little girl, and I wanted to protect you." His voice grew deep and gravelly with emotion. "I probably overreacted...okay, I did overreact by selling your horse, but I couldn't take the chance of losing you. I'm sorry I hurt you."

Her heart swelled with love. Her father rarely ever talked about emotions, and for him to do so now moved her greatly. "Oh, Father, you'll never lose me. I promise."

"Ah, daughter, don't make promises you can't keep. You're grown up now. Sooner or later, you'll find the right guy and things will change. Things always change."

Did he suspect something between her and Cord? Impossible. There was no way he could know what all had transpired between her and Cord. Her father continued talking while her thoughts spiraled back to that last toe-curling kiss. If they'd been somewhere more comfortable, she had no doubt things would have gone further—much further. But would that have been a wise decision? Perhaps not. Okay, definitely not. But at that moment, would that have stopped her? Heck no.

"Alexis, are you listening to me?"

"Um...yes." Thank goodness they were on the phone, because it'd take her father only one look to know she was lying. "Father, you should take some of your own advice. It's time you make some changes. You can't go back to your crazy work schedule. Your body needs a slower pace."

"I'm not ready to be put out to pasture. My mind is still sharp as a tack."

She couldn't argue. That's why she'd made sure to keep him away from the office. It wouldn't take him long to figure out the business was in trouble—serious trouble.

Her throat tightened, and she hoped her voice would sound normal. "Retirement doesn't mean you have to stop living. It means you'll have more time for hobbies. There are a million things you could try. It's time you seriously consider what the doctors have been telling you. I don't want to lose you either."

"I hear you." His voice suddenly sounded like that of an old man, something she never considered him. "Doesn't mean I have to be excited about the future."

"We'll be okay," she said, encouraged that he hadn't outright rejected the idea of retiring. "Change will only make us stronger. Now I'm off to talk to a rancher about some land."

With the town meeting not far off, she was running out of time to reason with Cord before the entire community was involved. In order to finalize this deal, she had to keep their interaction purely business. She wouldn't let herself get distracted by the temptation of his persuasive lips or magical fingers.

Who did she think she was kidding?

Alexis hadn't seen Cord in more than forty-eight long hours, and she'd barely thought of anything but saving the Brazen H and helping her favorite cowboy. She'd spent every waking moment of the last two days splitting her time between revamping her presentation to the town and researching an alternative site for the resort. Her presentation was almost complete.

She rushed to get ready to go see Cord, all the while going over everything in her head. The Arizona property had potential, but the owners weren't exactly jumping to sell. However, the paper she'd signed for Cord's bank remained valid for only forty-eight more hours—then the wheels of foreclosure would kick into gear.

In no time, she was driving toward the Brazen H. She could no longer go with her original approach to get the town to pressure Cord into selling to her. She'd already witnessed his difficulties with some of the town's residents. She didn't want to make him feel even more ostracized. And it was more important than ever that Cord be at the meeting. She wanted to show him that she was on his side and trying every which way to save his land and her company. After all, it didn't have to be Christmastime for miracles to happen, did it?

She pulled her rental vehicle to a stop by Cord's weathered barn. She didn't even waste her time checking the house. He wouldn't be there when there was work to be done. But with a sprawling ranch, Cord could be anywhere.

A young ranch hand stepped out of the barn. He was tall and lanky. Her guess would be that he had just graduated high school. When his gaze caught hers, surprise reflected in his eyes. She'd been around the Brazen H long enough to realize they didn't entertain many guests here.

She approached the young man. "Hi. Do you know where I can find Cord?"

"You the woman that wants to buy his land?" His face was devoid of emotion, so she wasn't sure what reaction to expect from him.

"Yes. I'm Alexis Greer." She held out her hand.

The young man pulled off his gloves, rubbed his palm over his faded jeans, and then shook her hand. "I'm Jesse."

"Nice to meet you, Jesse." She smiled, but he didn't return the gesture.

He stared at her as though trying to make up his mind about her. If this kid was having such a hard time trying to decide if he should give her the benefit of the doubt, no wonder Cord was so hesitant around her.

Jesse stuffed his hands into his pockets. "You're going to be talking at the town meeting tomorrow, aren't you?"

"Yes, I am. I hope you'll be there."

His brows gathered. "Are you gonna turn the town against Cord in order to get his land? 'Cause he doesn't deserve it. He's a good guy."

"I promise I don't plan to make things worse for Cord. I'd like to help him if I can. Do you know where he is?"

Jesse nodded.

"Would you mind telling me?"

He shrugged. "Cord just took off for the western pasture to check on the cattle. He won't be back for a while."

She knew she should leave and come back later, but she didn't want to—not until she talked things out with Cord. "Mind if I wait for him?"

Jesse shrugged again. "Suit yourself."

He strode back into the barn, leaving Alexis alone with her thoughts. There was another reason she needed to see Cord, and it had nothing to do with the land. Before her nerve failed her, they needed to have an honest conversation about what happened in the desert.

Cord had to understand her feelings for him were real and that they had absolutely nothing to do with whether he sold her the land or not.

For the first time in her life, she longed to toss aside her cautious tendencies. She wanted to live in the moment and savor more of Cord's spine-tingling kisses—more of all of him.

After their hike, she'd waited for him to think things through and understand her situation. He was a reasonable guy and would understand her need to do what was best for her father. For the last two days, she'd willed the phone to ring, but he hadn't called for any reason. Either he was nursing a bruised ego, or he was as confused as she was about where they went from here.

Unable to sit still, she paced across the lengthy porch, waiting for her cowboy—um, Cord to appear on the distant horizon. Seconds soon turned into a half hour. She needed something productive to do with herself to avoid becoming a ball of nerves.

Then a thought came to her, a way to soften him up. She recalled their conversation at the canyon about how he'd like to come home to her and a hot meal. In that moment, she wanted to be the woman be envisioned sharing his evening meals with while catching up on the day's events.

Her chest warmed at the thought of the surprise in his eyes and the smile on his handsome face. Anticipation fluttered in her stomach. Toss in a little of the wine she'd spotted in the kitchen and some casual conversation, and it'd be a perfect evening.

However, where exactly did she want this evening to go? She knew it should end with a tactful business meeting, but another part of her was eager for something more personal. They may not have forever, so why not make the most of the here and now?

She knew she was getting way ahead of herself. She didn't know how Cord would react to seeing her again, specifically with the town meeting literally on the horizon. And that wasn't the only problem with her plan. She hadn't exaggerated about her lack of experience behind the stove. Her idea of taking care of dinner usually consisted of ordering takeout.

Unwilling to give up, she knew she'd need help if she was going to make this meal a success. A recipe book would be a good start. Would a cowboy have such a thing? Probably not. But with the way he clung to the past, she'd bet he still had his mother's recipes.

She rushed into the kitchen and scanned the tidy counter tops. No books. She glanced in the cabinet drawers. No recipes there either. She was about to give up when she spotted a little rack of books atop the fridge.

She grabbed the first cookbook and flipped it open. She soon decided a casserole sounded the easiest. Mix everything up, toss it in a dish, and shove it in the oven. Even she could do that…she hoped.

Through a process of elimination, she settled on a taco casserole. It didn't sound so hard, and it had a Southwest flair. Who didn't love tacos? No one she knew.

She set to work, quickly learning that cooking kept you on your toes. Stirring this, chopping that, and mixing something else, but at last she got everything in the baking dish. She grinned like a little kid as she slid her creation into the oven, making sure to double-check the temperature.

She turned around, horrified at the mess she'd made of Cord's kitchen. Where had she gone wrong? Weren't casseroles supposed to be easy? She wiped her arm across her damp brow. If so, why in the world did she have so many dishes to clean?

She loaded up the sink with a fistful of utensils, a stack of bowls, a skillet, and a couple of cutting boards. The trick would be to get it all cleaned up before he got home. She turned on the hot water and set to work.

A full half hour later, the kitchen was spotless once again. The thought that she'd forgotten something niggled at her. She peeked in the oven to find dinner bubbling away. What was she missing? She bit down on her lower lip as her gaze darted around. For the life of her, she couldn't figure out what it could be.

She gave up worrying and walked out to the porch to look for signs of Cord. She wrung her hands together. She couldn't recall ever being this nervous about impressing a man in her life—not even her father.

CHAPTER EIGHTEEN

C ord stood by the barn door, his eyes glued to the beautiful sight waiting for him on the porch. He drank in the view of Lexi's purple T-shirt clinging to the swell of her chest and narrowing down to her waist before flaring out at her jean-clad hips. His mouth grew dry as he forced his eyes back to her smiling lips.

It'd been ages since he'd been able to come home to someone. He could get used to this—real easily. Not that he'd let himself. She'd already shot him down once. How many slap-downs would it take for him to learn his lesson?

She probably wanted to talk some more about the damn resort. His jaw tightened. The thought that she ventured here only for business dampened his anticipation.

"Wow-wee, looks like that cute missy is back." Manny let off a low whistle. "She still tryin' to get you to sell?"

"I don't know what she wants." Cord's heart beat a little faster as he stared at her. "But I'm sure going to find out."

He handed Manny his reins. "Can you take care of the horse for me?"

"Absolutely. Have fun. I know I sure would."

Manny chuckled the whole way to the barn.

Cord forced himself to walk casually to the porch. "Did we have a meeting planned that I've forgotten?"

She shook her head, her hair swishing around and framing her face. "I made you dinner."

"Dinner?"

"I thought you might like it after working all day. The food...I need to check on it." She raced across the porch like the house was on fire.

He followed her inside, smelling a foul stench. Was that dinner? She certainly hadn't been exaggerating when she'd professed that she didn't cook. In the kitchen, she rushed to the oven and yanked open the door. The smoke wafted through the air, setting off the smoke alarm. *Yep, that was dinner.*

She removed the baking dish and turned. "It was the right temperature. I know it. I double-checked."

Cord opened the windows and back door before fanning the smoke alarm to quiet it. "How long did you leave it in for?"

Dawning filtered across her eyes before a defeated look pulled at her face. "I knew I'd forgotten something. I'm hopeless."

Sympathy welled up in him. "No, you aren't. Everyone forgets now and then."

"I tried real hard to make a nice surprise for you."

She'd wanted to surprise him? But why? What was she trying to tell him? He'd never been good at reading women. He'd have to tread carefully or risk her stomping off like she'd done the other day. And he wasn't ready to see her go.

He smiled, not something he did often. "I'm very surprised. It isn't every day I come home to a pretty lady and a dinner."

She glanced down at the food and back at him. "I told you I was no good at homemaking. This is a disaster."

"No harm has been done. Just put the dish on the stove to cool." Even though dinner wasn't salvageable, he was still touched by the gesture. "I'll take care of it after I grab a quick shower. Do you mind waiting?"

She shook her head. "Want me to make something else? Like a deli sandwich? Surely I can't burn that."

At least she hadn't lost her sense of humor. "How about you go back out and sit on the porch? It's a lovely evening out. It'll take me five minutes to get cleaned up. By the way, what was dinner supposed to be?"

"A taco casserole. I found the recipe in one of your cookbooks."

He started for the bedroom, but then paused and turned back. "Just remember it's the thought that counts."

"That's good. I certainly wouldn't score any points for my culinary skills." She shook her head. "How could I have forgotten the timer?"

"I'm sure if you had remembered, dinner would have been delicious." He disappeared down the hallway.

He didn't waste any time before stripping off his grungy clothes and slipping into a cool shower. She hadn't mentioned anything about the land, so maybe she was just here to see him. But why? He scrubbed faster. Had she been thinking about that hot, steamy kiss they'd shared at the canyon? He sure hadn't forgotten it. No matter how hard he'd tried.

Less than five minutes later, clean and refreshed, he entered the kitchen to find Lexi seated at the counter. "Thought you'd be outside."

She shrugged. One look at her glistening eyes and red, blotchy cheeks, and he knew she'd had a meltdown while he was gone.

"What's the matter now?" He approached her and took a seat on the stool next to her.

"I tried to clean out the dish, and I can't even get the burnt food out of it. On top of ruining your dinner, I might have ruined your dish. I totally failed. I told you I wasn't good at this kind of stuff."

Cord pulled her toward him, and she willingly followed until she pressed against his chest, her face buried in his shoulder. His hand stroked her silky hair, and he wished he could hold her close all evening. There was something special about her, something that had him craving for any scraps of time she'd share with him. Did that make him pathetic? Probably. But he was beyond caring about his tattered pride. All that mattered now was Lexi.

"The dish will clean up once it soaks," he murmured, his chin resting against the top of her head. "I'm impressed you'd even consider entering the kitchen on my behalf. What gave you the incentive?"

"You did." She pulled back and looked up at him. "I...I wanted to make you happy."

His instinct was to pull her back into his arms and kiss away her worries, but something told him that wasn't what she needed just yet. "Talk to me, Lexi. What aren't you saying?"

"I've extended my trip here longer than I'd intended, and now my father is insisting I wrap up this deal and return to New York as soon as possible."

Her announcement came as no surprise, but it didn't lessen the blow of knowing that she would be leaving Whistle Stop. He didn't know why it should hit him so hard. After all, her life was in New York which might as well be the moon as far as he was concerned.

"We both knew you'd have to go back." Try as he might, he couldn't find a way to put a positive spin on it. He already missed her, and she had yet to pack her cute cowgirl hat and boots.

"I promised my father I'd quit stalling—"

"Stalling? Is that what you call what we've been doing?" Cord couldn't help but feel as though she'd diminished their relationship. "And why have you been dragging your feet?"

"Because I…I care about you." Her watery gaze peered at him. He steeled himself, resisting the growing urge to kiss her. She glanced away. "Because being here at the Brazen H is comfortable and relaxing. And…and most of all, because I've been waiting for you to change your mind about selling. You can't give up all of this." She waved her hands around. "It's too much of a sacrifice even if it's to save Haggerty. You have a little piece of heaven on earth. Why would you even consider letting the bank take it?"

"You care, huh?" He didn't even bother fighting the grin that pulled at his lips.

She elbowed him. "Is that all you heard?"

"Oh, you said more? I must have missed it." He'd heard her, but none of it mattered as much as knowing that she felt the same way about him. He reached out to her. They'd done enough talking—it was time for something more.

She sidestepped him and crossed her arms. When she tilted up her chin and her gaze narrowed, she reminded him of that businesswoman he'd met on her first day in town. "I promised my father I'd hammer out this agreement with you. Tonight."

He sighed and raked his fingers through his hair. "Do you honestly think there's anything left to say that would convince me to go along with your plan to develop my ancestors' land into some amusement?"

"Everyone has a price. I just haven't found yours yet."

He leveled a hard gaze at her. "And you won't either. I'm not selling."

"If you won't do it for yourself, do it for me. Help me save my father's company and keep him from ever knowing how close we are to declaring bankruptcy."

The pleading look in her eyes tore at him. For a moment, he almost caved in. He wanted so much to help her. In the next heartbeat, he realized he'd been in this situation before. Well, not exactly the same situation, but one quite similar. It had been a beautiful woman in a bad situation—his ex-wife. And look how that had turned out.

"Lexi—"

She held up her hand to stop him. He wrapped his fingers around hers. Her hand was small and soft. It easily fit inside his, and he never wanted to let her go.

"Don't say a word now," she said, as though with more time, he'd change his mind. "I want you to come to the town meeting tomorrow night and hear my proposal."

He shook his head. The last thing he wanted to do was be stuck in a room with a bunch of townsfolk who were going to turn on him and try to strong-arm him into selling Haggerty. "Lexi, you're asking too much—"

She pressed a finger to his lips, silencing him. She was right. They'd done more than enough talking. His immediate reaction was to stick out his tongue and suckle her fingertip, to give her a sample of what she was missing out on. His gaze caught and held hers. There was definite interest there. The temptation grew within him. What could it hurt? Maybe he was moving too slow, being too cautious.

Throwing caution to the wind, he parted his lips and swiped the tip of his tongue over the pad of her finger. There was a distinct inhale of breath, and her eyes dilated. Before he could wrap his lips around her digit, she pulled her hand away.

Color rushed to her cheeks. "I...we...um...think about it."

"I am." His voice was low and deep, filled with desire.

She clenched her hands together. "I meant think about attending the meeting."

She didn't fool him. She was turned on, too.

"I'll think about your proposition if you promise to think about mine." Her eyes widened, and he couldn't resist chuckling. "I meant about you buying the acreage I have for sale and settling down here. I might even be persuaded to share Midnight Star with you."

There was a glint of temptation in her eyes. "I'll think about it if you'll seriously consider my request."

"I said that I would." He walked over to the fridge and pulled the door wide open. "Now what should we do about dinner?"

"I don't know."

"There's leftover chile rellenos. I guess I should ask if you like them."

"I've never tried them, but I like to try different things at least once." Her cheeks lit up and she glanced away, but not before he noticed.

"Promises, promises."

The color in her face intensified, providing final proof of her wayward thoughts.

The fact she was also remembering their steamy clench made him want her all the more. He was ravenous, and his desire had nothing to do with food. He knew where this evening would lead, at least he hoped so, but he had to move slowly. He didn't want to scare her off. They might never have another evening like this one.

He pulled out a foil-covered dish. With her elbows resting on the center island, Lexi perched her chin on her palm, watching him as he shredded some Monterey Jack over the red sauce. He chopped a little fresh cilantro and sprinkled it over the top.

"You're the first man to cook for me. You know, I could get used to this special treatment."

He liked the idea of being the first to do something for her. "You could, huh?"

"Mmm...hmm. I find a man who pays such close attention to details extremely sexy."

She found him sexy? His shoulders pulled back, and his chest puffed up. Slow and steady, he reminded himself. He slid the covered dish into the oven, set the timer, and turned. "While that warms up, how about a drink? Would you like some wine?"

She nodded. "I'll get it."

He put a hand on her shoulder. "Tonight, I'm going to wait on you. Do you have a preference?"

She shook her head. "You choose."

"I have a perfectly good bottle of Chardonnay. It comes from a local winery."

"I didn't know New Mexico had wineries."

He located the bottle and handed it over to her to examine. "There are a number of them around the state. You should visit one or two before you leave."

Her eyes twinkled. "Are you offering to be my tour guide again?"

The idea certainly appealed to him. There was a lot he wanted to show her—a whole lot. "You have a knack for suckering me into showing you just about everything."

"Everything?" Her voice held a sensual tone to it.

They made idle chatter about his day as they worked together to set the table. The food didn't take long to warm in the oven. In no time, he carried the steaming dish into the dining room. He never bothered to eat in here when it was just him, but somehow, with Lexi here, he wanted to do things differently. Everything seemed fresh and new with her around.

Lexi's eyelids drifted shut as she inhaled deeply. "You made this all by yourself?"

"You sound surprised." Her eyes opened and met his. There was no denying it, he'd fallen under her spell. "I'm a man of many talents."

"So I'm learning."

He served up the food for both of them, all the while hoping she'd enjoy the taste as much as the aroma. There was a chance the chiles would be too hot for her. His fork hovered over his plate as she took a mouthful, chewed, and swallowed.

"This is delicious."

He expelled a long-held breath. "I'm glad you like it."

The easy banter continued throughout the meal. Leisurely evenings with Lexi could definitely become a habit for him—a habit he'd never want to break. Every muscle in his body tightened when he realized the feelings he had for her went so much deeper than he'd ever imagined.

The breath hitched in his throat. Could it be?

Was he falling in love with Lexi?

His mind raced. He'd sworn he'd never fall in love again. The price was too high. And yet every time he looked at Lexi or thought of her, his pulse raced. He couldn't get enough of her.

Why had he gone and fallen for a woman who would inevitably leave him? Or maybe that was the reason he'd let down his defenses with her.

She was a temporary fixture in his life. With Lexi, there was no future to contemplate. No big life questions to answer. There was only the here and the now. And he didn't intend to squander either.

CHAPTER NINETEEN

Wine? Check.
            Dinner? Check.
            Conversation? Check.
Surprisingly, after Alexis had charcoaled the taco casserole, the evening had still been an amazing success. Thanks to Cord. With the dishes cleared and the kitchen returned to order, Alexis had zero interest in returning to her motel room. There was nothing waiting for her there but more work. Besides, work and no play was making her very frustrated. Her throw-caution-to-the-wind attitude took over. There was no pressing reason not to enjoy a little more of this cowboy's company—especially since she'd be leaving in just a few days.

Cord led her toward the porch. He pushed the wooden screen door open and held it until she passed. His spicy cologne teased her senses. She knew if she were to stop in her tracks and turn that their bodies would collide. She savored the thought, but she kept moving.

"Hmm...there's something missing," Cord said. "Ah, I know. Wait here." He stepped inside the living room and turned on the stereo. He returned to the porch and sat next to her. "I guess I should have asked if country music is to your liking."

"It's my favorite."

A romantic ballad started to play and floated through the open windows. The intimate lyrics filled her mind with enticing thoughts. Her gaze shifted to his lips, and she longed to press her mouth to his. But she was hesitant, not exactly sure where they stood.

"It was a really nice evening." Her gaze met and held his. "Thanks for rescuing dinner."

"The company was my favorite part."

"It was? I…I mean it was for me, too." So then what had happened to all of the flirting he'd been doing in the house? Why was he suddenly acting like the perfect gentleman?

If only he'd make the first move.

Frustration and desire churned within her.

Fine. Nothing ventured, nothing gained.

Her heart pounded and her hand trembled ever so slightly as she reached out to him. Her fingertips ran along his jawline. "You are so handsome."

With the pad of her thumb, she gently rubbed over his bottom lip. Their gazes locked. Desire flamed in his dark eyes.

He captured her hand in his and moved it to his chest. "You realize that you're playing with fire, don't you?"

So he did still want her. Good. Detecting the pounding of his heart as he continued to clutch her hand to his chest excited her all the more. "If you're trying to scare me off, it won't work."

"Promise?"

She nodded.

"Should I be worried?"

His steady gaze continued to hold hers. If a person could ravish another with merely a look, this could be that moment. For so long now they'd been doing this dance of getting close and then pulling away. Tonight there'd be no pulling back on either of their parts. It was the only thing she was certain of at this point. And in this moment, it was all that mattered.

At last, she found her voice. It came out low and seductive—a new side of her. "You should worry. I have very definite plans for you."

His brows drew together as though he'd had an unsettling thought. "Not that I'm not flattered, because I am. But Lexi, this is already complicated. Are you sure you're prepared to complicate things even further?"

The echo of her father's cautioning voice combined with the memory of Cord's hesitant question balled her stomach up into a knot. She pulled her hand from his. Why did he have to pick now of all times to be sensible? Why couldn't he just go with the moment?

Part of her said life wasn't worth living without a few risks. Another part said she was being reckless and irresponsible. She was getting in far too deep with this sexy cowboy. She inwardly groaned. Why did she have to have an attack of conscience now?

She jumped to her feet and moved to the porch rail. The stars twinkled overhead as a gentle breeze rushed past her. In the distance, the moonlight lit up the paddock, giving it a peaceful glow—the opposite of the upheaval of emotions churning inside her. Why did everything have to be so difficult?

From the way she saw it, this was their last chance to be together, to see what might be between them. If she walked away now, they'd avoid further complications. But she'd be plagued by what if's and should have's. Could she run off into the night? The thought didn't appeal to her. Instead, she decided to let the night unfold one kiss at a time.

As though sensing her resolution, Cord moved to stand behind her. He leaned toward her, until his chest rested flush again her back. His breath tickled over her ear. Her every nerve ending tingled. He ran his warm hands down her chilled arms, and she began to relax.

Even if common sense dictated otherwise, she didn't want anything but to be wrapped in his warm embrace.

The full length of his hard body pressed against her, making her insides quiver with excitement. A moan swelled in his throat, the deep tones reverberating in his chest. She'd never met a man who intrigued her both mentally and physically.

"I can't remember an evening I've enjoyed this much." He lowered his mouth to her ear and murmured, "I'm glad you decided to come over and share the evening with me."

"Me, too. Whistle Stop is growing on me." She hoped her voice sounded steady, but she couldn't hear it for the pounding of her heart. "I understand why you love it here so much. With the continuous string of sunny days and the colorful citizens, what's not to love?"

He didn't answer. His fingers continued stroking her arms. Her head rested just below his chin, and their arms entwined. They fit together like two pieces of a jigsaw puzzle. She didn't ever want to walk away. She wanted him to continue to hold her like this—forever.

The thought of *forever* shook her to the core. Her stomach tightened. She was supposed to be here conducting business, not losing her heart to a man who made her want to forget her responsibilities and follow her desires.

She glanced up at the sky. A star caught her attention with its brilliance, twinkling like a diamond chip.

Twinkle, twinkle, little star. First star I see tonight, I wish I may, I wish I might, have this wish I wish tonight...to capture the heart of this cowboy who's holding me close.

"Do you think our fates are written in the stars?" She hoped the childhood lyric would bring her luck.

"I think we're the masters of our own fate by the choices we make in life. Right now, I choose you."

She turned in his arms. "I choose you, too."

Chest to chest, their lips were merely a breath apart. She didn't want to talk anymore. She lifted up on her tiptoes. Her lips tingled with anticipation. She pressed her mouth to his. His hands slid up her back as he deepened the kiss. A moan grew deep in her throat. No one had ever evoked such a powerful longing in her with a mere kiss—Cord's touch was most definitely magical.

Her arms slid up over his broad shoulders and slipped around the back of his neck. Her fingers stroked his neck and combed through his hair.

His eyes widened. "Your hands are cold."

She honestly hadn't noticed. Her mind had been on more important matters. "You know what they say: Cold hands, warm heart."

He smiled. "That's the thing about the desert. Once the sun sets, the temperature dives. You should get out of the cool air."

She swallowed hard. "Do you want me to go?"

"No...well, not unless you want to go."

Again, the warning voice in the back of her mind chimed in, willing her to go, to keep her heart safe from being broken again. But was that truly what she wanted? Would the memories be enough for her? Maybe if he didn't have his arms around her, she'd be able to think clearly. She pulled free from his hold and walked over to the porch swing.

"Would you like to go inside? I could light a fire."

"Not yet. This evening is so beautiful and peaceful. I don't get a chance to sit outside in the evenings very often. Can we talk?"

"Talk? Isn't that what we've been doing all evening?"

"Yes, but I meant about something a little more personal." She knew exactly what topic she wanted to broach, but she was still working up her courage. "You know...so we know each other better."

When he joined her, the swing seemed to shrink considerably. His thigh brushed hers, sending her pulse soaring, but it wasn't like having the entire length of his rock-solid body pressed up against her, driving her heart into overdrive. Just the memory of it warmed her chest. She had to think of something—anything—but how good he'd felt.

Cord stretched his arm out along the back of the swing. His fingers lightly brushed her hair, sending goose bumps down her spine. She'd never be able to carry on a conversation with him touching her. She attempted to wiggle over on the seat to give them each space, but there was nowhere to go. She turned to him. If she was going to get intimately involved with him tonight, she needed to know what she was getting herself into.

"Tell me about her."

Cord sat up a little straighter. "Tell you about who?"

"The woman whose clothes are in the barn, the one who made you afraid to become involved with other women."

Why anyone would want to hurt someone as thoughtful and caring as Cord was a mystery to Alexis. Then she realized that if she wasn't careful, she'd end up hurting him, too, whether she intended to or not.

Cord's voice interrupted her troubled thoughts. "You don't want to hear about her."

"Sure I do."

"I guess you'd say it started back when I was twenty-two...after my parents died in a collision with a tractor-trailer. It was up to me to keep the Brazen H up and running. After a while, rambling alone in this place got to me."

"I couldn't imagine the overwhelming loneliness. It isn't like you have any close neighbors or anything."

The muscles in his neck worked as he swallowed. "To make a long story short, I fell for a good-looking and outgoing young woman. Things moved fast—too fast."

"But she must have cared about you." Alexis couldn't imagine any woman in her right mind not falling for him.

He shrugged. "Maybe at first. I didn't want to be here alone, and she wanted to escape her family's poverty. So we eloped."

"Was it your idea?" She couldn't imagine Mr. Cautious taking such a big leap without lots of thought.

"No. But I went along with it. Things were okay at first, but it all changed after her artwork started to get noticed."

Alexis reached out and squeezed his thigh.

"After five or so years, Susan decided ranch life wasn't for her. She packed up her paintings and left, taking half of the ranch's equity with her."

So that's how he'd ended up in this horrible jam.

He sighed and ran a hand over the back of his neck. "I tried to reason with her, but she was too caught up in her rising career. She wanted to sell the Brazen H. She wanted—oh, it doesn't matter anymore. She didn't want to hear anything I had to say. And I couldn't do what she asked of me."

Alexis's body tensed. He might as well have been talking about her. Her only reason for being in town was to take away a part of his ranch. She was doing it mainly for her father and his company, but she doubted Cord would make the distinction. From his standpoint, she was no better than his ex. The thought lodged in Alexis's stomach like a jagged rock.

She glanced at Cord, seeing the same emotional turmoil on his face that she felt inside. She wanted to tell him it was different with them, but was it? Would she visit again after their business was concluded? Or would she find herself sucked back into the fast-paced life in New York—the life that left no time to think about a vacation?

"How about you?" he asked. "Ever had anyone special in your life?"

"I was engaged once," she admitted, not wanting to delve into those painful memories, but she realized it was only fair that she share since he had.

"What happened?"

Borrowing a phrase from Cord, she said, "To make a long story short, his work led him to the West Coast, and mine kept me in New York."

"Couldn't hack the long-distance relationship?"

"Something like that." She failed to mention that within two months of moving, her fiancé had had a new girlfriend—a girlfriend Alexis hadn't learned about until the woman answered the phone very early one morning.

Cord set the swing gently rocking. "Do you think you could ever be happy living somewhere other than New York?"

That was the million-dollar question. After spending time here in the Southwest, she'd fallen in love with the acres of sprawling red clay and living in the shadow of Roca Mountain. But there was something else more important to consider...

"I can't leave my father, not when his health is failing."

"Is he that bad?"

"If I don't convince him to retire..." She blinked, holding back the tears that stung her eyes. She couldn't repeat the dire prediction the doctor had given them should her father have another coronary episode.

"That's tough." Cord's fingers grazed down her cheek.

"What about us?" Her eyes searched his. She'd been dying to ask this question all evening, but she'd held back, fearing his answer.

"We can be whatever we want us to be."

"You want to give us a try?" Her throat tightened as she waited for his answer.

"Yes, I think I do." Desire burned in his eyes as his fingers traced the line of her cheek. "How about you?"

She stared straight into his eyes and nodded. "But the land deal—"

"Doesn't have to dictate our relationship unless we let it."

The word "how" hovered on her lips but was smothered when he leaned his head over to her. Her eyes fluttered shut as his mouth brushed hers. The slow, gentle kiss brought her body to life. Their problems faded into the gray, murky background to be dealt with later—much later.

His hands wrapped around her waist. Soon, she was nestled on his lap. His lips slid over hers. She exhaled a subtle moan. This was even better than her most steamy dreams. Those nighttime fantasies never made her heart beat so fast that she thought it might burst with anticipation like it was doing now.

In this moment, nothing mattered but the all-consuming hunger to taste more of his kisses. Cord took control, prodding and nudging her mouth to open up to him, to hold nothing back. His fingers tangled in her hair as his lips parted, inviting her tongue inside.

Mmm...he tasted of sweet berries from the wine. Yet his touch was far more intoxicating and addictive than the best bottle of grapes. He caressed the back of her neck. She slid her fingers beneath the collar of his black T-shirt. Her hand ran over his heated skin, and she was eager to feel more.

After witnessing his vulnerable side when he'd opened up to her, she found herself attracted to him inside and out. Oh, how she wanted to make love to him. Her fingertips explored the ridges and planes of his chest through the thin material of his shirt. Each stroke elicited another moan from him.

In the next instant, Cord got to his feet and lifted her in his arms. Her arms wrapped around his neck as she sent him a questioning look.

"I think we should finish this inside." His voice was deep and filled with passion. And his eyes promised that the night had only just begun. Excitement awakened every part of her body.

CHAPTER TWENTY

The sound of *Beethoven's Fifth* broke through Alexis's dream of being held in Cord's strong arms. She didn't want to wake up.

Not now.

Later. Much later.

The ring tone continued to play, rousing her back to reality. She blinked as the bright morning sun peeped in the window. And then her mind kicked into gear. This wasn't her motel room. The phone call disconnected, and silence fell over the room. The memory of the night before came rushing back to her. She had spent the night at Cord's place—in his arms—his very capable arms.

A smile played at her lips as she recalled how they'd been awake most of the night, getting much better acquainted. She grinned. It'd been the most amazing night of her life.

And she'd learned something—well, she'd learned a number of delicious lessons—but one in particular stood out. Memories of last night wouldn't be enough. She wanted more time. More caresses. More of everything. Eager for a repeat, she scanned the room for some sign of Cord. She frowned when she found herself alone. And then she spotted a scrap of paper with one word scrolled on it: *Kitchen.*

The handwriting was crude, almost as if a child had written it. How strange. She thought of dismissing it, but she felt as though she was missing something—something big.

She turned to her phone, knowing she needed to check her messages, but instead of reaching for it, she picked up the note. As she studied it, the wheels of her mind started to turn. She recalled the lack of reading material in the house. And then there was Cord's unwillingness to read the flyer about the town meeting.

Was it possible Cord couldn't read?

She glanced at the note again. Well, that wouldn't be accurate, but there was something not quite right about the situation. But what? She couldn't very well come out and ask him if he had a problem reading. She'd never want to hurt his feelings or make him feel small.

She'd known that feeling when her mother had left her father, but not before having a widely publicized affair with an associate of her father's. The kids had called her mother all sorts of horrendous names and said that Alexis was just like her. No, it wasn't the same as having a learning disorder, but in both cases they'd been made to feel like they were less than others.

Throwing on Cord's discarded shirt, she grabbed her phone and padded barefoot to the kitchen. Her stomach rumbled with hunger. Ever since she'd set foot in Whistle Stop, she'd been off her diet. At this rate, none of her business suits would fit. She had to do better. Eat less. And exercise more. In fact, she'd go for a run this evening. She'd been slacking off on those lately.

When she reached the kitchen, it was deserted. Cord must already be hard at work. She was sorry that she'd missed him. Too bad he hadn't woken her up before he'd slipped away for the day. She had just turned to head back to the bedroom when another note caught her eye. It rested on the island. She picked it up and found more of the crude handwriting, but she could make out the words. Following the instructions, she opened the warmed oven to find a foil-wrapped plate with scrambled eggs, a bagel, and a slice of ham. Her stomach rumbled in anticipation.

So much for her diet. Maybe she'd start it tomorrow. Yes, tomorrow sounded much more doable. She reached into a nearby drawer for a fork. She should have felt ashamed by the speed with which she inhaled the more-than-generous portions, but she was so hungry and it was so delicious.

Alexis had swallowed the last bite of ham when the back door swung open. She turned to find Cord smiling at her. Heat flamed in her cheeks. She must look a mess, and there he was all showered and dressed.

"Hey there, sleepy head. Glad to see you enjoyed the food."

She ran a hand over her hair. "It was delicious. Thank you."

He walked to the sink and washed up. After drying his hands, he moved to stand in front of her. "I could get used to this."

"Used to what? Cooking all of the edible food?" She meant to laugh and make light of this moment, but the intense way Cord was staring at her stole her breath away.

"No. I could get used to having you to come home to."

"You'd like that?"

"Definitely. Then I could do this when the mood struck."

When his head dipped so he could kiss her, she used every bit of willpower and leaned back out of his reach. His gaze connected with hers. Questions reflected in his eyes.

Now that she was fully awake and aware that the town meeting was today, she had to get something straight with Cord. "We need to talk."

"We will." He smiled that sexy look that always made her stomach quiver. "My lips will speak directly to yours." He leaned forward again, and using every last drop of willpower, she pressed a hand to his chest.

"I'm serious."

"I am, too." When she didn't give in, he sighed and straightened. "Okay, you win. We'll talk. But can you make it quick?"

"I will." She wanted him so much, but what she had to say was important. She didn't want to get swept up in the moment and forget about it. It also didn't hurt that in this particular moment he was in a rather agreeable mood. "Promise me something?"

His gaze narrowed. "Is this going to be something like, will I still respect you in the morning? Because I still think you are absolutely fantastic, and I must say you are quite stunning in nothing but my shirt."

Her heart fluttered, and she smiled. "I think you're fantastic, too." That didn't even come close to describing the depth of feelings she had for him, but she wasn't ready to delve into them. Not here. Not now. "But this is something different. I need you to promise me you'll go to the town meeting tonight."

He shook his head and started to pull away. "I don't think so."

Before he could get away, she looped her fingers through his belt loops and pulled him back to her. "Please do this. For me. I need you there."

"Even if I don't agree with what you're going to say?"

"Even if." Although she just might surprise him.

When Cord didn't say anything, she pleaded with her eyes, and then she stuck out her bottom lip in an obvious pout.

"Okay. You win."

Before she could celebrate her victory, he swooped down and claimed her lips. Even though they'd spent the night together, there was a reignited red-hot need in his kiss. *There isn't time for this.* Her hands crept around his neck. *There's work to do.* Her fingernails scraped gently up his neck. *There's the town meeting presentation to finish.* Cord's lips brushed along her jaw and down to the ticklish spot on her neck. *There's—*

Resistance was futile with Cord's lips creating the most arousing sensations, which fizzled and fried any further thoughts. There was absolutely no place she wanted to be but in his arms—

Beethoven's Fifth played.

Why now? Alexis pulled away from Cord. A frustrated groan vibrated in her throat. She couldn't just ignore her father, no matter how much she longed to do just that right now.

Cord sent her a questioning look.

"It's the second time my father has called this morning. It could be serious." She held up her index finger. "Just give me a second."

She slid off the stool and grabbed her phone from the counter. She pressed a shaky hand to her tender lips and swallowed. "Hi, Father."

"Alexis Anne, how could you have kept this from me?" her father's voice thundered through the phone.

A plea of innocence hovered on the tip of her tongue, but she didn't have a clue what she'd done to get into trouble this time. It could be any number of things.

Her father didn't wait for a response. "You had no right! I should have been told. You know it's still my name on the company."

Technically, it was his initials, but she wasn't about to correct him. His blood pressure was obviously high enough. "Father, calm down. Whatever it is, we'll work it out. It isn't worth risking your health."

"Enough about my health. I'm not senile or blind. You should have told me the company is in trouble. Serious trouble."

She glanced over her shoulder at Cord. "I can't talk about this now—"

"Don't put me off. I won't stand for it. We're going to have this out. You're still my daughter—my employee—you owe me answers."

Cord shot her an inquisitive look. She couldn't plead and cajole her father to calm down in front of Cord. And there was no way she could continue this romantic mid-morning tryst and leave her father to stew over the company's situation. Disappointment cut sharply through her. Her special time with Cord was over.

"Father, let me call you back in," she glanced up at the wall clock, "forty-five minutes."

"I'm coming out there." His voice brooked no room for argument. "If you aren't going to close this deal and put this company back on firm financial ground, I will."

"Just give me a few minutes to get back to my room. You don't need to fly off the handle. I'm negotiating with Mr. Lawson, and I've got the real estate agent inquiring about the property in Arizona. See? I am handling things—"

"I've seen how you handle things—with kid gloves where that cowboy is concerned. Now it's time for some serious negotiating. And since you aren't up to the task, I'll do it."

"Father, would you calm down?"

"Why should I? My daughter—my own flesh and blood—has been lying to me."

"And I would again if that's what it took to keep you safe."

"But you have no right—"

"I have every right. The doctors warned that the stress is too much for you, and you're proving them right."

"I...I am fine." His voice didn't sound fine. He sounded worn-out. "I just can't believe you'd turn against me."

"I love you. And I want what's best for you." She couldn't bear to think of losing him.

"And you think having me step away from HSG is for the best."

"I do." Her voice was calm and assertive. "Remember my horse—the one you got rid of because you couldn't bear to see me hurt or worse?—well, I guess I learned this protectiveness from you. And I'd do it all again if that's what it takes to keep you alive and well. Father, I love you."

"I love you, too."

"Let me call you back, and then we'll talk this out."

Her heart sank. Her romantic moment with Cord had come to a screeching halt. She wanted this time with him—a moment to love him before the world came crashing in on them. But it was too late.

♥♥♥

What was he thinking to come here?

Cord sat behind the steering wheel of his idling pickup as the citizens of Whistle Stop made their way to the historic dance hall now used as a community center. He'd occasionally attended these monthly meetings, but that was a long ways back—before his ex-wife.

His fingers tightened on the steering wheel. This was his town, too. And if they were going to discuss his land, he deserved to be there. Let them gawk at him and talk behind his back. He was used to it by now. After all, he had promised Lexi that he'd be here—he always kept his word.

He tried to remember how she'd gotten him to agree to this, and then he recalled how he'd found her in his kitchen in nothing but his shirt. He'd have agreed to almost anything in that moment. And they'd been just about to repeat their mind-blowing night of lovemaking when her father had interrupted. Cord hadn't been able to make out the exact words the man had said, but the tone of his voice hadn't been friendly. And Cord had noticed how the color had faded from her face.

His sympathy went out to Lexi. Cord was certain her father wasn't happy that she hadn't secured the land, but that wasn't her fault. As far as Cord was concerned, she'd gone above and beyond what was expected of her. And when he'd overheard that she was pursuing another property for her resort, he couldn't help but think that she was doing that for him. She really did care. But Cord never had a chance to discuss any of what he'd overheard, as Lexi had made a mad dash to make herself presentable and rushed out the door.

By now, the whole of Whistle Stop must know she hadn't spent the night in her motel room. He was certain that he and Lexi had provided the town with the juiciest bit of gossip to make the rounds in ages. *Two adversaries hammering out a deal between the sheets.* Cord's teeth ground together. Yet another reason for him to turn around and head back to the Brazen H.

And let Lexi face them all on her own—no way. He'd never let her face the town gossips alone. She deserved better than that, especially after she'd dismissed what she'd heard about him and given him a chance to prove himself.

It wasn't until he pried his fingers from the steering wheel that he realized how tight he'd been holding it. He leveled his shoulders, took a deep breath and switched off the engine. He was amazed as more and more residents showed up. This had to be right up there with the meeting about the mayoral election when some newcomer decided to run against their long-standing Mayor Ortiz—the town had been all abuzz.

Whistle Stop certainly didn't like change, and that was the reason half of the storefronts were vacant. Normally, he'd have told them that they were foolish to cling so tightly to their traditions and their famous line: *But that's the way its always been done.* However, in this particular instance, he was counting on the town rejecting Lexi's ideas—ideas of change.

He made his way to the door of the long adobe building with a red Spanish tile roof. As he stood in line to get in, he could feel the curious gazes leveled at him. He ignored them.

Once inside, he wasn't surprised to find every single wooden bench filled to capacity. People were milling around the sides, and even the back of the large room was standing room only. Luckily, he was tall and able to see over the crowd in front of him.

"Hi, Cord. I'm surprised to see you here." Mimi smiled up at him. Did she just bat her eyes at him?

He stifled a groan. "Hey, Mimi. I didn't know you came to these sort of things."

She tucked her arm in his. "I don't normally, but the whole town is buzzing with rumors about what that hotshot New York City woman is planning. I know that she wants to steal your land out from under you—"

"She does not." The wide-eyed stare Mimi sent his way had him regretting his severe tone. He cleared his throat. "I mean, she made me a reasonable offer."

"If it's so reasonable, why didn't you accept it?"

"I didn't want to."

How in the world had he let himself get drawn into this conversation with Mimi of all people? His gaze swept around the room. Lexi stood near the podium, and she was staring right back at him. Then her gaze moved over to Mimi and back to him. Her face was a mask of indifference, but her eyes told a different story. They were full of questions. When her attention turned to the mayor, Cord's gaze continued around the room, looking for an empty spot where he wouldn't be disturbed.

A hand waved. Was it waving at him? He peered closer and found it was Tony Granger waving at him. He pointed to a vacant seat next to him. It was an aisle seat and the second row from the back. Perfect for a quick escape.

"I've gotta go." Cord quickly detangled himself from a frowning Mimi and worked his way across the crowded room. "Thanks for the seat."

Tony slid over, giving Cord ample room to sit down. "No problem. I was saving it for my mother, but I see she already has a seat next to Mrs. Sanchez."

"Seats are at a premium tonight." Cord glanced around as the ceiling fans were switched on and all the windows and doors were opened.

"I don't think it'd be a stretch to say they are going to violate the fire code for the number of people in here tonight. Speaking of the fire department, I hear you're considering joining up."

"You did?" This was news to Cord. Then he recalled Manny mentioning the idea a couple of times. "Let me guess. Manny mentioned my name."

"He did. With men moving away from Whistle Stop to look for work, we're running short on volunteers. Would you consider signing on?"

It was on the tip of Cord's tongue to say he already had his hands full running the Brazen H, but he stopped himself. Tony had his own ranch to run, and so did a number of the other volunteers. Still, they somehow made time to keep their community safe. Maybe it was time he stepped a bit out of his comfort zone. Maybe he could be of value in this way to his neighbors.

"I'll give it some thought."

"Sounds good. Just don't take too long. We're going to be starting up classes soon."

The thought of classes made him uncomfortable. Would there be books to read? Tests to take? His thoughts turned back to school. His gut tightened into a knot, and his palms grew damp.

Before Cord could find the words to back out of volunteering without hurting his friend's feelings, the mayor banged his gavel on the podium, calling the meeting to order. Cord's gaze moved to Lexi. She sat rigidly in her seat, staring straight ahead. Was it possible he wasn't the only one to feel out of his depth at this meeting? Or was she having regrets about what she was about to do? Was she about to turn everyone against him to force him to sell?

CHAPTER TWENTY-ONE

How could she have forgotten how much she'd hated public speaking in college?

Alexis wished she were anywhere but sitting here in front of a couple hundred restless people. Cord was the only friendly face she'd located, but the last time she'd checked, he was occupied with Mimi Ortiz. Just the memory of that woman draped on his tanned, toned arm sent a stab of jealousy through Alexis.

Mayor Ortiz was long-winded as he went over a list of Whistle Stop's current events. He started by thanking the quilt guild for donating to their small hospital twenty-five hand-stitched baby quilts for new mothers. He then moved on to a request for more volunteers to help keep the library from having to reduce its hours. What really impressed Alexis was the fact that he was able to gain a couple of volunteers without a lot of arm-twisting. It gave her hope that the people of Whistle Stop would be receptive to her ideas about revitalizing the town—a place she'd fallen in love with, not to mention falling for one of its residents.

Much too soon, Mayor Ortiz introduced her. Alexis swallowed hard and got to her feet. She straightened her suit jacket and was suddenly plagued by second thoughts about her attire. She'd wanted to give off an air of confidence and leadership, but as she looked around at the roomful of jean-clad ranchers and casually dressed store clerks, she worried that they'd look at her as an outsider, an interloper. Which she had to remind herself that she was, even if she was starting to feel at home in Whistle Stop. It was more than she could say about her high-rise apartment in Manhattan, where she didn't even know most of her neighbors.

Alexis stepped toward the podium, stopping to shake the mayor's hand and to thank him for his kind introduction. She leveled her shoulders and turned to face the row upon row of curious onlookers.

She licked her dry lips and gripped the podium. "Hi. I'm fortunate to have met some of you, but for those of you I've yet to meet my name is Alexis Greer. I am the acting president of HSG Holdings. I must admit that until recently I'd never heard of Whistle Stop, New Mexico, and I wasn't sure what to expect when I arrived here. So imagine how surprised I was to be welcomed with open arms by so many of its residents—"

"Quit buttering us up," a man called from the back of the room. "Just tell us what you want."

Alexis kept the smile on her face. "Thank you. I'm just about to get to that. After spending more time in your lovely town than I'd originally planned, I'm certain that HSG and Whistle Stop can help each other." She grabbed the laptop computer that was set up with her slide-show presentation.

As if on cue, the lights dimmed and her first slide appeared on the large screen to her right. "HSG is proposing to build a resort on the outskirts of Whistle Stop. It'll mean lots of jobs—"

A cheer went up in the room. The energy that vibrated through the room was contagious, and Alexis couldn't help but smile. When a calm settled over the crowd, she clicked through some of the tentative sketches that her team back in New York had developed. She hoped they would impress her audience as much as they did her. Still, as nicely as the buildings were drawn, she realized that she no longer wanted to buy Cord's land to achieve her goals. But she had yet to secure an alternative location.

She wasn't even finished with her presentation—and the best was yet to come—when a woman called out, "I know you're trying to help us, but don't all of these wonderful new jobs hinge on Cord Lawson selling you Haggerty?"

"Yes, they do—"

The crowd all spoke at once. Alexis tried to regain control of the meeting, but no one paid her the least bit of attention as they all vocalized their opinions at once.

Alexis couldn't make out Cord's face in the shadows, but she could feel his steady gaze on her. She just hoped that he wouldn't leave before she got to the good stuff—the part that would show him that she did care about this town—and most of all him.

Mayor Ortiz took pity on her and moved to the podium. It took a few loud bangs of his gavel to restore order to the hall. "Ladies and gentlemen, I know there is a lot to discuss, but let's hear out our guest before making up our minds."

A man in the back stood up. "But if this all hinges on Cord's land, shouldn't he be up there, too? From what I hear around town, he shot down your plan."

This is where Alexis had to tread ever so carefully or risk alienating Cord. And even worse, creating more animosity between some of Whistle Stop's residents and Cord. That was the exact opposite of what she'd like to see happen.

"Mr. Lawson and I are still discussing a potential sale."

A woman near the front stood and turned to Cord. "Is that right? Are you going to sell?"

Alexis inwardly groaned. She hadn't wanted to drag Cord into the middle of this meeting. "How about I tell you the rest of my ideas?"

"We want to hear what Cord has to say."

"Yeah!" chorused a number of people in the audience.

"Cord isn't going to sell to you."

"That's right, lady! You're wasting our time. We've heard enough."

Again, the crowd erupted in boisterous conversation. Oh, this was a disaster. And then, above the din of voices, there was a loud and clear whistle. As the lights came up in the room, Cord was standing there with his hands pressed to his lean waist. All heads turned his way.

Alexis didn't have a clue what he was going to say. His face was devoid of expression as he stared directly at her. She knew whatever he said now would decide the course of the rest of the meeting. Her lungs burned as she held her breath in anticipation.

"You aren't wasting your time," he told the crowd. "I've gotten to know Ms. Greer, and she truly cares about the land, about Whistle Stop. She's trying in her own way to help the town. And this place could use some more people like her, people willing to go out of their way to help the town. You'd be wise to hear her out."

"Are you saying you're selling your land to her? You're going to help the community?"

"Yeah, Cord, are you going to help us?"

Cheers went up in the crowd for Cord to sell.

The mayor stepped up to the podium and banged his gavel, bringing peace back to the unruly crowd. But all eyes were still on Cord, whose face was hard as stone.

"Well, Cord?" the mayor prompted.

Cord didn't move. The only sign of life was a twitch in his jaw. The breath caught in Alexis's chest as she awaited his answer. She silently prayed that he'd made the choice to save his home.

"I'm still considering her offer. Now dim the lights and let her finish her presentation."

"We should have figured we couldn't count on you," a faceless voice called out from the back.

Alexis tightened her hold on the podium to keep herself upright. Had Cord just spoken up in public? And had he ridden to her defense like a knight in shining armor?

"Cord isn't going to sell. This meeting is nothing more than a pipe dream. And I don't have time to waste." A man got to his feet and started for the door.

There had to be some way to get the people to listen to her. She truly wanted to help, and she still had more to share, more that didn't relate directly to buying Cord's land. But others got to their feet and followed the disgruntled man out the door.

Instead of feeling like she was an outsider here, she imagined she was back in New York in front of the HSG board. They were a lot tougher crowd. So why was she letting these townspeople unnerve her?

She struggled to maintain a calm, collected composure, but she had to do something to ease the crowd's agitation with Cord. "Wait! Hear me out. I think I can help the town...even if the resort doesn't get built here." Her voice was clear, loud, and confident. "You're already here, why not hear what I have to say? It won't cost you anything. Consider it a thank-you to all of the kind people who've made me feel so welcome here."

When her gaze sought out Cord, she couldn't find him. The spot where he'd been sitting was now occupied by someone she didn't recognize. Where had he gone? She really wanted him to hear this part. She wanted him to know that she cared about a lot more than HSG's bottom line. She cared about Whistle Stop's future and his future.

With the people seated once more, she didn't have time to worry about Cord's absence. This was her chance to do something good for the community. She just hoped they'd listen to her.

"When I arrived here in Whistle Stop, the first thing I encountered was the abandoned train depot. I couldn't help but think that's a huge opportunity for Whistle Stop—"

"That train isn't going to create new jobs and that's what we need here. Not some dumb train stop." A man with a long beard got up and hustled his wife out the door.

Mrs. Sanchez stood and turned to face the crowd. "People, you're being downright rude to our guest. Maybe she's on to something here. Then again maybe not, but she's at least trying to find ways to help Whistle Stop." Absolute silence fell over the room. Mrs. Sanchez turned back to Alexis. "Please continue. Some of us would like to hear your thoughts. I know you've been working hard to prepare for this meeting."

Once Mrs. Sanchez took her seat again, Alexis glanced at her notes to find her spot. "I know my idea certainly isn't the entire answer to Whistle Stop's declining economy, but I think it could definitely play a big part in its recovery."

There were no interruptions this time, but there still was no sign of Cord. He was gone. Disappointment lodged in her chest.

"While I was investigating ways to get people to the resort other than by car, I checked into air and rail. I have a contact at the railroad office who is quite interested in the project. He said that, under certain circumstances, they'd be willing to add a couple more passenger cars and restore service to Whistle Stop.

With the train starting out in Albuquerque and heading south to make two round trips a day, that's four times it would pass by Whistle Stop. That has the potential for a lot of tourist dollars."

Alexis could see that she'd intrigued some people, but others were shaking their heads. She'd been in business long enough to know that there was no satisfying all of the people all of the time. She just had to hope that enough people found merit in her idea.

"What circumstances are we talking about for the railroad to add Whistle Stop back to their schedule?" The mayor peered at her thoughtfully, and there was genuine interest gleaming in his eyes. "And do you know if they'd still be interested in this venture if the resort isn't built here?"

Alexis started to feel more confident by the second. She turned so she could see the mayor, who was in one of the chairs behind her. "Actually, the railroad is quite interested with or without the resort. It'd be an additional revenue stream for them without a large capital expenditure. They seemed to think it could be a win-win for everyone."

She took a moment to take a deep breath. This next part...well, it was the hard part. She imagined there would be lots of resistance.

"As for the conditions that the railroad would place on Whistle Stop before they are willing to move forward...well, the stipulations are a bit involved. First, the train depot has been abandoned for some time and left to decay—"

"But isn't that their property?" called out someone in the audience.

"Yes, it is." She had to word this carefully. "To be honest, I didn't get into the reasons behind their requests. I was there to find out what it'd take to put Whistle Stop back on their map. That is all."

"I'm not doing their work for them! I've got enough of my own."

Alexis struggled not to lose her patience. "But think of what you'd gain in the long run."

"And that's all we'd have to do? Fix up the train station?"

"Not exactly." If they didn't like the thought of replacing a few broken windows and applying a couple of coats of paint to the train station, she knew they wouldn't go for the other demands, and that saddened her greatly.

"The town square, well, it needs work too." In actuality, it needed a lot of work, but she was doing her best to be as diplomatic as possible. "They'd also like to invest in the economic growth of Whistle Stop."

"Why?"

"Really?

"There has to be a catch." Shock and disbelief echoed throughout the room.

Alexis waited until people quieted down before she continued. "I was able to secure a promise that they'd help people reopen their businesses in exchange for a small, limited time stake in the businesses' profits once the train depot is operational again."

A roar of voices filled the hall as everyone vocalized their opinions at once. There wasn't much more Alexis could add to the conversation. She just hoped that they'd find a way to make it work. Whistle Stop was an endearing town, and she didn't want to see it end up like Haggerty—an abandoned ghost town.

She turned a pleading eye to the mayor to restore order to the meeting. He got to his feet and joined her at the podium. With a few bangs of his gavel, a hush fell over the crowd. Alexis thanked them for their time and wished them well with whatever they decided to do.

The mayor turned to her. "And you trust your contact?"

She nodded. "I do. I've worked with him before and he's very reliable. He's a high ranking executive who has the authority to make this all possible."

"Thank you." The mayor gave her a firm handshake. "You've certainly given us a lot to consider. And we appreciate you taking the time to come here and present it to us." He turned back to the audience. "Let's show Ms. Greer our appreciation."

The mayor clapped solo. Then Mrs. Sanchez got to her feet and joined him. Then a few more people got to their feet to clap. And then the volume swelled, and Alexis smiled. She was certainly going to miss this place—and one special cowboy in particular.

CHAPTER TWENTY-TWO

Alexis yawned for the umpteenth time the next morning.

Not even a coffee from the Poppin' Fresh Bakery was working its magic. She sat down on the edge of her bed and took another mouthful of the steamy brew. Between the stress of the town meeting, Cord walking out in the middle of her presentation, and the long string of questions by curious residents over coffee at Tilley's Café until late the night before, she hadn't slept much.

Her hand moved to the nightstand and grabbed her phone. No missed calls. No message from Cord. She was certain that he was upset about the meeting. But with the bank breathing down his neck to foreclose on his home, surely he'd come to his senses by now. No man would stand on principle or pride and let his home go into foreclosure, would he?

When she'd spoken with her father last night to update him on how the town meeting had gone, he'd asked if her heart was truly in seeing this deal through to the end—no matter how it ended. She'd remained quiet. She'd already deceived her father enough to last a lifetime, but she couldn't explain to him how Cord wanted her to move permanently to Whistle Stop. Or worse, that she was tempted by the idea.

Her father said they were out of time. She knew what that meant. And she knew what had to be done for all of their sakes.

She finished her coffee but still didn't feel up to taking a morning run. Instead, she headed for the shower. It did little to perk her up. The thought of what she was about to do left a sour taste in her mouth. She'd finished dressing and started applying her makeup when the phone chimed with the familiar classical tune. What did her father want this time? Hadn't they covered everything last night?

"Morning, Father. What's up?"

"I want to make sure you haven't changed your mind."

She stood on the cold tiles of the bathroom floor, staring at the dark circles under her eyes. Even concealer couldn't help her this morning. "I haven't changed my mind. I know what must be done. I'm getting ready to drive to the Brazen H right now."

She held the phone with one hand while she dabbed the round powder puff at the compact. Her father continued to rehash what they'd discussed the prior evening. Like she needed to hear it all again. It'd been all she'd thought about last night.

"I know, Father. I'll spell everything out for Cord. He'll see it's the only answer."

"He won't have a choice. You should have done this a long time ago and saved time."

"I thought I could reason with him. But cowboys, they're a different breed."

She ran the powder puff over her chin. The thought of tightening the screws on Cord made the coffee in her stomach slosh to and fro nauseatingly. He didn't deserve what was about to happen. He was a good, honest rancher who only wanted to save his family's land and live in peace.

She stabbed at the compact too hard, and it went sliding right off the edge of the counter. It clattered to the tile floor.

"I've got to go, Father."

She disconnected the phone and bent over. Some of the pressed powder had scattered, but it wasn't the bits of powder dotting the tiles that bothered her. She picked up the compact and held it in front of her. She stared into the cracked mirror. This was not a good omen. Mrs. Baker would insist Alexis was in for seven years of bad luck. Alexis wasn't so sure the stretch of bad luck would last that long, but she knew as sure as she was standing there that a bit of bad luck was due in the next seven hours.

She tried to tell herself she was being silly. She wanted to dismiss the superstition as a fun little saying, but she couldn't shake the black cloud dogging her steps. She wouldn't let it stop her. Today she had to do what she ultimately thought was best for Cord in the long term—even if it was painful in the short term.

With one last ace up her sleeve, she grabbed the phone. Her only hope was being able to secure that ghost town in Arizona. She selected the number for the Realtor pursuing the Arizona property. As the phone rang, she crossed her fingers for luck—if she'd ever needed some luck, it was now.

"Hello, Mr. Santos. It's Alexis Greer." She cut to the chase. "Have you been in contact with the owners of the Arizona property?"

The Realtor cleared his throat and paused, as though uncomfortable with delivering the news. "I thought your father would have told you. The Arizona property is now available, but it's more than you're willing to spend. And the sellers won't negotiate on the price."

She ignored the fact that her father had insinuated himself into this situation. She had bigger worries at the moment. "If they're stalling in hopes to get me to raise the offer, it won't work. I don't have time to play games. Did you tell them this is our best and final offer?"

"Yes."

"But they're asking far too much for that property." She muttered under her breath. "What about the 200 acres Cord has up for sale? Has anyone else shown an interest in it?"

Mr. Santos wasn't personally handling the sale, but the man had inside contacts who kept him abreast of the property situation. "No nibbles yet. Are you considering going ahead with the purchase?"

She liked the man, but when it came to business she'd learned long ago to trust very few. "It's still an option."

She quickly ended the call. With no options left, she dialed Cord's number and prayed he'd answer. If he had to hear the news, it was best if it came from her. After all, she was the one who'd located his ghost town in the first place. And then she'd been the one to sell the investors on Haggerty's merits. Guilt gnawed at her empty stomach.

When Cord answered the phone, she dispensed with the pleasantries. "I have something to tell you."

Her heart pounded in her ears. She was about to destroy any chance she'd have at a happily-ever-after with the cowboy of her dreams. This wasn't something to do over the phone. She had to face him. He deserved that much.

"I have something to tell you, too." His voice was warm and friendly.

"What would that be?"

"I'm glad you talked me into going to the town meeting last night. You came up with a really good idea about using the train to bring in more tourists."

"You heard that? But I didn't see you after my presentation about the resort. I thought...I thought you were angry about being pulled into the middle of the controversy."

"I stepped outside so things didn't get out of hand. But I did stick around long enough to hear your ideas of how to help the town. You really do care about Whistle Stop, don't you?"

"I do." *And I care about you.*

"Then come over. I think we need to talk." When she didn't respond, he added, "After we talk, I thought you might want to go for a ride. Maybe I'll even saddle up Midnight Star."

She closed her eyes, fighting back the storm of emotions colliding within her. Why did he have to wait until now to let his guard down?

"I'll be right over," she said, even though all she wanted to do was put off her part of the conversation for one more day…week…it'd never be long enough.

♥♥♥

If only there was another way…

Alexis searched her mind again for an alternative for what she was about to do. For the umpteenth time, she came up empty. Why did life have to be so unfair?

Her hand hovered inches from Cord's front door. Dread consumed her, making her empty stomach roll. She had an ultimatum for him—an ultimatum he wouldn't like, not one little bit. She took a deep breath and rapped her knuckles on the solid wood door.

When Cord opened the door, his hair was damp and unruly. Her fingers itched to reach out and comb through it. Her gaze met his and held longer than was necessary. She swallowed the lump that lodged in her throat. This was going to be so much harder than she'd ever imagined.

"Hi." He smiled. It was a real smile that lit up his face, not one of those forced smiles he'd used when they'd first met and he'd been suspicious of her. Now he trusted her.

That knowledge shoved the sword of guilt a little deeper into her heart. For a moment, she truly considered turning tail and leaving. How in the world was she supposed to do her job now when she knew it was going to destroy this relationship that she and Cord had worked so hard to build?

"Come on inside." He stepped back, allowing her entrance.

His pleasant mood was only amplifying her guilt. Once she got everything out in the open, he'd never again flash her one of those dynamite smiles that lit up his eyes. It'd taken them so long to get to this point. And in the next few minutes, it'd all be nothing but a bittersweet memory.

"Ladies should go first, so tell me what you want to see me about. Were you planning to sweet-talk me into another horseback ride?" His eyes warmed to a honey-brown shade.

When she caught herself smiling back, she gave herself a firm mental jerk. Now wasn't the time to get sidetracked. But maybe it wouldn't hurt just to see what he had on his mind. After all, once she said her piece, she'd never find out what he wanted. "What I have to say can wait. Tell me what you have on your mind."

He approached her and placed a hand on either side of her waist. "Well, if you insist. But first, I want to do this."

He placed a finger beneath her chin and lifted her head until her gaze met his. She wanted to fall into his embrace and promise him that they'd find a way to stay together. Yet, knowing it'd all be a lie, she didn't say a word. She had to do what was best for Cord, and that meant making sure he kept his ranch—at least most of it. After all, what was a sexy cowboy without horses and cattle?

Without waiting for her to speak, he brushed her lips with his. She forced herself to hold back. His kiss was gentle and loving. She should pull away, but she didn't have the heart to. She didn't want this moment to end—ever.

As though sensing her inner turmoil, he deepened the kiss. Against her better judgment, she responded. She craved him with every fiber of her being. His tongue traced her lips before plunging inside. She draped her arms around his neck. With a needy moan, he tightened his hold on her until their bodies molded together like two halves of a whole.

He lifted his head long enough to whisper, "I never knew a kiss could be this good."

"Me either."

Her body reacted to his with a will of its own. Wrapped in his arms, she wasn't a businesswoman trying to save her family's company or the woman trying to save the home of her very own cowboy. In this moment, she was merely a woman with an overwhelming desire to follow his kiss wherever it led her...but she couldn't.

What she had to say to him would prevent them from taking this relationship any further. And it wasn't fair to let him go on thinking they were building something special. Dread pinched her heart in its steely grip.

She forced herself out of his arms. "We need to talk."

Confusion clouded his eyes. "You mean about what you said at the town hall meeting?"

"Yes. And you aren't going to like it."

"Wait," he said, taking her hands in his. "I want to tell you something first."

She doubted anything he had to say would make her feel any better, unless he'd decided that building the resort was a good idea—surely she couldn't be that lucky.

His steady gaze held hers. "Whatever you have to say, we'll deal with it together. Because I love you."

Those three little words had the power to knock the air from her lungs. Surely she hadn't heard him correctly. Not now. Not today.

Happiness reflected in his eyes, and the lines of stress eased from his face. In that instance, she acknowledged that all of her stalling and trying to find a backup plan for the resort was due to the fact that she loved him, too. Her heart clenched, and she knew she'd never get a chance to say those words to him. She had to stop this madness. She had to do it now.

She stepped back. His admission drove home just how much she stood to lose this day. How in the world was she supposed to break the news to him now?

"I can't do this."

"Do what?" His brows gathered.

Ignoring the chain saw of guilt sawing through her heart, she blinked back the threatening tears. "I came here to tell you that…that if you don't agree to the terms of the sale, your bank will be notified that HSG's intent to purchase the land has been withdrawn. They'll put your entire property in immediate foreclosure."

His eyes darkened as his mouth settled into a firm line.

"After which the ghost town, this house…all of the ranch and your land will go up for auction. There will be no more extensions. No more chances to save your beautiful home. And no guarantee who will buy the Brazen H or what they will do with the place. Because by that point, it'll be too late for HSG to make the purchase. Our investors have lost their patience."

"No matter what I do, your company's determined to get their hands on my land." His voice was cold and cutting.

"I have tried to explain your situation to my father, but he's the final decision maker and: To him, business is business. And besides, this isn't just about my company getting what it wants. It's also about you getting to keep your home."

"You mean, your father doesn't have time for those things. You're here to do his bidding."

"That's not true. I'm here to do my job. I have to finish what I started. Believe it or not, I care about you, and this land deal is what's best for you."

"I don't agree." He crossed his arms and glared at her.

She withdrew the papers from her oversized purse. "Just sign them. It's for the best."

He waved them away. "I don't want them."

She paused and glanced down at the papers. Now wasn't the best time to broach this subject, but if it was part of the reason he was avoiding signing the papers, then it needed to be addressed. "Is it that you don't want the papers? Or is it that you have a problem reading, and that's why you're avoiding going over the offer?"

"What?" He glanced at the ground and shifted his weight from foot to foot. "I don't know what you're taking about."

Oh, yes, he did know what she was talking about. "I could go over them with you—"

"I told you I don't have a problem. I get by just fine."

She unfolded the papers and moved next to him. "Would you like me to read the whole thing to you? Or you could just let me know which words you need help with—"

He stormed over to the door. She thought for sure he was going to keep on going outside, jump on his horse and ride away. But he stopped. His shoulders slumped as though the weight of the world weighed down on him.

"If you must know, I'm dyslexic. I bet now you're happy that you didn't get further involved with a dumb cowboy."

"I never, ever thought you were dumb. You are very smart about so many things." Except when it came to letting go of the ghost town in order to save his home.

"I'm not like you. My choices are limited."

Then she understood the other reason he'd clung so tightly to the land. It was what he knew—what he could do without feeling inferior. Her heart went out to him. Suddenly so many things made sense to her. "Don't underestimate yourself. You can do whatever you set your mind to."

"Yeah, right. I'm a cowboy, and my livelihood depends on the land."

"Then help me save it. Look over the papers and then have someone in Whistle Stop go over them. Maybe your Realtor or an attorney—"

He turned to her. "I don't need anyone's help, because I'm not signing those papers."

She stepped forward. "Listen, I respect your undying loyalty to your heritage, but you're letting your pride overrule your common sense. Aren't you hearing me? Your home is about to be auctioned off to the highest bidder. You won't have any say in who buys it." She implored him with her eyes to listen to reason. "Please don't let that happen."

"You'd say anything now to make this deal, wouldn't you?"

"You act like you're the only one with something to lose here. Did you ever think that I might have something precious at stake, too?"

His gaze narrowed. "Your job at HSG?"

"No. My relationship with my father."

When Cord didn't say anything, she continued, "You've been so focused on your save-the-ghost-town-

at-all-costs campaign that I don't think you've listened
to one word I've said."

"Of course I listened to you," Cord blustered.

"No, you didn't. Sure, you listened when I told you
stories about my childhood, but not when I steered the
subject around to the land. Not when I tried to explain
that we both have a lot at stake."

He eyed her suspiciously.

She swallowed down her rising emotions. "My
father's entire life has been about building his legacy, a
legacy that he can pass on to me. It's all that matters to
him now, and I want...I *need* to make that happen. It's
all I'll ever be able to give him.

Worse than the anger was the wounded look in
Cord's chocolate-brown eyes. "How can you play on
my sympathies like this? I thought you understood that
I can't afford to cut this ranch practically in half. I'd
have to reduce my herd size drastically. I...I don't even
know if I could keep the ranch going. If I couldn't run
this ranch, I don't know what I'd do."

"We're both going to lose if we don't make this deal.
You're going to lose your home, and I'm going to lose
my family's company. Shouldn't *something* be saved?"
She longed to put her arms around him and offer some
comfort, but she knew that would be the last thing he'd
want. Her arms remained limp at her sides.

"You're no better than your father." He raked his
fingers through his hair, scattering it in an unruly mess.
"The other day when you were on the phone with him
you mentioned that you had an alternative building site
in mind, and I was foolish enough to believe you
understood my need to hang on to the land—"

"I said I was pursuing another site, but this morning
I learned that we couldn't reach an agreement with the
owner. There are no other alternatives. We have to
move ahead with our plan for Haggerty." Even though
Cord refused to admit it, she was saving his home. Too

bad the justification did nothing to comfort her. "I didn't want to do this, but my company is in major trouble. People will lose their jobs, employees who have been loyal and supportive for years."

"I know nothing about you." Cord's voice cracked with raw pain. "I thought I did. I thought we were building something real—something with a future. But the truth is, it's all been a lie."

The dark coldness in his eyes was killing her. "I'm sorry. This isn't how I wanted things to end."

His shoulders were held in a rigid line. A muscle twitched in his jaw. "You need to leave now."

She held out the sales agreement. "You have until tomorrow to sign this, if you want to keep your home."

When he didn't move, she placed the papers on the wooden stand by the door. "You'll sign them, won't you?" He glowered at her, but he didn't scare her. She knew he was a gentle giant even when he huffed and puffed. "Don't you understand that at least this way I could personally make sure the cemetery is protected?" she pleaded. "We could build a rock wall the whole way around it. And your home would still be yours, free and clear. Trust me. This is best."

"What about the ghost town? Would it be preserved just as it is?"

She shook her head. "Numerous upgrades are required before the insurance company will issue coverage. If you were to talk with the contractors and show them some of your old photos of Haggerty, they could attempt to rebuild it in a similar fashion."

"I don't intend to do anything to help you turn my past into some sort of tourist trap." He threw open the door. "Go home to New York."

The backs of her eyes burned with unshed tears. She swallowed down the rush of emotions. "You're going to lose your home, Cord. Is there some way I can make this easier for you?"

"Yes. Leave."

Regret clawed at her throat, choking her with its foul taste. Unable to speak for fear of losing control of her rising emotions, she turned pleading eyes in his direction.

"Just go. Get off my land before I call the sheriff." The ice-cold control in his voice chilled her to the bone.

Each step toward the door took effort. It was as though her feet were weighted down. Perhaps giving him some time to digest the news and cool down would be a wise way of handling this, but she was only deluding herself. Even if he came to his senses and signed the papers, he'd never forgive her.

She turned back. "I'll return tomorrow for the papers."

For an instant, the devastation showed on his face. He looked as though he'd aged ten years. Regret consumed her. She might be on the eve of saving her father's company and Cord's home, but she'd lost the only man she'd ever truly loved.

CHAPTER TWENTY-THREE

Cord slammed the front door, rattling the pictures on the walls. He strode into the living room. How dare Lexi march in here with her ultimatums? His hands clenched.

What in the world had he been thinking professing his love for her? Had he completely lost his senses? Hadn't one hasty marriage been enough for him to learn to be cautious when it came to women?

He glanced at the photos of his ancestors. His gaze settled on the photo of his wise grandfather, who had raised him to love the land. He could feel the man shaking his head at him in disappointment. Guilt settled over Cord like a soggy wool blanket, cooling his rising emotions. The image of Lexi filled his thoughts.

You've been so focused on your save-the-ghost-town-at-all-costs campaign that I don't think you've heard one word I've said about my father...

Her words echoed in his mind. His body tensed as his hands balled into fists. Of course, he'd listened. Hadn't he?

Was it possible he had such tunnel vision when it came to saving Haggerty that he'd never given any real consideration to Lexi's needs and the possibility she might end up losing her father and the legacy he'd built for her?

Cord dropped down on the edge of the couch and looked up at the family pictures on the wall. Conflicting emotions churned in his gut.

"What have I done?" He lowered his head into his outstretched hands.

Lost not only the family land...but the woman I love.

He recalled snippets of his conversation with Lexi about her company and the resort. Maybe he hadn't considered the people relying on her, such as her ailing father or her employees. He knew too well the burden of worrying about your employees and the need to make sure he could keep all his ranch hands on the payroll.

Cord raised his head, and his gaze landed on the picture of his parents on the mantel. He'd made such a mess of things. What would his mother tell him to do about Lexi—the woman with a successful career on the other side of the country? Did Lexi truly care about him, like she claimed? Or was she playing on his feelings to get what she wanted from him, like his ex did?

The questions continued to whirl through his mind at lightning speed, making his stomach feel sick. He had to get this right—too much was riding on what he did next.

He walked past the unsigned sales agreement and straight out the front door. He jumped into his pickup and fired it up. The back tires spun as he punched the gas. He knew what had to be done, and he didn't like it one little bit.

Questions and regrets trailed him into Whistle Stop. He stopped by the grain and feed store on the pretext of checking on an order. He then found himself walking from one end of town to the other. He swore to himself that he was only burning off some pent-up frustration, not trying to bump into Lexi.

When he ended up standing in front of the Green Chile Cantina, he didn't have any appetite, but he sure could use a cup of coffee. Deflated and weary, he entered the restaurant. A handful of tables were occupied, but with it being a few minutes past eleven, the other residents had yet to come calling for lunch.

"Just one today?" Ana asked as she approached him. Her eyes needled him for information...about Lexi, he was certain.

He nodded. "You know me, always the lone rancher."

She turned her back to him to grab a menu. "Too bad. Thought you and Alexis had something going on."

So did he.

"You don't have to worry about her. She's getting ready to head back to New York. She'll probably be on the next flight out of here."

"Really?" Ana led him to a corner booth. "That's interesting, because she didn't mention anything to me at bingo."

"Bingo?"

When had Lexi taken up spending her evenings with the locals? Why hadn't he heard anything about it? He needed to start getting out more. Maybe joining Tony with the volunteer fire department wouldn't be such a bad idea after all.

Ana laughed, drawing his attention back to her. "What's so funny?"

"The surprised look on your face. Is it that surprising to find out the woman likes bingo? Or are you worried she might like it in Whistle Stop and decide to stay on?"

"She can do whatever she pleases. Makes no difference to me." Not even he could buy into that lie. Everything Lexi did mattered to him.

Ana set a menu in front of him. "Ralph Vasquez wasn't feeling well, so Alexis agreed to fill in as the announcer. You know how important bingo is to the town."

"How'd you talk her into it?"

Ana rested a hand on her hip. "I didn't. It was her idea. And she spent an evening at the quilting guild. Don't say anything, but she still has a lot to learn about working a needle. But the ladies loved her, and they were happy to teach her the basics."

After he ordered a cup of black coffee, Ana left him alone with his thoughts. Too bad all of these revelations had come too late. Lexi probably already had her bags packed. And even if he had sympathized with her situation, it wouldn't stop her from returning to New York.

Maybe he'd subconsciously judged her by Susan's yardstick. Those two were nothing alike when he looked beyond their need to be successful—but who didn't want to be successful? It was all about how you went about fulfilling your dreams—there was a right way and a bunch of wrong ways to go about it. Lexi did it the right way. She didn't sneak around. She'd been honest about what she wanted way before they'd shared their first kiss. He'd known what he was getting himself into. And he'd let himself get in deep—real deep.

Now, could he say goodbye to Lexi? The thought of him going to New York taunted his mind. He'd always sworn he'd never leave Whistle Stop, but now he was seriously reconsidering his decision.

♥♥♥

Long before the sun climbed above the distant horizon, Cord's day started. In fact, he'd never gone to sleep. Instead, he'd lain in bed staring into the darkness, knowing that when daylight dawned he'd have to face facts and choke down his pride.

All morning, he moved through his chores, forcing one exhausted foot in front of the other. His movements were slow and clumsy as his thoughts continued to stray back to his argument with Lexi. The guilt over the way they'd parted ways weighed down his already beleaguered body.

When he was alerted to the fact a windmill pump in the southern pasture had quit working, he heaved a weary sigh. He didn't need any more problems. Losing Lexi had him tied up in knots. By the time Cord had dropped his wrench for the fifth time and busted a knuckle open, Manny pushed him aside.

"Go home, boss. I've got this."

He gave Manny a questioning look and saw his friend meant business. "Are you sure?"

"Positive. Go do what ya gotta do. Things will be fine here."

Cord knew he needed to step back and let Manny handle it. His friend had never let him down, and it was good to have someone watching his back. It made him wonder if Lexi had anyone watching hers. She was so busy trying to take care of him and her father that he didn't think she ever took time to think of herself. How could he have accused her of doing otherwise? Regret punched him hard in the gut. He'd been a bigger fool than he'd originally thought, and that was saying a lot.

He glanced at Manny who was already hard at work on the pump. "You're sure you have this?"

Manny nodded. "Go."

"Thanks. You're a good man."

Cord headed for the house. His decision had been made, and putting it off wasn't doing him or anyone else any good. He strode through the front door and immediately noticed how the silence engulfed him. He missed the blissful chime of Lexi's laugh and her endless chatter. She may not be the best cook, but she'd been willing to try, and that had touched him.

Why did her presence in his life have to be tied to the land? Why did being with her feel like he had to choose between his past and his future? He recalled the distant promise he'd made to his grandfather to protect all of this land, including Haggerty. *Don't worry, Grandpa. I'll take care of the land just like you and Pa did.*

Only Cord hadn't kept his word. He'd failed long ago—when he'd lost half of the ranch in the divorce settlement. Why hadn't he realized that before now? Whatever action he took now wouldn't change that sobering fact. Somehow, in accepting that he'd already failed to keep his word, it freed him up to follow his heart's desire—Lexi.

After a brief shower, he threw on his newest jeans and the shirt he'd set aside for those rare moments when he needed to dress up. On his way to the door, he glanced down at the stand where the folded papers awaited his signature. Time to put his feet to the fire and save what he could of his past and his future.

He carried the papers into the living room and sat down. With great effort, he started to read. He was pleased to find the document was written in straightforward language. His conscience said he should have an attorney go over it, but his heart told him to trust Lexi. He firmly believed that she'd never swindle him—or stand for anyone else to do it.

Cord walked to the kitchen, grabbed a pen, and took a deep breath. It was for the best. He pressed the tip of the pen to the paper. He noticed the slightest tremor in his hand as he scrawled his name on the appropriate line. When he finished, he expelled a pent-up breath.

He folded the papers—his proof that he'd heard her, truly heard her.

With his Stetson in hand, he headed out the door. He'd reached the bottom porch step when he heard a vehicle approaching. Could it be Lexi? He stopped and waited. The breath caught in his chest. Had she come back to give him another chance to get things right?

A black sedan pulled to a stop in front of him, and an older gentleman climbed out. The stranger stood as tall as himself, but the man's hair was a bit shorter and silver. The ill-fitting gray suit emphasized his skinny stature. When Cord focused in on the man's face, he had no doubt this was Lexi's father.

"Mr. Lawson, I'm Howard Greer." The man extended his hand.

"I know who you are." Cord ignored the man's outstretched hand. "What are you doing here?"

"I thought my daughter might be here. Seems she spends a lot of time with you riding around the countryside." He looked around as though Cord might be hiding her.

"She isn't here. Why don't you call her?"

The man sighed. "She isn't taking my calls. When I stopped by her motel, some gabby woman said my daughter wasn't in her room and she didn't know where Alexis might be."

"And you naturally assumed I'd what? Taken her hostage?"

The man's brows furrowed. "I didn't come here to argue with you, Mr. Lawson—"

"You shouldn't be here at all. You already caused enough trouble when you were on the East Coast."

The man pulled a folded white hanky from his pocket and ran it across his brow. "Sure is hot out here in the sun."

Cord, remembering the man's heart condition, relented and invited him onto the porch. After Cord retrieved him a glass of ice water, they both sat down.

Mr. Greer drank half of the water before setting it aside. "I flew out here to make sure you don't take advantage of my daughter."

"Me?" The man had to be kidding. No one could take advantage of Lexi. She was much too smart for that. "You're the one who won't let her use her own judgment to finalize this deal. You're the one making her miserable with ultimatums."

The man sat back as though the words shocked him. "You seem to know a lot about Alexis."

"We've spent quite a bit of time together since she's been in Whistle Stop. Lexi is a very strong, determined woman, who would do anything in the world for you."

Mr. Greer's eyes narrowed. "What are you implying?"

"That you need to let your daughter choose her life and not guilt her into doing what you want her to do."

Color filled the man's sunken cheeks. "She told you all of this?"

The dam on Cord's frustrations burst, and the words spilled out. "She'd never say it. She's too loyal to you. But she'd never leave you. She feels that without her around, you'll work yourself into the ground."

Cord paused, realizing he'd probably crossed a line. Lexi would be mortified if she knew he'd repeated the things she'd told him in confidence.

"And you know what my daughter wants?"

Cord wanted to say that he did, but he couldn't lie. "No, I don't. But don't you think you owe it to her to let her choose?"

♥♥♥

Caffeine from the Poppin' Fresh Bakery plus the sugar from not just one but two dark chocolate cupcakes pumped through Alexis's veins, bolstering her weary body. She'd almost requested a third cupcake, they were sooo good, but at the last second she'd latched on to a modicum of self-control. No amount of chocolate was going to drown her sorrows.

After procrastinating as long as she dared, it was time for her to face Cord. The coffee sloshed nauseatingly in her stomach. She desperately wanted to see where their future could take them, but first she had to stop him from losing the Brazen H. Just because her attempt to buy the Arizona property hadn't panned out didn't mean she didn't have another idea percolating in her mind.

The what if's and maybe's danced through her mind, keeping her up all night. By the time the sun had crept over the horizon, she'd had a new plan. It wasn't a perfect plan, but it was better than nothing. However, there was one major hitch—her new idea would still leave her father's company in a tough spot...

The words *her father's company* profoundly struck her. Was this truly how she looked at HSG—as her *father's* business?

She didn't have to even contemplate the answer. Deep inside, she knew she'd followed in his footsteps because it was what was expected of her—not because she'd chosen the path herself. As much as she loved her father, she didn't love running HSG. Did that make her an ungrateful daughter? A bad daughter?

Even so, could she keep on doing what was expected of her? When was it appropriate to follow her heart? Something told her that it'd never be the right time where her father was concerned. This meant she must now mark her line in the sand. She either chose her future with Cord or chose her preordained future at HSG—if Cord agreed to the sale.

The decision nagged at her as she drove down the familiar two-lane highway toward the Brazen H. She knew the answer her heart craved, but she didn't know how her father would take the news.

If the resort didn't go through, HSG would no longer have the working capital to stay in operation. The business's assets would be sold off. Her father would be forced into retirement. At least money wouldn't be an issue for him. He had plenty in savings to live comfortably the rest of his life.

At last convinced she knew what was best for all of them, she turned onto the gravel road to Cord's house.

She slowed down when she noticed an unfamiliar black sedan in front of the house. Who would be visiting Cord?

Her gaze moved to the porch where Cord was shaking hands with...with her father? She blinked. Her mouth gaped open. What was he doing here?

Her father accepted folded papers from Cord—the sales agreement. Her heart slammed into her ribs, knocking the breath from her lungs. Her father had flown out here because he hadn't trusted her to finish this deal. She threw the vehicle into park, but she didn't bother to cut the engine. She wouldn't be here long enough to bother.

Cord turned as she marched up the steps to them. She lifted her shades, resting them on her head. She shot Cord a don't-you-dare-mess-with-me glare. She'd deal with him later.

She turned to her father, taking in his drawn face and sunken cheeks. The strong man he'd once been was now reduced to the stature of a man twenty years older than he was. His gaunt appearance only fueled her anxiety over him traveling so far and all alone.

Howard Greer smiled. "Daughter, I'm glad you're here. I was worried about you."

"You were, huh?" She planted her hands on her hips. "So now it's my fault you ignored the doctor's orders and hopped on a plane."

"I thought you might need me, and I was right." His brows furrowed, and his eyes darkened, which always happened when he'd reached the end of his patience.

"Why is that? Oh, never mind. It doesn't matter." Her concern came out in anger—anger over his risky behavior. Already on emotional overload, she didn't stop there. "You aren't supposed to be working or traveling. I'm the one handling the business now."

"Daughter, if you'll calm down, I'll explain. The doctor released me to resume normal activity—"

"And the first thing you decided to do was jump on a plane and come here to undermine my efforts to secure this deal."

"I was worried—"

"About your company. I know. It's all you talk about. Well, for months now I've been worried about you, but you don't seem to get that."

She swung around to Cord. Her fingers pointed at him. "And you, why would you cave in to my father after all I did to close this deal?"

"What are you talking about?" Cord stepped toward her but she backed away. "I didn't cave in to him."

She yanked the document from her father's hand and shook them at Cord. "I talked to you—no, I *begged* you to sign these papers and save your home, but you flat-out refused."

"I...I had to think things over. It was a big decision for me. Surely you understand—"

"Funny how all of your clarity came about when my father shows up." Her hands pressed to her hips.

"That's not true—"

"I bet if I look at these papers, they'll be signed."

"Wait." Cord reached for the papers.

"I've waited too long already." She moved out of his reach and unfolded them. The blue ink of Cord's signature stood out. He'd at last agreed to sell Haggerty. A convergence of conflicting emotions dammed up inside her.

"Lexi," Cord's brown gaze pleaded with her, "we need to talk about this. Alone."

"No, we don't. There's nothing left for us to discuss." She was incensed to think he'd undercut her in front of her father. "And, Father, you obviously don't need me. You seem determined to do what you please, whether it's good for you or not. Well, don't expect me to stand around and watch you work yourself into an early grave."

"I won't…I…I'm not."

"You are, and you're too stubborn to realize it. You can do it alone, because I quit." She looked at one stunned man and then the other. "You both are the most pigheaded men I've ever dealt with. You deserve each other."

She tossed the papers at her father before turning on her heel and marching down the steps. Once inside her vehicle, the cold air from the vents fanned her hot face. She yanked the gearshift into reverse, not giving either man the slightest glance. Whatever they decided to do was no longer her problem.

She tramped the accelerator. The time had come to reevaluate her life. She could start over anywhere in the world she wanted. She was free. She should be jubilant. Relieved.

She glanced at her reflection in the rearview mirror, catching sight of the damp streaks trailing down her cheeks. She was something all right. Disappointed. Crushed.

CHAPTER TWENTY-FOUR

Cord's hands clenched as Lexi's SUV roared down the lane. In her wake, the billowing dust cloud obscured the last sight of her—or was it the steam from her boiling temper?

He couldn't believe he'd handled things so badly. He'd meant to say he loved her and to beg her forgiveness, but he hadn't been able to bring himself to grovel in front of her father. Cord's body tensed. He'd once again let his foolish pride trip him up.

"What are you doing, boy?" Mr. Greer moved to stand by him at the porch rail.

Cord, still lost in his thoughts, looked at the man in confusion. "What?"

"Are you just going to stand there and let her get away?"

"She said she doesn't want anything to do with either of us."

"And you believe her?" The man shook his head in disbelief. "My daughter has been deeply hurt in her life. When her mother left, Alexis was devastated. Not only did she have to deal with her mother's absence, but then exaggerated rumors about her mother spread like wildfire. Alexis's peers overheard those vicious lies and taunted my daughter mercilessly…"

Mr. Greer's face grew ashen. His head lowered, and he shook it. Cord stood there, utterly stunned. Alexis hadn't mentioned any of this to him.

"I...I failed her." Mr. Greer's voice grew emotional, and his shoulders slumped. "My ex-wife's affair took me by surprise, and then her legal battle for the company sucked up most of my attention. My daughter was left to fend for herself, and I'm afraid she learned to hide her heart behind walls that are so high you'll need climbing gear if you hope to scale them."

Everything the man told him filled in the blanks about Lexi's past. Cord longed to race after her, but he held back. He needed to be prepared if he wanted to get past her now reinforced walls.

Cord started for the front door—but then he paused.

"What is it, boy?"

Cord turned back. "No matter what she says, she loves you."

"I know." The man's eyes were shiny with emotion. "I love her, too, even if I don't always show it."

"My going after her will only hurt her more."

Mr. Greer's gray brows scrunched together. "I don't follow."

Cord shifted his weight from one foot to the other. The admission would cost him dearly, but he had to do his best to help mend the relationship between father and daughter. "Lexi didn't mean it about quitting HSG. She was blowing off steam. She won't leave you alone at the company. She's told me that numerous times. After she cools off, she'll be back at work."

The man's face grew solemn. "That's one of the things I wanted to tell her. After I'd gone over everything at HSG and took stock of the challenges awaiting me, I had a long chat with my doctor."

Mr. Greer turned and rested his palms against the porch railing and stared out at Roca Mountain. Would he just spit it out? What had he decided? Something told Cord this decision was going to greatly impact his life. For better or worse remained to be seen.

"And..." Cord prodded, unable to stand the suspense.

"And my daughter will no longer have to worry about me or the company. I also think it's time my girl has someone of her own to lean on. Someone who's dependable and will put her best interests first." Mr. Greer turned and looked Cord squarely in the eyes. "I think you're that man. Now quit standing around. You have a woman to track down."

In Cord's book, those words qualified as a father's approval. He turned toward the front door.

"You're going the wrong way if you want to catch her."

Cord turned back. "I figure I'll need some special climbing gear if I'm going to scale those walls around her heart."

The man chuckled. "And I've got a plane to catch. Tell my daughter I love her and I'll talk to her soon."

"Will do." In his rush to get to Lexi, Cord almost forgot to do something very important. He extended his hand to Mr. Greer. "Thank you."

The man's eyes opened wide, and then a smile eased the ingrained lines on his face. "My daughter does have good taste." He gripped Cord's hand with a firm grip. "Just remember to send me an invitation to the wedding."

"If she'll have me." There still remained one huge question in his mind. Would Lexi forgive and forget? Cord didn't waste any time standing around debating the answer. Only the woman herself could let him know where he stood.

His hurried footsteps thundered through the house as he ran to the study. In the cabinet beneath the bookcase sat the safe. Inside were his mother's diamond and turquoise-inlaid wedding rings. He grabbed the diamond solitaire and stuffed the little box in his pocket.

He headed for the door. He'd find everything else he needed to scale the wall around Lexi's heart in town. He took the steps two at a time and strode to the pickup. He didn't have time to waste—he couldn't be too late to set things right with her.

♥♥♥

This had to be a nightmare.

But try as she might, Alexis couldn't dismiss the fact that the two men she cared most about in this world had just let her down. How could they have done that to her?

Alexis wheeled her rental vehicle into the motel parking lot, turned off the engine, and sat there for a moment. Her heart was still pounding, and her hands were shaking. She needed to calm down—big-time. A Choconut Bar sprang to mind. And just as soon as the thought occurred to her, she realized that the last thing she needed was more calories.

As it was, she'd have to get up earlier when she got back to New York so she could spend extra time at the gym. And then her dinner choices would be relegated to the salad section of the takeout menus. Definitely not a regime she was anticipating, but a girl's got to do what a girl's got to do. And right now, circumstances dictated that she wallow in the rich chocolaty taste of her favorite candy. Her dieting could just wait another day. After all, these were extraordinary circumstances.

She debated whether she should drive the short distance to the Hitchin' Post or walk. The answer was easy—she'd walk. It wasn't far, plus the fresh air and sunshine might help improve her sour mood, though she doubted it. She'd just stepped out of her vehicle when Mrs. Sanchez came rushing over.

"Are you all right?" The woman peered speculatively at her through her black-rimmed glasses. "An older gentleman was here looking for you. But don't worry, I didn't tell him anything."

"No worries. It was my father. I just saw him." She might as well tell her now. "I'm leaving."

"Leaving?"

"Um, yes. I'll be over to settle up my bill as soon as I run a quick errand." She didn't have the nerve to say that her craving for a Choconut Bar was greater than her willpower.

"But why?" Mrs. Sanchez's round face creased with worry lines. "What happened? Is it the resort?"

Alexis shook her head. "I don't know what's going to happen with it. It's not my problem anymore."

"But...but you worked so hard to make it all work."

"I'm not a part of HSG anymore. I just quit."

Mrs. Sanchez's mouth gaped. She looked as stunned as Alexis felt. And now that she'd actually uttered the words that she'd quit her job, she realized there was no need to rush back to New York. She was no longer needed there. But she couldn't stay in Whistle Stop either. This was Cord's town, and it was much too small to avoid each other indefinitely.

The thought of never seeing Cord again spiked her anxiety. She desperately needed that chocolate. "I'll be back to pay my bill."

For the first time since she'd met the woman, Mrs. Sanchez stood there, speechless, and merely nodded. The events of the day played over in Alexis's mind as a gentle breeze brushed over her skin and threaded through her hair, scattering it about. How could she have been so foolish as to think she and Cord would be together? When was she ever going to learn that the people she loved would invariably let her down?

She took the long way around town, enjoying one last look around. When she reached the Hitchin' Post, she pulled open the glass door, and the little bell jingled over her head. The backs of her eyes stung, and she blinked. After today, she'd never hear that bell again or talk to these wonderful people. Whistle Stop had grown on her more than she'd ever thought possible.

She moved to the candy rack and went to grab a Choconut Bar, but found the box empty. Where had they gone? The box had been nearly full the day of the town meeting. She knew because she'd needed a little chocolate to take the edge off her anxiety before standing in front of the town and pitching her ideas.

She stepped up to the checkout counter. Sam gazed at her empty hands with a puzzled look on his face. "Hey, Lexi. Can I help you?"

"I hope so. You seem to have run out of Choconut Bars. Please tell me you have more in the back."

"Afraid not. Ever since you've come to town, I seem to sell more of those than any other candy. But don't you worry. Sam has you all taken care of." He smiled proudly. "I ordered twice as many. They should be here in a day. Two, tops. I put a rush on them just for you. It's my way of saying thanks."

"Thanks? For what?" Had she missed something?

"It's just that it's been awhile since anyone has taken a special interest in Whistle Stop and gone the extra mile."

"But I didn't do anything." Not really. Certainly not like she'd hoped by building the resort and providing more jobs for the families of Whistle Stop.

"You did more than you think." He glanced around as though making sure they were alone, then he leaned across the counter and lowered his voice. "You got that lazy, complacent town council to sit up and take notice. I'm telling you, good things are coming to Whistle Stop, and we'll all have you to thank."

Alexis smiled and blinked back another wave of tears. She sure hoped Sam was right. Whistle Stop was a great place to visit and to live. Too bad she wouldn't be around to see the changes.

She thanked Sam and rushed out of the store before she dissolved into a messy puddle of tears. She definitely had to leave—the sooner, the better. Saying good-bye to everyone was just too painful.

Not ready for another farewell with Mrs. Sanchez, Alexis headed for her motel room to pack. She'd just placed the empty suitcase on the queen-size bed when there was a knock at the door.

She took a deep, calming breath. Hopefully, it wasn't her father or Cord. She wasn't ready to deal with either of them. She looked through the peephole and then swung open the door.

"Mayor Ortiz, hi. Can I help you?"

"Do you have a moment to talk?"

She had absolutely no idea what they'd talk about, but she had to admit she was curious. And it'd be a nice distraction from her own problems. "Sure. Come on in."

Leaving the door wide open, the mayor stepped into the small room. His gaze came to rest on the suitcase. "So the rumors of you leaving Whistle Stop are true?"

She nodded. "They are. My job is done here. I'm sorry, but I'm no longer working on the resort project, so I can't tell you how it's going to work out."

"The town council and I would like to thank you for working so hard on the town's behalf to make the resort a possibility. We owe you a debt of gratitude."

Why did everyone keep thanking her? She didn't deserve it.

"But I didn't finalize the deal. It's still up in the air." She had no idea what her father and Cord had decided to do.

"Perhaps we don't need the resort. Maybe the sole purpose of the resort was to bring you to our town. The older I get, the more I find that fate works in very unpredictable ways."

"But if it wasn't the resort, then what was the point of me being here?"

"That's easy. To wake up a town that had grown accustomed to moaning and groaning about the economic decline and the continual erosion of residents." He smiled at her and took her hand in his. "Thank you for waking up this foolish old man and making me see all of the opportunities that I was letting slip by."

"You mean about the railroad and restoring the town square?"

"Yes." He squeezed her hand. "I've called a special meeting of the town council to follow up on what you've started. In fact, I came here to invite you to the meeting. Your input would be most welcome. But I see I'm too late." He released her hand. "If you change your mind, the meeting is tomorrow evening at six at the community center."

"I'm sorry, but I really do need to get back to New York." She wanted to go to that meeting more than she let on. She had a lot of ideas about festivals and hot air balloon rides. There were so many things they could do to draw the community together while also entertaining visitors.

"You will always be welcome in Whistle Stop. Maybe sometime in the future you can visit and see how we're doing with the town's makeover."

"I'd really like that." But she didn't imagine it would ever happen.

After a brief hug, the mayor headed for the door. When it closed, Alexis felt more alone than she'd ever felt in her life. At least she could cling to the fact that her time here had done some good. She had no doubt the mayor intended to breathe new life into Whistle Stop. It wouldn't dry up into a ghost town like Haggerty had.

If only her broken heart could be so easily restored. Even though it felt ripped in half, it still beat out Cord's name. She couldn't imagine that ever changing, no matter how far she traveled or how much time passed.

CHAPTER TWENTY-FIVE

With a brown paper bag gripped in one hand, Cord took a deep breath and rapped on Lexi's motel room door. His body tensed as the seconds ticked by. He sensed her standing on the other side of the door with stubbornness written all over her adorable face.

He knocked again, louder this time. "Lexi, open up. I'm not leaving here until I see you. I'm prepared to stand here all night if that's what it takes."

When she at last opened the door, he made sure to prop his boot in the doorjamb.

She frowned at him. "Do you have to yell?"

"I had to make sure you heard me."

"Well, we have nothing left to say to each other. Now go away." When she pushed the door to close it, the door came to a halt against his boot. "Move."

"Not until you give me a chance to explain."

"Save it. I'm not interested. Now go away."

"Not yet."

She let go of the door handle and crossed her arms. "Talk fast. I have to check out in a few minutes."

He glanced over his shoulder. The couple in the next room who were loading up their white minivan kept shooting him strange looks. This wasn't the right place for this conversation.

"Please let me inside."

Her lips pursed in contemplation as her gaze strayed to the nosy couple. When she retreated into the dimly lit room, he followed. She stopped next to the bed where her suitcase was propped open. She kept her back to him as she folded a pile of colorful tops and placed them neatly in the already-full case.

"Lexi, stop packing and look at me."

She sighed but turned. "Time's ticking."

Her cool tone added to the nervous tension plaguing him. "I need you to listen and believe me."

"Believe you about what? Are you going to try and tell me that my eyes were playing tricks on me and that wasn't your signature I saw on the sales agreement? Or that my father twisted your arm and made you sign it?"

"No. I'm not going to tell you any of that. You're the reason I came to my senses about the sale. The honest-to-goodness truth is I signed those papers before your father pulled in. If you don't believe me, ask him."

A flash of surprise lit up her eyes.

He'd made his first chip at her steely resistance. He couldn't let up now. Time to break out the first tool he planned to use to make cracks in the reinforced wall surrounding her heart. He moved to the bed and dumped the contents of the paper bag. Choconut Bars showered down all over the blanket.

"What in the world?"

"It's a peace offering."

When their gazes collided, her eyes dimmed and she pursed her lips. "Chocolate can't fix this problem. We're over. You've got the money to save the Brazen H, and it's time for me to head back to New York."

"Whistle Stop could be your home, if you wanted it to be. Or…or I could give New York a try."

"What are you saying?" The rigid line of her shoulders eased.

He took a deep breath. "I don't want you to leave…not without me. I've gotten used to having you around. And when you aren't there, it's lonely. I...I miss you when you're not there."

"You miss me?" Her eyes rounded as the thought settled in.

"It's true. I can't imagine my life going back to its solitary existence." He stepped toward her. His fingers slid around her arms. His thumbs stroked her smooth skin. "Don't you understand what I'm trying to tell you?"

She took a moment and then shook her head, but her gaze never broke with his.

"I love you, Lexi. I think I lost my heart to you the day we visited Haggerty. And then when you started having a reaction to the scorpion sting, you scared the life out of me." Remembering the ring in his pocket, he yanked it out. Not giving her a chance to say anything, he dropped to one knee. He opened the box and held it out to her.

Her mouth gaped. "Cord...I..."

"Shh...just let me say this before I get too nervous and forget." He swallowed and tried to gather his jumbled thoughts. "Lexi, I love you and I want you to share my life, my home, and my future. Will you consider being my best friend for life?"

Her eyes shimmered, and a tear splashed onto her cheek. Her gaze went from his face to the box and back to him.

Her trembling fingers grasped his hand. "You're sure about this?"

"I've never been more sure in my life. If you think you could be happy with this cowboy, please wear my ring."

She started shaking her head.

No? She was saying no?

His gut twisted into a painful knot. This wasn't how it was supposed to go. He sensed her working hard to rebuild the wall between them, but he refused to give up. They'd come too far to let their future slip away. She loved him. He knew it. She just had to admit it.

He got to his feet. "If it's your father, you don't have to worry. He gave us his blessing before he left."

"My father…he knows you were going to propose?"

"Yes. He encouraged me."

Her fingers reached out to Cord's face. They traced down over his jaw, and he waited, wondering what she was about to do. His heart hammered. His muscles tensed. He forced himself not to pull her to him. This had to be at her pace. He couldn't rush her.

"You're so sweet." She shook her head again and backed up. "But I can't accept this. Not like this. It won't work."

"It can if you'll just believe in us as much as I do."

She swiped at her cheeks. "I've got to go."

Her words slugged him in the gut, knocking the wind from him. He'd put himself out there, put his feelings on the line, and she'd rejected his proposal— she'd rejected him.

His chest ached as though his heart had been ripped from it and lay bleeding on the floor. The searing pain of loss surpassed anything he'd ever endured.

"Don't let me stop you." He strode out the door.

Unable to believe it was truly ending this way, he paused at the door and turned back. Lexi closed her suitcase and lowered it to the floor. The finality of her with her bag in hand drove home the reality of the situation.

He'd lost the thing he loved most—Lexi.

Alexis passed through the airport's security checkpoint. She had a plan, a way to make things work for her and Cord, but as things stood, she couldn't accept his proposal. He'd sacrificed too much to make it work between them. And some day he'd realize this, and he would grow to resent her. She wouldn't be able to bear losing him.

Before that happened, she needed to fix this for him, for herself—for them. The first thing she had to do was catch up to her father. As soon as she'd arrived at the airport, she'd called his cell phone, but it went to voice mail. Then she'd had him paged. She'd waited, but he didn't respond. Her heart pitter-pattered as her gaze scanned the multitude of people. He had to be here somewhere. But where?

Her mind was still busy ironing out the details of her plan. She was certain withdrawing her trust fund was the right decision. This was most certainly an emergency, but she needed to do one more thing.

She braced herself for the argument of her life once she located her father.

"Alexis?"

She turned, and her gaze landed on her father. In the end, he'd been the one to find her. He strode up to her. Before she could say a word, he enveloped her in his arms, and the tension melted away. This was her father. The man who'd always been there when she needed him.

He released her and stepped back. "Before you say anything. I want you to know that I didn't fly here to undercut you. In fact, Cord had those papers signed before I got to the ranch."

"He told me."

Her father's brows rose. "So he caught up with you, yet you're here. What happened?"

She bit down on her bottom lip to keep control of her emotions. This was her chance to make everything right—or as right as they could ever be. She had to hold it together until she got it all out.

"He proposed."

"You're here, so I'm guessing you turned him down. Why, Alexis? I know you care about him. Otherwise, you wouldn't have stalled on this project and defended him countless times. That's why I came here, to make sure the man who stole away my little girl is good enough."

The air trapped in her lungs. Had she heard him correctly? It took her a moment to breathe again. "You came all this way for me?"

Her father nodded. "Cord's a good guy. He'll do right by you. So if you turned him down because you don't love him, that I can accept. But if you turned him down because people you've loved in the past have let you down, then you aren't being fair to yourself or him."

Alexis shook her head. "It's not that. I love him, but I have to make things right between us, or else we won't have a chance for a happy future."

The crowd of people thickened, making it harder to talk. Her father grabbed her hand and led her off to the side where black-cushioned seats lined the wall.

Once they were seated, he held her hand. "And what will it take to set things right?"

Alexis sucked in a deep breath and blew it out. She launched into the biggest, most important negotiation of her life—one that would dictate the terms of her future.

CHAPTER TWENTY-SIX

Alexis hadn't even been gone a day, and Cord was utterly miserable.

None of the ranch hands would get near him—not even Manny. He couldn't blame them. He was in a foul mood, and everything grated on his frayed nerves.

Being absolutely no help to anyone or anything, he'd taken off on horseback. He'd hoped riding astride Midnight Star with the wind in his face would lessen the sting of Lexi's rejection. It hadn't worked. If anything, the silence had him missing her even more.

Now back at the barn, it was long past dinnertime. With his horse tended to, he headed back to the house. He was partway up the porch steps when he thought he heard an approaching vehicle. He refused to give in to another one of his deluded fantasies that Lexi had changed her mind and come looking for him. He assured himself he was hearing things…again. Even if it was a vehicle, it wouldn't be Lexi. She was on a plane by now, jetting across the country.

He'd reached the front door and grabbed for the doorknob when the sound of the engine was so close he was certain it wasn't his imagination. Whoever it was, he was in no mood to talk to them. He didn't care if it was rude, he started inside.

"Aren't you even going to hear me out?" a familiar voice called out.

Lexi? Hope and anticipation swelled in his chest. He spun around, finding her standing in the driveway. She'd returned. He blew out a long-held breath. He refused to get his hopes up too high. She could be here for anything.

She climbed the steps, holding some folded papers.

His excitement skidded to a halt. "Are those more papers you need me to sign before you leave town?"

She glanced at her hand and then back at him. "Is that what you want? For me to leave? Have you changed your mind about us that quickly?"

"You know what I want," he ground out. "And you turned me down."

"I never turned you down. If you'll remember, I said I couldn't accept your proposal under those circumstances. We had too many things stacked against us."

"And hours later, it's that much different?" He stifled the urge to pull her into his arms. He was still wary of her intentions.

A tiny smile pulled at her lips as she shrugged. Now he was certain she was up to something, and he wasn't sure if he liked it or not.

"Okay, Lexi. Spit it out. What has changed?"

"I officially quit my job. Now you can ask me that question again."

She what? She had? When? Life suddenly hit warp speed, and he was having problems hanging on for the ride.

"Slow down. Let me get this straight. You actually quit HSG? I never thought you'd leave your father alone to run the company."

"I've proven myself in the business world, but I don't want it to be my entire life, like it was for my father. I need more."

A surge of excitement raced over Cord. He struggled to remain still and not smother her with kisses. He needed to be sure she'd thought this completely through.

"And you think living here at the Brazen H is going to give you that fulfillment?"

"I'm here to stay. If you'll have me."

"But what about your father? How can you leave him when he needs you?"

"That's something I wanted to discuss with you. What would you say to having a permanent houseguest?"

"Your father?" Cord didn't hide the shock in his voice.

She nodded and smiled. "When he figured out I wasn't as devoted to the business as he'd always been, he decided to sell the company to an associate who has made offers for it over the years. So he and I, we come as a package deal."

"You do, huh?"

"Yes, we do. I hope you can make room for both of us. We could build on or—"

Cord pressed a finger to her tempting lips. "We'll work something out."

Her eyes grew round. "Are you sure...really, really sure you don't mind taking us in? I couldn't stand it if you changed your mind later."

Cord smiled as his hand cupped her cheek. "I want us to be together, and I'll do whatever it takes. I promise."

He proved it by pulling her into his arms, lowering his head, and pressing his mouth to hers. Her skin was still cool from the car's air conditioning. Her curves fit snugly against him, sending his heated blood pumping hard and strong.

When his tongue swept inside her mouth, she tasted fresh and minty. He moaned, wanting nothing more than to pull her into the house and continue this kiss for the rest of the night. Her kisses and touches were the only nourishment he needed.

Not wanting to break their embrace, he stepped toward the door, taking her with him. Even though he'd have no problem continuing this reunion right here on the front porch, Lexi would probably be mortified if one of the ranch hands happened upon them. He was fumbling with the door handle when she pulled back. Her lips were rosy and swollen. Her eyes questioned what he was doing.

"Let's go inside where no one will disturb us." He pulled on her hand, but she wouldn't budge. "Come on, don't you want to celebrate privately?"

"First, I have one more surprise for you." She handed over the papers.

He frowned. "You sure know how to dampen a guy's enthusiasm. You couldn't have waited to finalize the sale of Haggerty until later?"

She shook her head as she smiled. Her eyes glittered with happiness. Didn't she understand that even though he'd consented to the sale, the reminder of parting with a piece of his heritage still hurt?

"Open it." She practically bounced up and down in anticipation.

What in the world? He unfolded the document and noted the bank's name at the top—the same bank that held his mortgage. When he noticed it was marked *Paid in Full*, he started at the beginning and scanned the page. Lexi patiently waited while he made out the highlights.

"What about the resort? What about Haggerty?"

"Seems my father still has a lot of pull. He convinced the investors to spend the extra money to buy the Arizona property."

Cord glanced at her. "You did all of this for me?"

Her eyes lit up and then she nodded.

"How did you pay off the loan?"

"I had a little bit of rainy day money set aside." She pressed her fingers to his lips, holding back his protest. "Daddy pulled a few strings. This is just a copy. The official paperwork won't come through until later this month. Consider this a wedding gift."

He moved her hand from his mouth. "Does this mean you're proposing?"

"Most definitely."

"Shouldn't you have a ring for me?" He smiled, teasing her.

"Quit joking around. This isn't funny." Her face sobered as her gaze held his. "Cord, will you marry me?"

He grinned. "Considering you're now part owner of this ranch, I guess I'd better accept."

She playfully slugged his arm. "Couldn't you just say yes?"

He cleared his throat. "Yes, Alexis Greer, I'd be honored to be your husband."

She squealed and jumped into his arms. Her lips pressed to his. Cord's chest swelled with love and a happiness he'd never encountered before. No life experience had ever fulfilled him as much as making Lexi's dream come true—and he'd only just begun.

COMING SUMMER 2015...

A MOMENT TO DANCE
A Whistle Stop Romance, book #2

Tony Granger meets up with Whistle Stop's newest schoolteacher, Ella Morgan, and instantly the sparks fly. Add in one determined little boy, a cute puppy and a dance contest and you never know what will happen next. But most importantly, will Tony and Ella be able to let down their guards long enough to help each other?

OTHER BOOKS BY JENNIFER FAYE

Best Man for the Bridesmaid
(The DeFiore Brothers – book #2)

Planning her sister's Italian wedding only reminds Jules Lane of how far away she is from finding her own true love. And worse, she's doing it alongside the brooding, mouthwateringly handsome best man, Stefano DeFiore. Having seen the destructive power of love, Stefano has no time for weddings—but Jules's smile is captivating. Making her feel like the most beautiful woman in the world is one thing, but can he give this blushing bridesmaid a happily-ever-after of her own?

The Playboy of Rome
(The DeFiore Brothers – book #1)

Lizzie Addler's dream of working in Italy is about to come true—that is if she can convince passionate Italian chef Dante DeFiore to keep his side of their bargain. Dante might be hotter than the Italian sun, but he's as cool as ice toward Lizzie. Dante hasn't the time to pander to Lizzie's dreams of culinary fame—he has a restaurant to run! But as Lizzie proves herself to be a spectacular addition to his kitchen—and to his life— Dante wonders…can he keep her forever?

A Princess by Christmas

Prince Alexandro Castanovo arrives in snowy New York intent on protecting his royal family from scandal. And when Reese Harding—down-to-earth and heart-stoppingly beautiful—finds room for him at her inn, it seems like the perfect twist of fate. Not long ago Reese's world came crumbling down, shaking her foundations. But this enigmatic stranger intrigues her! She's learned to be wary of secrets...but when she discovers Alex's true identity, might there be enough magic in the air to make this regular American girl a princess by Christmas...?

The Return of the Rebel

Being promoted should be a dream come true, only it means working closely with Cleo's childhood crush, Jax Monroe. Jax may no longer be the rebel she remembers, but he still gets her heart racing like no other. Jax cares too much about Cleo to let her get too close—but keeping his distance is proving impossible! As Jax reveals the extent of what he's been through, will Cleo show him that some things are too precious to put off until tomorrow?

Safe in the Tycoon's Arms

When billionaire Lucas Carrington returns to his New York mansion, he never expects to find beautiful stranger Kate Whitley making herself at home. Invited by his aunt to stay, he soon discovers she's a woman in need. She's raising funds for her sick daughter, so he agrees to let her stay—temporarily! Kate may not belong in Lucas's high-society world, but she sees there is more to this tycoon than the headlines suggest. Yet with so much at stake, can she trust herself and her heart with New York's most sought-after bachelor?

Snowbound with the Soldier

It has been seven long years since Kara Jameson last saw Jason Greene. Returning home as a wounded war hero, Jason looks a shell of the man she once knew. Yet her heart still skips a beat as if it was yesterday. Stepping back into civilian life, Jason looks to Kara for help. But there's too much water under the bridge—not to mention too much lingering attraction. But it seems that the mountain weather has other ideas, and when Kara and Jason end up snowbound together they are forced to confront the ghosts of Christmas past.

Rancher to the Rescue

Jilted at the altar, celebrity chef Meghan Finnegan flees the scene – and the baying press – only to run straight into the muscled torso of Cash Sullivan. The former rodeo champion knows what it's like to have your life crumble in the spotlight, so he offers Meghan a place to lie low at his ranch. Fresh air, no paparazzi and the brooding rancher's lazy smile are making Meghan not want to leave her sanctuary. But she and her unborn baby can't stay here forever...can they?

Dear Reader:

I hope you enjoyed your visit to Whistle Stop, where anything and everything can happen. Every time I write a new book set in Whistle Stop, it's like going home again. The characters have grown into great fictional friends that I just love to watch as they find their own happily-ever-after.

Cord and Lexi were amazing to work with, and don't worry, you'll be seeing more of them and how their journey continues in other Whistle Stop books.

Next up is *A MOMENT TO DANCE* where you'll get to know Tony much better. He's a cowboy by trade and the town's fire chief. He'll be the first to admit that he hasn't always made the right choices in the past and now they've caught up to him. He's doing his best to right the wrongs, but he's in over his head and sinking fast as he learns the ropes of being a single parent to his orphaned nephew.

Ella is the new schoolteacher in Whistle Stop. She's hoping this small town will give her a chance to wipe her slate clean and start over. However, when these two meet for the first time, sparks fly...and not in a good way. But when there's a little boy and a puppy involved, well...things never go according to plan. ;-)

Happy reading,

Jennifer

ABOUT THE AUTHOR

Award-winning author, Jennifer Faye pens fun, heartwarming romances. Step into the pages of exciting destinations with rugged cowboys, sexy tycoons & enchanting royalty. Jennifer won the 2013 RT Book Reviews Reviewers' Choice Award for Best Harlequin Romance. She also has been named a RT Book Reviews TOP PICK author and has been nominated for numerous awards. Now living her dream, she resides with her patient husband, amazing daughter (the other remarkable daughter is off chasing her own dreams) and two spoiled cats. She'd love to hear from you via **www.JenniferFaye.com**

Subscribe to Jennifer's periodic newsletter for news about upcoming releases and other special offers.

You can also join her on Twitter, Facebook, Goodreads or Tsu.